*In the darkness,
may you always
find starlight.*

ev

1
ROCKWELL MANOR

It was a brisk autumn afternoon in the Northern Province of Bellaton. Ana and Adam zipped down the lane in a sleek hovercar. In all official records, this road did not exist. Nor did the very township itself that they had passed miles back. Generations of Rockwells had been sure of that. They had many enemies. Almost as many as Ana.

Ana's family was one of seven royal lines on Bellaton, or they had been. Until every member was picked off one by one in a series of accidents, illnesses, and outright murders. She was the last remaining member of the Halt line. And she wasn't safe.

At the end of the last school year, her own adviser had attempted to kill her with an arrow dipped in poison.

Ana stared out the window at the umber rolling hills and forests of scarlet and deep crimson leaves. If she really craned her neck, she could just barely see the metallic road below. The hovercar operated on a magnetic propulsion system that required no wheels.

Ana wanted to roll down the window to get a better view, but as she reached for the button, the driver turned around. "Best to leave the windows up," he said in a low gravelly voice.

Well, he was more of a bodyguard, she supposed. Although he sat up front, the car appeared to be self-driving.

"We're almost there," Adam said in a hushed tone.

Ana could sense his anxious energy, and she snuggled closer, lacing her fingers through his. "I can't wait to see it."

"It'll be hard to miss," he said pointedly.

Ana knew Adam was nervous about showing her his house. He had already explained that it would be different. Bigger than she expected. And his dad could be a little... well, she had met his dad. She knew exactly how he could be.

Ana wasn't worried. She thought Adam was being a little silly. She had seen the academy and the capital. She knew his house would be large and magnificent. In her mind, she was imagining something like the White House—a palatial home with columns and flags.

It had been difficult to leave home again. Ana and Adam had lounged around Earth for several weeks—eating at Frank's diner, hanging out with Ana's brothers, swimming in the lake, and working on their suntans. Ana didn't need a job. Money was, at the moment, not an object.

She and Adam had been excused from end of year exams, as were all involved in the challenge. Time to rest and recuperate from the terror they had faced. Counseling had been offered. Ana snorted. All she needed was tape recorded sessions falling into the hands of her enemies. Still, it was luxurious and languid. Everything a summer should be. It felt like the end of an era when they had boarded the spaceship a few days ago.

The hovercar approached a tall iron gate and paused by a sizable guard shack. A uniformed officer exited the building, and their bodyguard got out to talk to him. Ana couldn't help but notice the turnstile was in the up position. She looked over at Adam and waggled her eyebrows. "I bet this thing can go pretty fast, huh?"

His eyes flashed like lightning in a bottle. He leaned forward and pressed the boost button, grabbing onto a nearby headrest. The hovercar lurched forward. They achieved 0 to 100 mph almost at once.

Ana screamed like she was on a rollercoaster as her head was sucked back to the seat. She was now regretting not taking Adam to a theme park.

The car slowed to a stop in the shadow of a large estate—a cross between a castle and a prison. It loomed ahead, many stories tall, the portrait of a gothic tale. Its roofline stabbing like unhappy swords into the clear, autumn sky. Despite its name, Rockwell Manor was no manor house at all. It was a massive compound.

The walls were constructed from enormous gray stone blocks. The roof of obsidian. Turrets formed in sections. Perhaps the most disturbing addition from Earthen architecture were the demonic-looking gargoyles on the roofline.

She sucked in a breath. "Whoa."

"I told you," Adam said, crossing his arms over his chest.

"I can't believe I'm saying this, but I think you undersold it."

He grunted.

"Let's, um, let's go in," she said, regaining her composure.

The hovercar lowered obligingly to the ground, allowing them to step onto the metallic road.

"I can't believe we just passed through security like that," Ana said, sliding out of the car.

Adam gave her a half-hearted smile. "If one of us didn't have Rockwell DNA, we would have been automatically reduced to vapor."

Ana's eyes bulged. She looked around as if attack robots might soar at her from the rooftop. "Are we safe?"

"Of course. I'm a Rockwell."

She drew her shoulders back, determined to put Adam at ease. She could handle whatever his creepy house had to throw at her. "Well then, Mr. Rockwell, I think it's time we see your—ahem—estate."

He rolled his eyes and nudged her playfully in the side. "Fine. But stay with me and don't touch anything. There are a lot of dangerous objects and security measures. Don't do anything... hasty."

She looped her arm through his, and they marched up the stairs to the front doors of Rockwell Manor. Ana started to step forward onto the large black welcome mat, but Adam pulled her backward. "Don't step there."

She looked at him in confusion. "On the welcome mat?"

"It's rigged with explosives."

Maybe, she had been wrong to downplay Adam's warnings about his house. So far, not that she was counting, but it could have killed her twice.

He led her over to the second window and a gas lamp that glowed silver. Adam reached for the base of the lamp and slid it upward. A scan was activated around them. The gas lamp returned to its original position, and the glass windowpane disappeared.

Ana peered inside, careful not to breech the interior. "Is it safe to step through?" she asked. She wasn't taking any chances anymore. The manor was not only uncharted but rigged with booby traps and security measures at every step.

"Yeah, come on in," he said, stepping in and reaching a hand out to her.

She stepped through to join him. "Wow," she breathed.

The entry was thirty feet high and illuminated by the light of a chandelier made entirely of sharp, silver swords that had been welded together. It might have been her imagination, but she could have sworn she saw a glint of dark dried blood on the point of one of the swords. The walls themselves were a light gray, and they too were covered with artfully placed swords.

The floor was gray stone. The only spot of warmth in the

entire room was a small round rug that had been placed in the center of the room. It looked more like an armory than an entry for guests.

"Home sweet home," Adam said, forcing a smile. "It's better once we get inside, I promise."

He accessed a panel and began entering some sort of information.

Ana spun around, looking at the towering walls. Captivated, she reached out to touch a sword. Adam, still busy with the access panel, noticed out of the corner of his eye.

"No," he shouted, jerking her toward him.

The sword, once suspended on the wall, now shot outward in a stabbing motion in the spot where Ana had just been standing.

They were both breathing hard when the opening to the house appeared. Together, they stepped into an elaborate dining room.

"The security is much lower in here. Only a very small handful of invaders have ever made it to this point. You can touch things now," he said. "Just don't try to open any closed doors, and don't touch any security panels. If something looks locked, leave it."

Ana was still thinking of the chandelier. "Was there blood on that chandelier?"

Adam didn't meet her eyes. "Yes. It lowers."

Several staff members hurried forward to greet them, sinking into deep bows and curtsies. They were dressed in matching cream-colored uniforms with golden accents, reminiscent of the Bellaton flag. A man stepped forward and inclined his head. "Welcome home, Young Master Rockwell."

"Hi, Giles. Is my dad home?"

Giles gave his most pleasant smile. "The esteemed general is away on urgent matters. He sends his regrets for not greeting his son and favored daughter-in-law."

Adam rolled his eyes. "We're not engaged."

Giles did not reply, a sure indicator he had received this form of address from the general himself. He sidestepped the issue. "The general, in his wisdom, has also asked that Lady Halt be assigned a personal maid to attend to her needs for the duration of your stay."

A shaking young woman with red curly hair stepped forward and curtsied. She couldn't have been any older than Ana.

"You're very kind, but I don't need any help."

The staff exchanged horrified glances. The maid nearly dropped her tray.

"No help?" echoed Giles as if he had failed to understand her words. "I can find another maid if she is unsuitable."

Adam nudged her in the side. "Just give in on this one," he whispered.

"Oh, no, she's fine. Um, help will be great."

The staff seemed to normalize once more.

"Excellent. We shall retrieve your baggage and prepare Lady Halt a place in the East Wing. The Floral Room is available," Giles said.

The young woman curtsied again and left the room.

Floral. That sounded promising. Ana had been expecting the "Sharpen your Pickaxe" Room or the "Conquer an Empire" Room.

"It's only a few doors down from me," Adam assured her.

Giles said, "We have prepared a welcome dinner, of course. It will be ready at seven, if that is agreeable to you, young master."

Adam nodded. "Very good. Thanks, Giles."

The staff scurried out of the room and into what Ana supposed was the kitchen.

Finally, they were alone in the room. "You know I don't need a maid."

"I know. But my father will insist. It's easier to just roll with it. Otherwise, he'll fire the staff for being inattentive."

Ana frowned.

"Want a tour?" Adam offered, changing the subject.

Ana looked a little uneasy.

"I swear no more scary stuff."

"Okay then."

They spent the rest of the day roving the enormous compound. There were countless bedrooms and hallways. Adam zoomed past these which he considered "mostly boring" —past three sitting rooms, a swimming pool, and even a weapons range. He finally slowed as they neared his favorite spot— the hanger.

The hanger was the size of three football fields and several stories tall. The inside was filled with immaculately maintained aircraft. Adam sighed when he walked in, as though admiring lovely jewelry or perhaps a puppy he hoped to take home from the pound.

Bright yellow lines divided off large parking spots, and white lines provided aisles. Adam toured Ana down several rows, cautioning her to remain inside the white lines. She didn't need to be told twice. She had seen enough of Rockwell Manor to realize they didn't appreciate anyone touching their things.

There were more than fifty craft here, and everything was unusual and impressive to Ana's untrained eye. In the center of the hanger loomed the largest of them all—an enormous black triangular craft. It reminded Ana of the diagram she had seen on the S.S. Beatrice.

"Are all spacecraft triangular?"

"Not all. But they do have good stability."

"I think the ship I came in on was a triangle."

"Yeah, an old model. Kinda clunky. Made of a different alloy than the one here. Much heavier and larger but with less space inside."

There was nothing small about the ship in the center of the hanger. Of course, Ana had never really seen the exterior of the S.S. Beatrice. It had been covered with dirt when she had banged on the hatch one year ago. And, of course, she had left the ship in a large box to avoid being detected.

"Is this one for cargo too?"

"It could be. It's pretty versatile. But most likely no. It's currently set up for long space travel—a luxury liner."

They passed several sleek jets like the one that had taken them to the ball last winter. Then, they passed an empty spot.

"Did someone take that one out?" she asked.

Adam smiled impishly, drew his gun, and fired just inside the yellow lines. Suddenly, the outline of a craft appeared, illuminated with an electric glow like an eel striking its prey. "Stealth craft," he explained.

"Cool," Ana said. "I wish we could get closer, but I don't like the looks of that defense system."

"If you like that, you'll love the one that will take us back to the Academy when the school year starts." He picked up his pace. His hands were in his pockets, and he had a big smile on his face.

THAT EVENING, Ana got ready for bed, letting the cold water run until it turned warm. She splashed the water on her face. General Rockwell's words turned over in her mind.

As she slid under the covers, thoughts of Madame Bali danced behind her closed eyelids. A cramp was beginning to form in her left arm. She rolled over, grabbing for the other pillow, which was still fluffed to perfection. Her hand grazed against a slip of paper.

Confused, she opened her eyes and felt around again in the

darkness. She grabbed the paper and climbed out of bed. She flipped on the lights. Scrawled in thick black ink was:

Anabella,

You didn't really think I was gone, did you?

Yours Forever,
M.B.

ANA'S EYES widened in horror, and she felt her breath catch in her chest. M.B. Madame Bali. The adviser who had betrayed her. It couldn't be. She was dead. She flipped the note over, hoping there would be more written on the back. It was blank.

Then, an icy chill shot down her spine. What if she wasn't alone? What if Madame Bali was still in the room watching her? She whipped her head around. She saw nothing but the canopy bed and curtains. She rushed over and brushed the curtains aside, as if Madame Bali might be hiding behind their floral cloth.

No, she was still alone in the room. The bed. Under the bed. A tingle of fearful anticipation shot through her, but she leaned down slowly and peered under the bed. There was nothing. Not even a dust bunny.

She walked over to the adjoining bathroom and peeled back the floral shower curtain. She was, waiting at any moment, for someone to jump out at her. A ghost. A human. She wasn't sure.

But the bathroom was empty too.

She turned around the room once more and checked under the bed a second time. There was no one here. Just the note. Ana inspected it, looking for any clue. The paper was plain white. Nothing out of the ordinary. The ink was black and thick like it had been written with a high-quality ink pen. The sort you re-filled. She didn't know what she had been expecting, a fingerprint, a web address maybe?

The most chilling part of the note was the thing she did recognize. The handwriting. It was absolutely, 100% identical to Madame Bali's. There was no doubt about that. Did that mean? Could Madame Bali still be alive?

No, it wasn't possible. General Rockwell had said she was dead. Then again... was General Rockwell above suspicion? Was he above lying? Ana snorted. Certainly not. He had no qualms about setting up his son's engagement without his knowledge.

Ana looked at her infotab, hoping to see a message from Samuel. She hadn't spoken to him since his arrest. After the challenge, she had demanded he be freed from prison and made her adviser. But before they could be united, she had been whisked off to Earth. Not that she was complaining.

Now, more than ever, she really wanted to talk to him. To tell him what had just happened. He was the only one paranoid enough to believe Madame Bali might be alive. And right now, she felt like she needed someone to affirm that she wasn't going crazy.

But there were no new messages.

She chastised herself. She had only been back on Bellaton for eight hours. She'd hear from Samuel soon enough. For now, it was enough to know he was free and that they'd be together soon.

2

SAMUEL'S BOUNDLESS BOOK COLLECTION

The cheerful spring sunshine bathed Samuel in its warm glow. He lay on a grass-covered knoll with a book in his hand, rapidly turning the pages with interest. Nearby, birds chirped, and flying lops scurried in the bushes. Other than that, the park was still. There were no other people here.

The book was interesting. It was about Bellaton's star portals—one of the planet's most enduring mysteries. The portals enabled rapid space travel throughout this galaxy and many neighboring ones. However, as much as the Seven liked to deny it, they had no idea how the portals worked. They also had no idea who built them. Another fact they liked to deny. The Seven were the greatest civilization to ever live on Bellaton. To dispute this was a death sentence.

Many mathematicians had postulated theories over the years on how the portals might work, but so far, each had been proven wrong. Finally, several decades ago, the engineers had grown impatient of waiting for answers. They were granted permission from the Council to do destructive testing on one of the sites. It had been destroyed.

Still, this particular book was working through a theory Samuel had never considered before. He was just about to get to the crux of Dr. Emanuel's theory when the book vanished. Samuel was staring at empty space now. His hands were empty. The book was gone.

Samuel roared in frustration.

Of course, the book had never existed at all. At least, not in a physical form. A few feet away, on a park bench, a new book materialized on top of a small stack.

Samuel was in prison. More specifically, he was in a simulation. And while this park looked like paradise, it was hell. One designed specifically for him.

The disappearing books were one of the rules of the simulation. Samuel had been making a mental list.

The sun always shined—day and night. This made it very difficult to sleep, of course. On his first night in the simulation, he had crawled under the park bench to try and escape its relentless rays. But it had made little difference. Now, he had lost track of any semblance of the passage of time.

The park never changed. The trees, grass, and bench always remained. The animals moved, scurried, and chirped on a set pattern. He could make minor changes, like when he dug up some grass, but it always reverted.

There were always books. They sat in a neat, immovable stack at the edge of the bench. He could move them, but they would always reappear. When he got to the good part of a book, it always, ALWAYS disappeared. A new one would arrive to take its place.

He was never hungry or thirsty. Somewhere, outside of the simulation, his body's nutritional needs were being met.

Samuel paced for a few minutes, trying to work off his frustration. He knew he needed to calm down. He knew who had designed this prison—his own family. And he also knew, he was being watched. When they sensed he was beginning to break, that's when someone would finally arrive.

So, he sat in the dirt under the large tree. He drew in the dust with his finger, thinking about the unsolvable star portal equation. He needed to keep his mind active.

In the back of his mind, his worst fear wasn't that his family would come to interrogate him. It was that no one would come. Ever. That he would never leave this place.

He knew, if he stayed here long enough, there would come a time when he wouldn't remember the walk down the long beige hallways or being forced into the room that now held him captive. No, he would forget the outside world altogether.

He lived in the park.

He had always lived in the park.

There was nothing but the park.

FIVE PARTIAL BOOKS LATER, Samuel lost his temper. He grabbed the stack of books and tossed them off the bench. He slammed his hands against the edges of the simulation. He couldn't feel the pain, but he knew somewhere, his fists were bloody and bruised.

A crack of blinding white light appeared next to the tree. Two people entered, a tall, lean woman and a man with a gaudy ruby ring. The man had black hair with a tough of grey at the temples and a stern expression. The woman was ringing her immaculately manicured hands.

Samuel let his hands drop to his sides. "Hi, mom. Hi, dad."

3

DINNER WITH THE GENERAL

When Ana and Adam arrived at dinner, they found a large, muscular figure waiting for them at the head of the table. General Rockwell was home.

"It's about time," he said. "You're nearly two minutes late."

Ana checked the nearby clock. It was 7:01:47. She repressed a laugh. General Rockwell would never survive her family dinners. They usually took turns bringing fast food home, and they never started at a specific time, just when the food arrived. Fletcher was developing a flair for cooking, and on their parting night, he had created his pièce de résistance—a supreme pizza covered with buffalo chicken fingers and topped with blue cheese and crumbled Doritos. Ana had choked down half a slice. Adam, on the other hand, had asked for the recipe.

Adam held out Ana's chair, and she sat down. He sat directly across from her.

A servant immediately stepped forward to pour ice water into their goblets. Ana took a long swig. She was thirsty from another day of exploring the grounds.

"The staff said you wouldn't be home tonight," Adam said.

"Yes, well, I had a meeting with the council, but it ended…abruptly."

Ana looked up. "Was there an argument?"

"A difference in opinion on the case of your Madame Bali."

"You said on Earth that she was dead."

"And so she is," he growled. "The gall of attacking my son and killing a Rockwell. My only regret is we didn't make it a public execution."

Ana had the slightest suspicion that General Rockwell may have killed her himself. She flinched but pushed forward with her questioning. "Does the council have any more information about who hired her or why she, um, wanted me dead?"

"Nothing to be shared with a teenager."

Ana fought the urge to put her hands on her hips. Instead, she kept them demurely folded in her lap. She could feel herself shake a little with repressed fury.

General Rockwell appeared to mistake this for fear. "You're a Rockwell now. You don't need to worry about such pathetic threats. We will eliminate them. With prejudice. That is the last Rockwell blood that will be spilled in this matter."

His tone was gruff, and his eyes were stony. This was no idle threat. Ana wondered if she could get any more information from him. She had to be careful in how she asked. He would never tell her anything if he thought she was nosing into Council affairs.

"Thank you, General. I feel safer knowing that." She didn't really, of course. She had been watched for an entire year and nearly killed on numerous occasions. She had lost a friend. She wasn't giving this up until she knew everything.

He nodded. "Remember my promise, Ana. As a Rockwell, no one will lay a hand on you."

She nodded. "Just one more thing I was worried about. Why did Madame Bali do it?" Ana had been thinking about this all summer.

General Rockwell narrowed his eyes. "I thought Adam would have told you. Money. We found several ID cards with untold amounts of cash on them."

Of course, Ana did know this. Adam had said as much. She just wasn't sure she believed it. "Couldn't the money have been put there after her death?"

"Enough questions. The woman is dead, and our security is tight. There's no need for you to dig into this worthless urchin's past."

Ana knew the topic was closed. She had pushed her luck enough already. She had, however, gleaned one useful piece of information. Madame Bali, whatever her real name, was not from one of the Seven families. General Rockwell had called her an "urchin." That implied she was an ordinary citizen.

She had also learned that the Rockwells would be upping security at the academy this year. What would that look like? She thought of the manor's security. All this security might be the death of her.

The staff brought out tray after tray of food. Ana had thought the academy's food couldn't be topped, but she had been wrong.

The red-headed maid's hands shook as she lowered the main course onto the table, the tray rattled terribly, and Ana feared she might drop the dish. She longed to reach out a hand to support the tray but held back.

General Rockwell watched the maid like a crocodile until she disappeared back into the kitchen. "Well, son, you've been gone nearly one lunar cycle; let's hear some of this Earthen linguistics and culture you've been studying."

Adam stopped carving his meat and winced. They hadn't gotten around to studying linguistics or culture, unless you counted swimming by the lake, eating junk food, and watching movies.

General Rockwell read his body language. "I should have

known." He looked at Adam appraisingly. "I bet you neglected your routine too. Slow and fat isn't a good look on the battlefield."

Ana had seen Adam shirtless at the lake. There was nothing fat about him. He was muscular and toned in a way most boys his age would envy.

Adam looked indignant. "No, sir. I ran and swam every day. I studied Earthen culture too."

Ana's eyes widened. He was clearly lying.

"Show me."

Adam affected his best Southern dialect. "Hold your horses. Lord willing and the creek don't rise, I'll top my current course record."

General Rockwell squinted.

Adam grinned and continued, "If the heat don't get ya', the humidity will. I reckon I was slow as molasses, fightin' through all them no see 'ems"— He looked at Ana for confirmation. She nodded.— "but once I got here, I shot off like a cat on a hot tin roof."

"What? I don't understand anything you're saying."

Ana whispered something in his ear.

Adam crossed his arms over his chest and grinned back at his dad. "Well, bless your heart."

Giles leaned over at that moment to spoon some relish on Adam's plate. "What a kind sentiment, young master Rockwell."

Ana tried to disguise a laugh as coughing, hiding her face behind her linen napkin.

Adam's dad looked at her suspiciously but let the matter drop.

THE FOLLOWING evening concluded with another formal dinner. Perhaps, here, they weren't considered formal at all. Perhaps, this was ordinary.

General Rockwell, at six feet tall and a larger build, moved with the stealth of a panther. His path crossed that of the young redheaded maid. She was holding a glass bowl full of a bright gelatin-looking substance. She noticed his towering shadow before she heard him. She jerked in surprise, and the bowl sprung from her hand. She clutched at it desperately. It shattered on the ground, and she dropped to try to retrieve the pieces. An instinct. A bad instinct. The glass shards ripped her pretty hands to pieces. The blood refracted on the polished surface.

"Jumpy, are we?"

"No sir," she said, still scrambling to pick up the broken bowl. "I'm sorry about the bowl, sir."

"The bowl is of little consequence, although I'd thank you to take better care. My greater concern is why I have a staff member who is so…alert. Do you have something to hide?"

"No, sir. Of course, not, sir."

"Hmm. And how long have you served in our home?

"One year, sir."

He didn't recognize the maid after a year, Ana thought. What a jerk.

And then, without warning, the girl flew through the air, immobilized by a beam of blue light. Just like Ana had seen in the challenge.

She hung above the table.

Ana slid her chair back in horror.

Adam tried to clutch her hand, to stop her from getting up.

She shook his hand away. "What are you doing?" she demanded.

Adam winced.

"Running my household," the general replied.

"By stringing up your staff?"

"By any means which I deem necessary. If you can't stomach it, then you can be excused."

Ana refused to leave the room.

"If you're so concerned, heal her yourself." He waited, a knowing smile crossing his face.

It chilled Ana to her core. Did he know? Could he know? Adam didn't know. How could his dad? He wasn't even there, and she had hidden the plant from the cameras. She was sure of it. "I-um- I can't. Not on command like that."

Rockwell raised an eyebrow. "I see. Well, in that case," he turned his attention back to the maid. "Go and clean yourself up and try not to drip blood on the rug in the foyer. Adam's mother is especially fond of it."

"Yes, sir," she said, cupping her hands to try to prevent dripping and fleeing the room.

"And girl?"

The maid turned, frozen in terror. "Yes, general?"

"Breathe a word of this incident, and it will be your last."

"O-of course not, sir." She curtsied and fled the room, clutching her hand.

A horrible silence hung over the dining room.

Adam looked at her out of the corner of his eye.

Ana had lost her appetite, but she quickly sawed the last two bites of food and chewed them up. Then, she stood, "May I be excused?"

Rockwell lifted another eyebrow. "As you wish."

Ana fled after the maid.

BACK IN HER ROOM, Ana found her maid was already turning down the sheets. Her hand was wrapped in a hasty bandage. When she heard Ana enter, her eyes darted from side to side, as if looking for an easy escape route. She reminded Ana of a squirrel stuck in the road with an eighteen-wheeler oncoming.

"I'll just be leaving, miss," she mumbled, ducking her head in deference.

"No, it's okay," Ana said, holding a hand out. "Please stay."

The girl froze in place as if glued to the floor. "Of course, Lady Halt. As you wish."

"What's your name?"

"Tiffany."

Ana nodded. "I'm really sorry about what happened back there."

The girl hung her head and began anxiously fluffing a pillow. "It was my fault. I'm sorry I disappointed General Rockwell. Giles says I lack the proper spirit of staff. My anxious behavior unsettled the master of the house."

"But you didn't do anything wrong!" Ana exclaimed. "This is ridiculous. Why don't you work somewhere else?"

Tiffany's eyes widened once more. "Are you firing me?"

Ana held out a hand. "No, no, no," she assured her quickly. "I just- why don't you work somewhere safer?"

The girl looked puzzled. "Safer than the Rockwell Manor? It's the safest place in the world."

"Perhaps for the Rockwells," Ana muttered.

"What's that, my lady?"

"Nothing."

"This is one of the best positions I could hope to receive. I have no formal education. I don't come from a connected family. I'm no high born. Here, I am safe and protected by the walls and earn a good wage. My sister, she's much younger than me, she'll be able to go to a good school with the money I send back."

Ana nodded. She understood this. Wasn't this what Ryker had wanted to do for her? "You're a good sister," she said.

Tiffany looked taken aback. "Thank you, lady. That's very kind."

"I am sorry about your hand though. I haven't completely mastered my healing gift yet. Please don't tell anyone."

In truth, after everything that had happened during the Challenge, Ana no longer believed in the Halt family gift. She had tried so hard to heal. Yet, she had never managed it. There was only one conclusion. Ana came from a long line of liars.

It made sense, really. How many lies had Ana told since she got here? How many secrets was she keeping from her own friends? Her mom had been a liar, too. For fifteen years, she had somehow "forgotten" to tell her daughter she came from another world.

How many generations of Halts had been pressing medicinal herbs and pharmaceuticals into the mouths of the sick and the dying to keep this charade going? The thought of it made Ana feel nauseous.

"My lady?" the maid prompted.

"Oh, I'm sorry. Did you say something?"

"Just that I would never utter a family secret, especially one that might bring you harm."

Ana smiled at her. "Thank you."

After Tiffany left, Ana paced across the cold marble floor. When General Rockwell had attacked the maid, Adam had done nothing. Worse. She thought of his green eyes flashing toward her, his hand reaching out to stop her from getting up. He had tried to stop her from helping.

Ana couldn't help but think that Samuel would have done things differently. She lay down in her bed, carefully running one hand under the pillows and sheets, searching for another note. She breathed a sigh of relief. Nothing. At least something had gone right tonight.

4
DEAL WITH THE DEVIL

Ana woke the next morning and walked quietly past Adam's door. After the events of last night, she was hoping to avoid him for as long as possible. She couldn't believe what a coward he had been! Letting his father abuse a maid in that way. He didn't stick up for Ana either. He hadn't even come by her room to apologize.

It was at this moment that she realized how truly isolated she was here at Rockwell Manor. She was hidden by tons of stone, acres of land, and more militaristic enforcements than anywhere she had ever seen in her life. If Adam wasn't on her side, she had put herself in a very bad situation.

Still, she was more angry than frightened. She made her way into the kitchen. A dark-headed woman leaned on a tabletop and let out a great yawn. A large, burly man was stirring a large bowl.

"Hi," she greeted.

They both jumped, startled at her sudden presence in this sacred space. The slouching maid straightened into a standing position and curtsied. The burly man stopped stirring to bow.

She still hated when people did these things, but it no longer surprised her. "Sorry to interrupt your work. I was wondering if you had something I could eat. Nothing fancy," she quickly added, realizing they would probably start whipping up a five-star breakfast if she didn't stop them.

As expected, the man said, "I'd be happy to fix you a full and hearty breakfast, lady. Would you like to sit down in the dining room? I could have it ready in no time."

"No, no. Just something small. I thought it'd be nice to walk the grounds. Maybe a cup of coffee to-go and a granola bar or muffin or something."

He frowned. "To-go?"

"In a mug is fine. Anything really."

Still looking taken aback, he handed her a small basket with a cloth napkin wrapped pastry selection and a tall mug of coffee. She was Little Red Riding Hood, and she had already met the Big Bad Wolf. She was hoping the Wolf, or the General as he referred to himself, was out on business this morning.

"To-go," he said.

"This is perfect. Thank you."

She made a beeline for the back door, but just as she turned the knob, she heard Adam's cool baritone. "Avoiding me, huh?"

She looked over her shoulder and saw he was only a few feet away. Damn his stealth.

"I don't blame you, really. I'm sorry about last night."

She looked at him with hard eyes. "You didn't do anything."

"I know. I'm sorry. I should have defended you. It was wrong to put you on the spot like that. You don't have anything to prove to anyone, especially when it comes to healing."

"And the maid?"

"If I had defended her, my father would have lost his mind. If there is one thing he believes in, it's a hierarchy. He's at the top. I'm below. And that maid? Well, she's so far down the ladder, she may as well be underground."

Ana opened her mouth to protest. "You may not be aware of

this, but I used to be pretty close to that maid in the social strata."

"I didn't say that's how I see things. If I had gotten involved, that maid would have been fired on the spot." He frowned, a shadow casting across his forehead. "You promised when we came here that you wouldn't judge me based on him or this house."

Ana paused, letting her anger flow out of her in a long stream of air. "You're right."

"Let's get out of here for the day."

She nodded. Anywhere but here sounded good.

They ducked back into the kitchen, so Adam could grab his morning glass of Grasshopper's Revenge, a thick, gloopy green drink. He said it was packed with nutrients, but Ana thought it tasted like grass. Together, they headed out the back door. The walk was quiet at first.

"Did I mention I'm an idiot?"

She smiled and nudged him in the side. "No, but it's good to hear you admit it."

He took her hand in his, and they continued on together. They walked across a long expanse of manicured lawn toward a hedgerow twenty feet high.

Ana pushed him up against a large concrete wall between two shrubberies and kissed him.

"Mmm," he moaned. "Does this mean I'm forgiven?"

"What do you think?" She kissed him again.

If Adam's house was oppressive and gothic, Holden's was the antithesis: a sunny, picturesque home with a big tree in the front yard.

Holden was waiting for them on the front porch.

"Alarms go off?"

Holden tapped his temple. "Something like that."

Last spring, Holden had displayed the family gift of foresight. Something he had been hiding for a long time.

The three of them sat around Holden's round kitchen table.

"So, what happened after the challenge?" Ana asked Holden eagerly.

Holden scratched his head. "Didn't you hear?"

"Adam's dad wasn't feeling very chatty."

Holden's lip twitched upward. "My uncle isn't a chatty man."

"So, spill. What do you know?"

"The council called for a full inquest into the situation. They've instituted a media blackout on the topic. A few hours after the challenge, all of the interviews were scrapped, and none were allowed to re-air. Of course, everyone watching live saw everything."

"And the inquest? What does that mean?"

"It means they searched the dome. They've interviewed everyone in the dome as well as everyone on the committee. I imagine anyone who set foot on Obsidian in the last year will be contacted. I expect they'll want to interview you and Adam too."

"What did you tell them?"

"The truth."

"All of it?" she asked, raising a knowing eyebrow.

Holden knew exactly what she meant. And so did Adam. It had taken Holden until the end of last year to finally work up the courage to tell Adam about his gift. Only after his secret had nearly exploded their friendship.

Holden, like a small number of others in the Rockwell line, could see the future. In Bellaton, each of the Seven noble families had fantastic, inhuman abilities that ran in their blood. They called them "gifts." In some families, like the Rockwell's, the gift was rare. But in Ana's family, it was quite common. Not that she would know. She had been faking hers for the better part of six months now.

"Well," Holden relented. "Not everything. They did forensics on the body, I'm sure. The Nobles hinted at it, but there have been no press releases. The adults all know. Well, those in the inner circle anyway. My mom told me Madame Bali wasn't registered."

"So, she's a career criminal then?" Adam asked.

"No way," Ana said.

"It's all being kept very tight-lipped."

LONG AFTER DINNER, when most of the household had gone to bed, Ana opened her door quietly and padded down the long hallway. She had been thirsty for the better part of an hour.

She tiptoed into the kitchen, where a maid fetched her the water. As she exited the kitchen, she noticed a glow of light coming from a door just to her left. She wondered who would be awake at this time of night. Was this room for staff? Adam had warned her about opening closed doors, but this one was cracked. It was harmless, she assured herself. She'd just have a quick peek and then be off to bed. She leaned in to look through the crack and spotted General Rockwell, sitting at a large command desk in the center of the room. All around him, a holographic projection played. One she recognized all too well.

He was watching the challenge.

More specifically, he was watching Ana hovered over Adam's lifeless body, the plants in her hand, preparing to save him. She sucked in a breath, and General Rockwell turned his head.

"Ah, Anabella," he said in a rich pleasant tone. "Why don't you come in?"

This honeyed tone to his voice terrified her more than his usual bark.

Seeing no other option, she opened the door and stepped inside. "Sorry to disturb you, General. I was just getting a glass of water." She held up the glass in her hand to prove her point.

"Nonsense. I was just watching the footage from the Challenge." He looked at her, carefully gauging her response.

She swallowed.

An uncomfortable silence fell between them as General Rockwell continued to measure her facial expression.

Attempting to lighten things up, she asked, "Do you have any, um, additional information that you've learned? Any lead on Madame Bali's employer?"

"No, but I've stumbled upon something…interesting. No matter what angle I play this video at, I can't seem to see the moment you healed Adam. I wanted to watch it in its full glory."

She nodded, willing herself to remain calm.

"Now, I believe you, of course. But the other families, I'm not sure they would. After all, there are several restorative medicines that could render similar results. I may have to defend you against the whole council."

Ana gulped.

"I would, of course. Since you're family."

"Of course," she echoed feebly.

"There's another video I've been watching that might interest you."

The holographic projection vanished like vapor. It was replaced with the image of a bright spring day and a long, dark-haired young man sitting in the dirt reading. Samuel. Her heart skipped a beat.

Why was he watching a video of Samuel? She didn't dare to ask. To show that she cared.

"Let's skip past this part. It's a bit boring."

They fast-forwarded past hours of Samuel reading and

drawing mathematical symbols in the dirt. Finally, the General hit play.

Samuel shouted in heart-wrenching agony. His eyes were wild. Not in his usual catlike way. Instead, they were that of madness. He slammed his fists against the edge of a perimeter that she hadn't realized was there.

He was trapped.

"Where is he?" she gasped, panic rising in her chest.

"Prison, of course."

"You mean he's not free?"

"You didn't really think the council would free him just because you said so?" His voice was gruff, but his mustache twitched in cruel amusement.

"Well, I guess," she faltered. That's exactly what she had thought. She had proven herself the rightful heir, hadn't she?

"The boy is guilty of treason, or so his family says. And, honestly, that's good enough for the council. We let each family handle their own internal issues."

"But we can't leave him in there. You have to help," she blurted. She regretted the words the moment they left her mouth.

General Rockwell controlled his expression, maintaining a veneer of neutrality, but Ana could see it was taking some effort. "I wouldn't meddle in another family's affairs," he paused for effect. "Unless I had a really strong incentive to do so. I mean, technically, Rockwells do control most of the corrections facilities. It wouldn't be too difficult. But oh, the paperwork would be very annoying."

"I'll make it worth your while."

"How so?"

She gritted her teeth. "What do you want?"

"A daughter-in-law."

"Fine."

"A compliant one."

Ana's arm twitched. She would love to punch that smirk right off his arrogant face. But instead, she bit her lip, forced her arms to remain by her sides, and nodded.

"So, we have an agreement?"

"Yes."

"Then, I'll travel to the capital tomorrow and begin the paperwork."

Ana felt a wave of relief wash over her. She hurried back to bed. Samuel would be safe soon. It was the least, the very least, she could do.

5
THE RING THE SEA SPAT OUT

The Rockwell topiary garden was filled with dangerous animals— slithering ancient jasper, monstrous bears with fangs, hulking wolves with intelligent eyes, and many more. Luckily, most of them were merely carved into the foliage. The only real animal she had spotted so far was a flying lops that landed gracefully on top of a shrubbery.

It was an unseasonably warm fall day in the Northern Province. Adam led Ana along a manicured stone path to a long table setup with crisp ivory linens, candles, and more food than she could ever eat.

"All of this is for us?" she asked.

He shrugged noncommittally and pulled out a chair for her.

She sat down and noticed there were extra place settings. "Is your dad coming?"

At that moment, Holden stepped out from behind a shrubbery of an ancient jasper, running one hand through his tousled blonde hair. "Surprise," he said sheepishly.

Ophelia was close behind. "Surprise!"

Ana leaped up from her chair to greet them.

Holden swooped her up into a bear hug. "Happy birthday!"

Ophelia gave Ana a small, tight embrace. "I'm so glad to see you."

"Me too. I was worried about you."

Adam clapped Holden on the back and moved to hug Ophelia. But to Ana's surprise, Ophelia stepped back.

She rounded on Adam, and her ears tinged pink. With all the fury of a tiny mouse, she stabbed an accusing finger at Adam. "You! You shot me in the foot!"

Adam put his hand on the top of her head, accentuating their stark height difference, and mussed her hair. "Sorry, O. Had to do it. Safeties were down."

She glared up at him. "I could have helped."

"Maybe. Couldn't risk it."

She gave an impish grin and waved her hand. The terrible topiaries grew out of their grisly shapes and into tall, ungroomed shrubberies.

Ana laughed.

"Alright, alright, you could have helped. I'm sorry," Adam relented. "Can you put them back now? My dad is going to be furious."

Ophelia relented. She walked closer and touched each bush until its foliage formed into a series of oversized flying lops.

"Well, it's something, I guess," he shrugged. "Are we good now?"

They were interrupted by the redheaded maid who had hurried over to fill water glasses and check if the food was to everyone's liking. Ana invited the maid to join them.

Adam's eyes widened, but he didn't say anything.

The maid, looking terrified, politely declined and hurried back to the house.

"I almost forgot." Ophelia stepped behind the shrubberies and brought out a small animal carrier. She unlatched the gate and released a black and white tuxedo cat. He stalked around the table, glaring at Ophelia for the crime of his imprisonment.

"Petrie!" Ana gushed. Food forgotten, she rushed over and scooped him up. "Hello, sweet baby," she cooed.

He bumped his big, furry cat head under her chin.

Ophelia smiled. "He was an absolute angel."

Adam scrunched his eyebrows like he was watching an insane person.

"Thank you so much for watching over him for me." With a small frown, she added, "Madame Bali didn't turn out to be the best caregiver."

They were all quiet for a moment.

Ana poured herself a glass of bright blue tea and selected an assortment of finger sandwiches. When everyone's plates were overflowing, Adam raised his water goblet. "To Ana, the best thing to come to Bellaton."

They clinked glasses and spent the rest of the brunch eating, joking, and smiling.

After brunch, they decided to visit the closest town to do some back-to-school shopping. The trip took about an hour by hovercar, and Ana watched as the leaves turned from scarlet to green as they left the mountains and headed south. Adam and Holden tried to speed up the ride by punching the blast button no less than three times.

"If only I could get underneath this thing and make some adjustments," Holden lamented.

When they arrived, the car dropped them in the center of a small but modern town. The buildings were no more than two stories but made of modern design—glass and obsidian.

"Let's divide up," Adam suggested. "The girls can go clothes shopping, and Holden and I can duck into that video game place."

"Don't you need clothes too?" Ana pointed out.

"I have a personal tailor."

Ana rolled her eyes. "Why didn't I see that coming?"

Holden laughed, and they went their separate ways with an agreement to meet up in an hour and a half in this same spot.

Ana and Ophelia were supposed to be going to a nearby clothing store, but they weren't making it far. Ana kept getting sucked into every outdoor display.

"Here, try these sunglasses," she called to Ophelia. They were large round pink rimmed glasses, which she thought were extremely vintage.

Ophelia frowned. "It's still light out."

Ana crinkled her brow. "Well, yeah, that's sort of the point."

"Why would you want to wear sunglasses during the day?"

Ana pulled a red cat-eyed pair with a diamond glistening at the temple. She put them on. "Woah!" she cried. To her surprise, two suns shone ahead, and blinding brightness filled her vision.

Ophelia still seemed perplexed. "They're meant to be used at night. You know, sun-glasses," she emphasized.

Ana took the glasses off, blinking rapidly as her eyes adjusted to the ordinary daylight. "On Earth, sunglasses reduce the sunlight to make it easier on your eyes."

"Oh, we have something like that too. We call them Right-Light Glasses. They adjust to meet your ideal light needs."

"But why are there two suns?" Ana wondered, thinking of the sunglasses.

Ophelia laughed. "Oh, that. They're designed on Galari Four. They have two suns. It's an homage to their creator. It is a bit weird at first."

"And what are these?" Ana asked, looking at the next rack. She picked up a pair with rainbow lenses and a thick frame that blocked light on the sides. They were almost goggles, really.

"Virtual reality glasses."

"I thought you guys used neural net, like for video games."

"These are different. They're only good for one type of experience. It's why they're so cheap."

Ana shrugged and pulled on a rainbow pair. She opened her

eyes, and she was on a round laser disc, floating above a rainbow. She was soaring forward, surfing a rainbow. She threw back her head and laughed, sticking out her hands to keep her balance.

She pulled them off her head, breathing hard. "That was amazing. How much are these?"

Ophelia gave a small smile. "You know all of this is banned on campus, right?"

Ana frowned and reluctantly placed the rainbow glasses back on the rack.

They left the sunglass stall and passed more kiosks, including neural implants. "Learn the secrets of the universe in seconds!"

Ophelia steered her past.

"But I could get straight A's!" Ana protested.

"Be careful who you let into your brain."

"Blubber Be Gone," read the product label in bright red letters. "Work off your fat while you sleep!!"

"I heard they found an army of them working at a factory while they were sleeping," Ophelia whispered.

Ana dropped the package.

"Let's do some clothes shopping, okay?" Ophelia said.

Ana nodded.

THE SHOPKEEPERS AGREED to send their packages straight to the academy. Ana and Ophelia met back up with the boys.

"There's something I have to do," Ana said. "Do you mind waiting with Holden?"

"Not at all. I'd like to get a drink and sit for a while anyway."

Ana grabbed Adam by the hand and pulled him away from the cafe.

He let himself be dragged for about a block before asking,

"Ana? What's all this about? Did you forget something at the store?"

"No, it's nothing like that. I, just, your dad—"

"What about him?

"He wants us to get engaged, right?"

Adam shifted uncomfortably. "He hasn't exactly been subtle about it, has he? But that doesn't mean—I saw how upset you were at the capital—I can hold him off for a while. Don't worry."

"It's okay. You don't have to."

His eyes widened. "What? Are you saying you want to marry me?"

Ana's stomach lurched. That wasn't what she meant at all. She was doing a terrible job explaining herself. She was so embarrassed she felt she might melt into a puddle of goo. "It's not that either."

Maybe she was imagining it, but behind his disappointment, he looked a little relieved.

"I'm sorry I'm not saying this well."

"It's fine. Just say it."

"Your dad wants us to be engaged. He told the media. The whole school probably thinks we're engaged anyway."

"True. You'd be a lot safer if people believed the rumors, you know."

"And who cares what people think as long as we know what's real."

"So," he fixed his green eyes on hers and smiled. "What is real?

She hadn't expected him to turn the conversation on her. Usually, Adam told her how he felt, and she had kissed him in return. Now that she thought about it, maybe she hadn't been so good at verbalizing her feelings. She owed him this. "Well, I like you…a lot." Her cheeks burned red.

"Is that so?" he asked with a cruel grin. "I was beginning to wonder if you kissed all of your other friends too."

She hit him in the arm. "Obviously not," she muttered. "I'm just not the best with feelings."

"Well, for the record, I like you too. A lot." He grinned.

"Stop teasing."

"Fine." He got down on one knee on the empty sidewalk.

She started to panic.

"Anabella Halt, will you be my girlfriend and also pretend to be engaged to me so that my lunatic father will leave us alone and also protect you from your enemies?"

She burst out laughing and pulled him to his feet. "Yeah. That sounds pretty good."

"Well, I guess we better get a ring then."

She gasped. "What? You can't be serious."

"I am. If we're really going to pretend to be engaged, we need a ring. If we don't pick one, my dad will just start sending jewelers."

"When you put it like that—"

ADAM LED her back toward the main square.

Part of her was soaring, Adam understood her feelings. He returned them. They were officially dating now. But the other part of her was feeling wary. Could it really be this easy? Could she have Adam in the way she wanted and also protect the people she cared about? It seemed too good to be true.

A few minutes later, they had reached their destination. Nestled between an intergalactic travel agency and an upscale tailor, there was a jewelry shop with big glass windows. Adam opened the door, and they entered a room as chilly and dazzling as an icicle. The walls were a frosty, glowing white, and an enormous chandelier hung in the center of the room, refracting piercing, white light.

She ran her hands along her arms to warm them.

A saleswoman moved to greet them. The woman's eyes

narrowed with a measure of suspicion as she took in their ages. “Hello, I’m Izemena. Is there something, in particular, you’re looking for today?”

Ana felt like an imposter. This store was so fancy. What were they doing here? She assumed Adam would buy the ring, but maybe she was wrong to assume that. They weren’t even really engaged. Even the shopkeeper seemed to realize they had no business being in a place like this.

Adam stepped forward and shook the saleswoman’s hand. “I’m Adam Rockwell, and this is Anabella Halt.”

The woman’s expression transformed. “I thought you looked familiar! You certainly take after your father. And, of course, I watched the challenge live. I was rooting for both of you. I’m so glad you’re well.” She reigned herself back in. “What can I help you with today?”

“We’re here to buy an engagement ring.”

Izemena attempted to repress a squeal of delight, but it only came out as a squawk. “How thrilling. I watched the challenge, and I can’t think of two people more suited for one another! It would be my absolute honor to help you find the perfect piece to denote such a momentous occasion.”

“Thank you,” Adam said with a serious expression.

Ana, however, was trying not to laugh. It was as if the woman had swallowed a dictionary.

“We have a unique assortment of both antique and modern jewelry. If there’s something you want that we don’t have, please let me know. Our laboratory can create anything you desire. We merely need your specifications.”

“That’s good to know. I think we’ll look around first, if that’s okay.”

“Certainly. Take your time.”

On each side of the room, there were cases of jewelry displayed. At first, Ana was nervous to get too close to them; they appeared to be made out of some sort of forcefield rather than glass. But Adam assured her they were stable enough to lean on and smudge-proof.

"Pick anything you want. You may as well enjoy yourself."

"Don't I need to get a diamond?"

He screwed up his face into a look of sheer bewilderment. "Why would you get a diamond? They're not even in the top ten most valuable stones. I mean if you want one, sure. But it might look cheap."

She laughed. Diamonds were cheap here.

"As long as it doesn't have any rubies. It's bad enough you picked that guy as an adviser. What's his name again?"

Ana rolled her eyes. As if Adam didn't know. "Samuel. And I don't like rubies anyway."

Izemena returned. "Can I get you something to drink?"

Adam looked at her, and she nodded. She had always seen on television where bridal parties got to drink champagne while they tried on wedding gowns. Against her better judgment, a part of her was really having fun.

He answered for them. "Sure. Two Northern Fizz?"

"But you don't drink," she said.

"It's non-alcoholic. A Northern specialty. I think you'll like it. It's got a refreshing taste."

Her eyes fell on a round stone that glimmered with a thousand colors, every time she tilted her head it changed. Right now, it was a brilliant deep red and turquoise like the deepest seas. It was a veritable kaleidoscope reflecting in its cut. Surrounding it were little triangles cresting the appearance of a sun.

Ana sucked in a breath and reached out a hand to touch the glass without thinking.

"Want to try it on?" Adam asked, leaning against the glass casually as if he went ring shopping all the time.

Ana pulled her jaw off the floor. "No way, it's too big. I bet it's really expensive. We should look at something simpler."

"Expensive and showy is kind of the point. Besides, it's obvious you like it."

"I do not. I—"

He smirked. "There's a speck of drool on the case."

"There is not," she said, crossing her arms over her chest.

"There is so."

There was. She followed Adam's pointing finger to a spot on the glass, where a small droplet of water rested.

"I didn't do that!" she said indignantly. "It's from the drink."

He smiled and nudged her. "Ana, why don't you just try on the ring? It's what we're here for, right?"

The shopkeeper swooped over with a smile. "What a gorgeous couple and so young. I love young love. Like the bud of a flower."

The ring's stone was dark. Something about it was alluring, calming.

"Ah, the sea's stone."

When Ana placed it on her finger, the stone came alive. It glowed like a thousand suns on her finger. It was unlike anything she had ever seen. Like a sun going supernova.

"It's perfect," Adam said, looking not at the ring but at her face. "Let's get it."

ANA AND ADAM walked hand in hand down the sidewalk. Ana felt strangely nervous, she had been made brand new and others would see.

They spotted Holden and Ophelia ahead under a cloud of mist. Ana stepped through it, feeling instantly refreshed. It smelled like oranges.

"Hey!" Adam called, and she noticed his voice didn't sound as casual as it usually did. Maybe he had that weird new feeling too.

Holden noticed the faint blush on Adam's cheeks at once,

and it wasn't long before his eyes traced their way to the source — Ana's ring finger. He smiled. "Congrats."

Adam opened his mouth and then shut it. He looked taken aback. "How did you..."

Holden tapped his temple. "I saw it a long time ago, but I didn't know how far away it was or if I was misreading something."

Ophelia looked up from a tall frosty glass. "Huh?"

Adam released Ana's hand, and she held it up. "We're engaged. Sorta."

Holden scrunched his face. "Sorta?"

Adam spoke up. "Dad sort of demanded it. And you know what it's like trying to say no to him."

Ophelia's brow crinkled. "So, you don't want to be engaged?"

"Well, it's not that." Ana's cheeks turned fire engine red. "We really, um, like each other, and we want to date. But the engagement thing is more of a maybe one day."

Holden's smile slid from his face, and he gave Adam a serious look. "And you think that will work?"

"Not forever. But it buys us some time."

An awkward silence hung in the air.

Ana broke it. "Besides, how cool is this bling?"

After everyone had left the hovercar, Holden pulled Ana aside. He handed her a small bag from one of the gift shops. "This is for you."

"What's this for?" she asked.

"Consider it a birthday gift."

She opened the package and found the exact same pair of red sunglasses she had tried on at the kiosk. The ones Ophelia had said were contraband. "What? How did you?" She laughed. "Your visions must really be getting stronger."

"Do you like them?"

"Of course. They're awesome."

Adam nudged him. "Hey, where's my gift?"

A smile tugged at Holden's lips. "What? Ana isn't enough."

Adam looked flustered.

"I'm not sure why, but it's important that you have these. Keep them with you."

She shrugged. "But they're contraband."

"Nobody will search your bags. Just don't wear them in the hallways. Off campus should be fine."

She tucked the sunglass case into her messenger bag. "Thank you."

6
GREEN, GOLD, & OUTGUNNED

The last days at Rockwell Manor were better than the first. Ophelia and Holden decided to stay until the beginning of the school term, and Ana was delighted to have a roommate. She had been uneasy sleeping in her room alone since she found the note.

That morning, at breakfast, General Rockwell commented on Ana's ring, which he called "a tremendous thing of celebration" and "the merging of two great dynasties." Although he did add, "I've never seen a ring like that, a bit cheap looking," but he quickly redirected. "Ah, the stone is hardly of importance. Well done, son. Many congratulations."

Holden shifted in his seat, looking uncomfortable. Ophelia managed a small smile.

When General Rockwell wrapped up his speech, he drained his cup of coffee, and with a knowing look at Ana, he announced he was leaving for the capital. Ana hoped it was to fulfill his end of their agreement.

"Important business," he boomed. "I'll just leave you kids here to celebrate. We'll formalize the rest later."

Ana winced. She wasn't sure she liked the sound of that. What more did she have to do?

If Adam had noticed anything amiss, he didn't say so.

THAT EVENING, Ana and Ophelia were getting ready for bed. Ophelia pulled back the duvet. Ana ran a quick hand under the pillows, checking for any notes. To cover, she lifted the pillow into her arms and began fluffing it.

"Is everything okay?" Ophelia asked.

"What do you mean?"

"It's just—you've fluffed that pillow already."

Ana bit her lip. Should she tell Ophelia? What if she sounded crazy? Then again, she had physical proof. Why should she sound crazy? "Okay. On my first night here, I found a note."

Ophelia stopped. "What kind of a note?"

"One from someone who is supposed to be dead," Ana said in a rush of air. "I'll show you."

Ana hurried over to the spot where she had hidden the note. Just inside her duffel. She ran her hand around the inside pocket, but it was empty. All she felt was slick nylon. Frantically, she dumped her clothes onto the floor.

"Is something wrong?" Ophelia asked.

"The note. It's gone. It was right here."

"Are you sure you didn't put it somewhere else? Maybe, in your dresser or something?"

"No!" Ana said too loudly. "It was here. You believe me, right?" She was being defensive. She knew it. In foster care, there had been many times Ana had been blamed for things she didn't do. Times she had been accused of lying.

Ophelia put a hand on her shoulder and her eyes widened innocently. "Of course, I believe you."

Ana nodded. What had gotten into her? Of course, she could trust Ophelia. She had been one of her first friends in Bellaton. She had agreed to fight by her side in the dome. She had even watched Petrie after the challenge.

"What did it say?"

The words were carved into Ana's brain. She recited them for Ophelia. "Anabella, you didn't think I was really gone, did you? Yours forever, M.B."

Ophelia sucked in a breath. "That's freaky. Do you really think it was from her?"

"I don't know. The handwriting looked like hers, but I guess there is some way to copy that here, right?"

Ophelia nodded. "Have you told Adam yet?"

Ana grimaced. She should have told Adam, shouldn't she? They were dating. Engaged even, if you asked General Rockwell. "Not yet," she admitted.

Ophelia cocked her head to the side and frowned.

Ana hurried to explain. "We had kind of a rough start once we got here." She told Ophelia about the maid.

"Mmm, things must be difficult for him."

"For him?"

"The General obviously expects things, and so do you. It will be difficult to make you both happy."

Ana fell into silent thought. She had never thought of it like that. It would be almost impossible. What was she asking of him? She'd wanted him to stand up to his father, but maybe it was more than that, really.

They climbed under the covers, and Ana turned off the lights.

Ophelia whispered in the darkness, "You don't really think she's alive, do you?"

"I honestly don't know."

"Why would General Rockwell lie? Didn't he say he saw her dead?"

Why indeed? Ana wondered.

THE NEXT DAY, they boarded the Rockwell jet to return to school. Ana was relieved to put Rockwell Manor in her rearview mirror and anxious to be reunited with her other friends, especially Samuel.

As they soared through the air, Ophelia had fallen asleep, and Holden had joined the pilot in the cockpit. Adam was reading on his infotab with one arm draped lazily around her shoulders. She got out her infotab too.

As she opened it, her application faded, and the screen went white. How strange. Words began to appear. She wasn't in the message application. She tried to exit but couldn't. It was as if someone had taken control of the screen.

Dearest Anabella,

My heartiest congratulations on your engagement. Here's a small token of my affection and esteem.

A photo appeared on the screen. It was of her and Adam in the dome. He was cradled in her lap. Her eyes widened. What was this? She tried tapping the screen again.

Then, another photo appeared and replaced the first.

It was from the night of the Winter Ball. She was in the revealing lilac dress that hugged the curves of her body, and she was pressed into a tall guy with dark hair. Her arms were wrapped around his neck, and they were kissing.

Ana gasped.

Beside her, Adam didn't look up from his book.

She tapped the screen frantically, willing the photo to disappear. Her heart was pounding in her chest. What if someone saw it? What if Adam saw it?

A new message appeared.

Which boy was it you wanted again?
M.B.

Ana's face turned pale. How could someone have this picture?

What if Adam saw it? What if they sent him a copy too? Should she tell him about the kiss? It was so embarrassing. And it really meant nothing. After all, Samuel had turned her down cold. She and Adam were together now. Well, sorta.

IT WAS midday when they arrived. They walked down the long corridor, and Holden turned into the austere Rockwell dormitory, marked by gray block walls and weaponry. Then, they dropped Ophelia off at her dorm, which was surrounded by trailing vines. Ana had Adam walked until the walls turned to sandstone with shells poking out. They reached her door, and Ana leaned in to kiss Adam goodbye.

He gently pushed her against the wall, deepening the kiss. When he pulled back, she was breathing hard.

"Are you sure you want to leave?"

He laughed, and she could feel it against her chest. "We have to get ready for the parade," he said, trailing kisses on her collarbone.

She closed her eyes for a minute, but then she felt Petrie down by her legs, clawing at her pant leg. She opened her eyes.

Behind Adam's shoulder, a Rockwell guard approached. "Um, Adam," she muttered.

"Yeah?"

She cocked her head toward the rogue guard. Adam pulled back from her and whipped around.

For the first time in her life, she saw Adam's cheeks tinge ever so slightly red. He straightened himself and said, "Guardsman, explain yourself."

The guardsman swallowed, looking embarrassed himself. "Sir, I have been assigned to sentry duty."

"At this door?" Adam asked.

"Yes, sir. My orders are to keep the Lady Halt safe at all times and to make sure no one passes through this door without authorization."

Adam's mouth grew tight at the corners, and he looked at Ana questioningly. "What do you want to do?"

"Can't you just send him away?" She turned to the guard. "No offense. It's just that I've been burned before."

He didn't move or reply. He just stood like a statue.

"It'll be easier to just let him stand here," Adam whispered.

"He won't come in, will he?"

"Not if he wants to live," Adam said, loud enough for the guard to hear, shooting him a deadly glare.

"Soldier, you are to stay outside of this room at all times. You are not to step foot inside unless you are clearly called for by Lady Halt herself. Do you understand me?"

The soldier looked uncomfortable. "Sir, I have been instructed to guard this door and escort Lady Halt on any excursions off campus."

He turned to Ana. "Can you live with that?"

She frowned. "For now, I guess."

He gave her a chaste peck on the forehead. "See you at the parade."

. . .

ANA SHUT the door behind her, leaving the guard in the hallway. She secured the deadbolt, although she knew the lock had very little application here. The real lock was DNA-based.

She felt relieved to be in her own dorm. She had lived here longer than her apartment. And while Hugh's house, the one she had grown up in, was wonderful, she felt too old for it now. Too grownup. Like sleeping in your room from when you were five with frills and princesses.

She inhaled the familiar scent of her dormitory. Petrie slunk past her to explore.

Looking around the room, Ana was filled with a familiar wash of memories. When Ana had last left her dormitory, there had been dirty dishes in the kitchen sink, clothes strewn on her bedroom floor, and more. No more. The dormitory was totally sterile. Everything was in perfect condition. Too perfect.

The drawers were neatly shut. Her clothing was crisply folded. The closet doors were shut. Her bed was made. There was no dust. The curtains smelled freshly laundered. If only they had put this sort of effort into her first arrival. She snorted.

She checked for her anti-listening devices, the ones Shay had provided her last year. They were missing. They had swept her entire dormitory. Her hope sank like an anchor in the sea. She had hoped when she returned to school that her questions would be answered. She had planned to search Madame Bali's room and find the answers she needed. But as she looked around at the perfectly neat room, she knew the chances grew lighter and lighter until, like a feather, they blew away.

How could she have been so stupid? Why hadn't she realized General Rockwell and the other council members would have turned this place over? They had no respect for her privacy or possessions. Not if it interfered with their goals.

Holden had told her there had been an investigation, that he himself had been interviewed. And somehow, it hadn't occurred to Ana that they would search this dorm, and the evidence would be gone. She thought of the paper left under her pillow. M.B.

Would she ever find out who sent it?

SHE WALKED BACK to her bed and flopped down. She sunk into her mattress. It felt so good to be back. She wondered briefly when this place had started to feel like home. When she had arrived last year, she had been backed into a corner with no other options. But now, she was glad to be here. Glad to be back in her own bed. Even a little glad to be back in Bellaton. And soon, she would be reunited with her friends.

Ana's rest was short-lived. From somewhere in the room, her infotab blared loudly. It took Ana a few minutes to locate it at the bottom of her duffel bag. She had a video call from an unknown number. Her heart skipped a beat. What if it was from Madame Bali?

She sucked in a breath and pressed accept.

Ms. Kandinsky's harsh voice barked from the speakers, and her silhouette formed above the screen in 3D. "Dollface! Good to see you. You had an old woman worried."

"Ms. K?" Ana said

"Who did you think it would be? The Easter Bunny?"

Ana rolled her eyes. "It's good to see you too. Are my brothers okay?"

"You worry too much. Then again, hundreds of people want to kill you."

Ana frowned.

Ms. K barked out a laugh. "Lighten up, kid; it's dark humor." She waved her hand. "I'm calling you about the welcome parade. Zora and Michael will be there any minute. I've vetted them. They're solid as a rock. Don't worry your pretty little head."

"Didn't you vet Madame Bali, too?"

"Way to sock an old woman in the gut. I tried, kid. The real

Madame Bali was a longtime supporter of your family. Rock solid. Her fakes were good. Really good. I'd wager she had powerful help. Now, I can't stand around and yap all day."

"See you."

"Maybe sooner than you think."

The screen went black.

FIFTEEN MINUTES LATER, there was a knock at the door. Ana got up to open it and found Zora and Michael standing just beyond the doorway. She also saw the now familiar face of the guard, staring at this crowd of unwelcome visitors with suspicion.

"Lady," he said, "I caught these interlopers in the hall. They say they're here to see you, but judging by the state of them—"

Ana held up a hand. "No, no, they're here for me. Please let them in." She glared at him as he was now standing between her guests and the doorway.

Reluctantly, he stepped to the side, allowing Zora and Michael to enter.

"Ana," a familiar voice said in its soothing cadence, "it is good to see you."

"You too," Ana said, giving Zora a hug.

"I am glad you feel that way. I was concerned after Bali... that you might believe I..."

Ana cut her off. "No, Zora. I trust you. With Bali, there were signs. I just didn't look for them. I regret that.

"No regrets today. Only dresses. Beautiful dresses."

As if on cue, Michael stepped past them with a rolling luggage rack. This year's model was more compact; however, once he got inside, he pressed a button. The luggage rack expanded to three times its current size.

"Wait until you see what we have planned this year," Zora said, excitement spreading across her face.

Michael nodded. "Yes, this year's plan is far more established. We didn't have the time or the resources last year as we didn't know about your impending arrival. However, this year we've been able to coordinate with emissaries from the island, local people as well. I think you'll find it all very satisfactory."

Zora laid the infotab on the table, and a hologram formed above. There were graybeasts. Not just one. A small herd in formation. A tiny version of Ana sat atop the largest one in the center. An ornate saddle had been placed on its back. More than just the cloth she had sat on the year before.

Then, there were men and women in colorful clothing. Large tropical birds of paradise perched on leather straps on their arms. A cart made of shells and brilliant tropical flowers strung into lines. It was all beautiful—bright, tropical, and filled with abundant life.

"Wow!" Ana gasped. "You pulled all of this together?"

Zora and Michael nodded, exchanging pleased looks.

"Last year, we were in hiding," Zora said. "This year, you are a queen."

Ana tried to return the smile. She didn't feel like a queen, even now. Then again, perhaps queens were always being spied on, arrange into marriages, and nearly killed. "It looks amazing," she said out loud.

"Wait until you see the dress," said Michael with a grin.

Despite her worries, Ana felt herself grin. Michael's enthusiasm was contagious. She followed him over to a corner of the room and began to sift through the gowns hanging there.

A knock came at the door. Ana opened it, and the guardsman handed her a large box with a satin bow. "This arrived for you, lady."

Ana did not accept it. "Who sent it?" she asked. She was suspicious of gifts after what had happened last year. She had received a tracker bracelet and poisoned chocolates. Now, she was doubly paranoid. What if it was another note from M.B.?

"It's from the General," the guard said.

Ana accepted the package, thanked the guardsman, and closed the door. Zora and Michael gathered to see what had arrived. Ana carefully untied the bow and opened the box. She moved a thin piece of tissue paper to the side and unveiled a dark green dress with golden cordage. At first glance, it looked more military than ballgown.

A SMALL CARD rested on top of the garment in an ivory envelope. Ana picked it up and read it silently to herself.

Don't forget our bargain.

Loyally Yours,
General Rockwell

SHE STRUGGLED to maintain a neutral facial expression. She didn't want her guests to know the true nature of her relationship with General Rockwell. For their own safety.

She sighed and pulled the dress from the box. It was rigid, boring, and drab. Everything a good Rockwell wife would be. The kind of thing the type of daughter-in-law General Rockwell had requested would wear to the proceeding.

Michael grimaced.

"Well," she said, "Not exactly cheerful, is it?"

Michael scratched his chin. "No, I certainly wouldn't say cheerful."

"Ana, do you wish to wear this?" Zora asked. "Michael and I had something very different in mind, but we will follow your lead. We had hoped this year to make up for your hastily executed entrance last year. With great difficulty, we've been able to assemble more people from the island, several unique birds, and three graybeasts. However, if this is something you want to do…" she trailed off.

Until Samuel was safely returned, Ana couldn't in good conscience ignore General Rockwell's request. No matter how much she wanted to. It was just a dress, after all. But first, she had to break the news to Zora and Michael that all of their beautiful plans would never happen.

Ana pulled herself upward and said, "Yes, I'll wear the dress. It's just a dress. And if it means that much to General Rockwell, I will wear it. After all, Adam and I are engaged."

Zora's mouth dropped open. "You're what?"

"Engaged," Ana said, holding up her hand to show the ring.

After a moment of immense struggle, Michael composed himself into the portrait of celebration. "Congratulations, Ana! I am so pleased for you. Adam seems like a remarkable young man."

Zora squinted her eyes, studying Ana with care. "If this is what you want—"

"It is," Ana said firmly.

IT WAS a beautiful day for a parade. The summer sun was shining overhead, and the ocean breeze blew gently across Ana's face. She and her team weaved in and out of the parade participants, searching for their spot in the lineup.

The cobblestone streets were already crowded with spectators. The locals were dressed in their brightest and finest clothing. Their smiles and laughter were infectious, and Ana found herself wanting to join them.

She imagined what today would be like if she weren't the last heir to the Halt family council seat, if she were just an ordinary girl in the crowd. She imagined meeting her friends and milling around the carts and shops.

Adam would probably buy her a flower from the crowded flower shop. She could imagine him pinning it to her dress. His warm hand sliding gently against her collarbone as he secured it into place. Ophelia would laugh and tuck tiny roses into her blonde braids, creating a circlet like a crown. Baylan, who had finally graduated after the challenge, would probably take the day off work to meet them. He, Holden, and Ja would definitely be at the food carts.

Ana and her team were squeezing through neat lines of Rockwells, already in formation and ready for the parade to begin. Ana brushed against one of her guards. General Rockwell had assigned two for the parade.

"Excuse me, lady," he said.

Her mind jerked back to the present, and she offered the guard a smile. "Sorry. I wasn't paying attention."

Ana looked back up and gasped. Zora and Michael hadn't been kidding. This year, far more than empty cobblestones awaited her. There were a dozen men and women with thick leather straps on their arms. Large colorful birds perched on their shoulders. An adult graybeast stood in the center with a saddle and blankets on its back. The blankets were stitched with glimmering shells. Behind him were two adolescent graybeasts. Ana could tell because they were still a very faint lilac down, not yet gray. Their handler, a young woman, was scratching the smallest one's chest. It shivered and purred.

Ana beamed at Zora and Michael. Who cared if she had to wear a boring green dress when she would sit amongst so much beauty and color? Maybe today wouldn't be so bad, after all.

Ana allowed herself to be lifted onto the back of the graybeast with no complaint. She wasn't afraid this year. She stroked its long trunk and listened to its otherworldly purr. From atop the graybeast, she looked down at the Rockwell soldiers. A familiar boy with dark hair and handsome green eyes stood in the back row. He waved. She returned his wave and blew a kiss.

He smiled.

As the procession moved forward, Ana had to admit she was thankful not to be behind the Nobles this year. While their performance had been strange and entertaining, it had also been loud and unnerving. She certainly wouldn't miss the mechanical spiders. She wasn't looking for any surprises today.

She moved along at a pleasant clip. People on the sides of the road waved and called to her. This year, no one hurled fruit or insults. The people seemed to actually want her here. Her remaining tension evaporated.

Finally, she reached the center square. Just like last time, her graybeast stopped in the center. She waved down at the people below and tossed vibrant flower petals down. Along her left and right flanks, the handlers released their birds into the air. The birds rose into the air in a rainbow of color, circling and performing spectacular feats of aeronautics. Even Ana, unable to help herself, stared up at the sky in delight.

Kids in the crowd pushed forward to get a better view. Adults moved to allow them to pass through. People pointed up at the birds, and their eyes sparkled in delight.

There was a stir in the crowd as a man pushed his way to the front. A woman screamed as she was knocked sideways. There were other shouts of indignation. Ana's eyes locked on the man as he made it to the front row and raised a silvery weapon. He pointed it directly at her.

Her breath caught in her throat. But then, one of her guards grabbed her saddle strap, and she was jerked down from the graybeast. She fell nearly fifteen feet and collided hard with the cobblestone street. The breath was knocked out of her, and she gasped in a desperate breath.

Meanwhile, through the legs of the graybeast, she could see Rockwell soldiers swarm the crowd. They slammed the shooter to the ground. At first, Ana was relieved. Then, they dragged him back to his feet, pointed his own gun at his head, and pulled the trigger.

At the sound of the gunshot, the crowd screamed, and chaos broke out as people looked for a shooter and ducked for cover. The man crumpled in a heap on the ground, blood pooling around him.

Crying children were pulled away from the terrible scene. The crowd began to disperse until there was a ten-foot perimeter around where the man lay.

Ana just stared. The man had seemed dangerous. Likely, he would have even killed her. But the way the problem had been solved didn't sit well with her. There would be no information from the man, no trial, no questions. Only a brutal and public execution.

"Are you alright?" the guard asked, looming over where she was curled on the ground. "Are you injured?"

Ana, who had been clutching her arm, let her hand drop. "No!" she said at once. "I'm fine." She wasn't sure that was true. Her left side had taken the brunt of the impact. She felt as if she had been pounded with a meat tenderizer. However, admitting it would be a death sentence.

During the challenge, Ana had healed Adam using petals from a Fleur laboratory. Then, she had lied to the council. She had claimed she had healed him with her family's gift.

If Ana had the gift, she could heal herself. If she couldn't, her lie would be revealed. Lying to the council was treason. The sentence was death.

So, she composed her face and looked up at the guard with a soft smile. "Thank you for pulling me out of the way. Can you please help me back onto the graybeast?"

And he did.

She tried not to wince as he touched her bruised side.

Soldiers were now forming a roadside blockade, standing

between the crowd and the street. One of the soldiers shouted, "Nobody leaves. Remain where you stand."

A woman with two young children attempted to slip backward toward the buildings and away from the street, but she didn't make it far. A soldier grabbed her shoulder and jerked her backward. As Ana looked over the frozen crowd, she saw many of their eyes were bright with fear.

The procession continued. Ana rode the rest of the way with clenched teeth and an aching pain in her arm and side. She smiled and waved like a marionette.

7
HOME

Ana sighed in relief as the strong, iron gates closed behind her. She was grateful to be ensconced in the lush, protective grounds of the academy. She moved a few paces forward to join Adam. He hurried toward her.

She tapped her feet gently on the graybeast's head. He obliged her and sunk into a kneeling position. Then, he lowered his head, and Ana slid down his strong trunk.

Adam reached out two hands to steady her on her landing, and one of them jostled her injured arm.

She bit her lip to stop herself from screaming out in pain.

"Are you okay? I heard you fell from the graybeast."

"I'm fine. Don't worry." It was a lie, of course. She wasn't okay. Not even a little bit. Someone had tried to kill her…again. She was frightened. She was in pain.

"You're bleeding," he said in a low voice, pointing to her arm. The cobblestones had left little indentures and minor cuts. "Are you having trouble healing?"

"Nothing to worry about. There are just so many people here."

He wrapped an arm around her shoulders. "I'm sure you'll be able to heal it once you're back in your dorm and everything is quiet."

She nodded.

He offered to walk her back to her room, but she insisted he stay and enjoy the celebration. It's what the General would expect. Besides, if he came with her, he might want to watch Ana heal her arm. Something she couldn't do.

Ana hoped that rest and a blast from a cryocanister would be all the help her body needed. She hoped there was nothing seriously wrong with it.

IN HER BATHROOM, she pulled off the hideous green dress and went to assess the damage. In the mirror, she could see her left side was bright red and swollen. There would be bruises tomorrow. She took a damp washcloth and blotted her arm, removing blood and dirt. She was lucky it wasn't worse. She was lucky nothing was broken.

She pulled on a silk top, jeans, and a lightweight cardigan. The dormitory air conditioning was pumping, and she was feeling a little chilly. Besides, she'd need to cover her arm until it healed.

When she returned to the living room, she spotted Samuel lying on the couch. At the sound of footsteps, he shot straight into a standing position.

For a moment, she forgot all of her problems. She let out an earsplitting squeal and launched herself at Samuel. She wrapped her arms around his neck, ignoring the pain in her arm and side. He returned her embrace, and she noted the feel of his body pressed to hers. No space between them. Like that night at the bar. She felt a tiny stab of guilt.

She stepped back and looked at him. Samuel had always been lanky, but now he looked stretched. His cheeks were a little too thin. Though a broad smile covered his face, his eyes had bags underneath them. But even more disturbing were his eyes themselves.

"Your eyes!" she gasped. "What happened to your eyes?"

"Well, hello to you too."

"Hi," she murmured.

Ana had long thought of Samuel by his trademark eyes that looked like those of a cat. Amber that reflected in the darkness. Eyes he had modded so he could read late at night. So very Samuel. These eyes were brown and unfamiliar.

What had they done to him?

Samuel tried to look nonchalant, but he didn't manage it. His hands balled into fists at his sides, and his knuckles turned white. "My parents decided to change them back," he gritted out.

"Without asking you?" Ana asked.

"I don't think they cared much about that," Samuel replied.

"How long were you in that horrible park?" Ana asked.

His eyes narrowed with suspicion. "How did you know it was a park?"

Ana shut her mouth. The last thing she wanted to do was tell Samuel *how* she had gotten him out of prison. He wasn't going to be happy about it, and the longer she could put it off, the better. She also realized she didn't want Samuel to know about her engagement. She wondered why she felt that way.

She changed the subject. "Why didn't you just give them what they wanted? What did they want?"

"My pledge of loyalty." He paused. "And you."

Ana closed her mouth. "Oh. I'm sorry."

"Me too."

After a long pause, he said, "Let's forget about that for now. How was the parade?"

"I got shot at. Don't worry. I'm okay, and they murdered the suspect in cold blood on the street."

"Welcome to the Bellatonian Justice System."

Ana was beginning to get a very clear picture of this justice system, and it wasn't pretty. Samuel had been dragged from his home with no warning, no trial, nothing. He had been secretly imprisoned in a way that likely qualified as torture. He hadn't seen darkness in months. He couldn't mark time. He was alone. It was enough to drive most people mad. Then, they had altered his body without his consent.

Ana had the idea that this might be standard for political prisoners. When she had looked out the window, she noticed how unnaturally empty the streets were and she had seen other faces peeking out from windows. Frightened.

Madame Bali, by all appearances, had been summarily executed. No questions. No trial.

Now, the shooter, she felt little sympathy for him, but he too had been executed on the spot in front of a live audience, including children.

Bellaton had wealth, technology, and power, but it was brutal. Justice was the will of the Seven.

She shook her head to clear these dark thoughts. "Where are you staying?"

"Here. If it's okay with you?"

"I thought you couldn't stay here because of decorum." She made air quotes around the word "decorum."

"Screw decorum. Someone tried to kill you, and my own family arrested me. Decorum is out the window. We're doing things differently this school year."

"What's that supposed to mean?"

"You'll see."

"Cryptic, as always."

He shrugged.

"Fine. Keep your secrets." Not like she didn't have plenty of her own. "Let's turn this place over. If Madame Bali left something behind, I want to find it."

"I'll help, but I don't think you're going to find anything. When Madame Bali entered that dome, I don't think she had any plan of returning to this Academy."

Ana sighed. "I think you're right. But we have to look."

He nodded.

They started in Ana's room. Just in case new spy devices had been placed.

"What's with all these boxes?" Samuel asked, wading through the mountain of her new school clothes, still in their original packaging.

"New clothes," Ana said.

He opened a box and peeked inside. "I like them. Less floral."

"Thanks. You paid for them, after all. By the way, I've been wanting to ask you... how do you have so much money anyway?"

"Well, when I took the papers from my father, it's not all I took."

"You stole from your parents? No wonder they're so mad."

"Ana, you can't steal from crooks. I... reallocated it. Like in that Earth story. What was it called? Robin Hood?"

"You reallocated it to yourself?"

He shrugged. "That's about the size of it, yes."

"I don't think that's exactly the same as Robin Hood..."

"Eh, who cares. They had it coming."

They moved on to Madame Bali's room.

"It looks like this place has already been searched and cleaned."

"Maybe they missed something."

"Unlikely."

She hoped beyond hope that she might find some clue left

behind. Had Madame Bali expected to return to this dorm room, or had she always known that the dome would be her last stop? Did she know what she did there would be irreversible? That there would be no coming back?

Ana pulled the scarlet comforter onto the floor until it pooled into a giant heap. Then, one-handed, she began working on the fitted sheet beneath. She struggled until finally frustrated, she tugged with all of her might. Suddenly, the sheet came loose, and Ana soared backward.

Samuel caught her.

Together, they removed the rest of the sheets and pillows from the bed, shaking each thoroughly, just in case something might fall out. Ana tried to conceal the fact that she was babying her left arm by taking on a new task.

She lay on the floor on her stomach and swept a hand under the bedframe. Maybe something had fallen.

Samuel rifled through the closet.

Finally, Ana reached the bedside table. She ran her hand to the back of the top drawer. Nothing. Then, she checked the bottom drawer. She pulled the top one out in frustration, but it stuck halfway. In frustration, she jerked it. The drawer loosened, and the table toppled over with a loud crash.

On the floor, a few feet away, was the source of the jammed drawer—a porcelain hair barrette with a white blossom.

Ana ran her fingers over the smooth porcelain finish. Had this belonged to Madame Bali? Had she meant to hide it, or had it merely fallen between the drawers?

"I think this is a sign it's time to stop," Samuel said.

"Yeah but look." Ana held out the barrette.

He accepted the barrette and looked at it. "No hair left in it to DNA test. Still, we could try having Ms. K run it through the lab. She's back on Bellaton, you know."

A few minutes later, Ana was yawning again. They agreed

they were both too tired to go on. Exhausted, they went their separate ways.

Ana flopped down on her bed, the porcelain flower still in her hand. She ran her fingers over its cool surface before setting it down on the bedside table. Where had this hair clip come from? Had it belonged to Madame Bali? Had it meant something to her?

8
TERRA

After only a few minutes, Ana was asleep.

A small girl stepped into an elaborate garden. Her thick, dark hair was pinned back with a porcelain flower. Her hand was safely tucked into her father's. She was twelve and too old to clutch her father's hand or shrink like a violet every time she heard a sudden movement. But she clung to his hand all the same. The world was a dangerous place.

"Run along, Terra," he said, releasing her and giving her a little push forward. "Go explore the gardens. Mr. Gentry and I need to discuss a few things."

Mr. Gentry was the head of the household staff at the Fleur Estate. He was a short, dignified sort of man who looked as though he had never laughed in his life. He would be her father's boss.

She bit her lip and took a slow step forward. And then another. Each step was a battle. A step away from her father's towering bear-like protection. Of course, Mr. Rorre wasn't really towering at all. He was an average height, but he seemed so to Terra. He seemed larger than life.

Just like the memory of her mother. When Terra thought of her for too long, she thought not of the smiling woman who whistled when she came home from work. Instead, she thought of the night she died— the dirty alley, the surrounding men, and the blood.

Her heart hammered in her chest like a hummingbird's. She felt, at this moment, as if she would die. But there were no threats here. Only sprawling beautiful gardens, tall hedgerows, and a manor house just to her left.

She closed her eyes for a moment and calmed down. Yes, the gardens were quite beautiful. She cheered herself up. She and Father would be very happy here. They were far from the dark dangers of the city. They would start a new life here.

The sheet-drenching nightmares couldn't last forever. Could they?

Her thoughts flickered as she saw a woman in her fifties with deep auburn hair and fair, freckled skin shake hands with her father. They talked for a moment, and her father turned and pointed at Terra. He smiled with pride.

The woman left the head of household and Terra's father and walked straight toward Terra.

"Hello there," she said in a posh voice, moving to stand beside Terra. "You must be Terra. I've just met your father."

Terra shrunk a little as the woman talked. Meeting new people was difficult. She strained to give a polite answer. "Why yes. We're ever so grateful to come. Thank you for giving father a job."

"Of course," said the woman with a surprised smiled. "I'm sure he will do a wonderful job."

Terra nodded. "He's a very hard worker."

"I hear you're from the city."

Terra's eyes widened, and her heart picked up its pace once more. "Yes, ma'am."

She pointed to the porcelain flower in Terra's dark hair. "Do you have an interest in gardens too?"

"Oh yes," Terra said. She looked at the grounds. "You have the loveliest gardens I have ever seen."

The woman laughed, and a large smile spread across her face.

"Why, thank you. That's the finest compliment I could receive. I do it all for my husband, you know."

Terra's eyes widened. "Do you work in the garden, too?" She was shocked that such a glamorous, wealthy woman would work in the gardens and get her hands dirty.

"Of course. In fact," she pointed to the flower bed just to their left, "I planted those creeping tulips myself just last weekend."

"I wish I knew how to grow things." She stopped at the expression on the woman's face. "Why are you smiling? I don't like it when people laugh at me."

The woman turned to face her. "You remind me of my daughter. She has passed on now, but she loved flowers. She was about your age when she died."

Terra nodded solemnly. She had almost died minutes ago in the empty garden with the butterflies fluttering around her and the sun shining on her cheeks. The world was a dangerous place.

"I'm sorry," Terra muttered.

"As am I," said the woman. "But I'd be delighted to teach you as much as you'd like to know about gardening. I am a Fleur, after all. In fact," she said, lowering her voice and with a sparkle in her eye, "my mother had the gift."

Terra gasped. "Really? And you?"

"I'm afraid not. I've had to learn the old-fashioned way."

"Oh." Terra was disappointed. She'd always wanted to see the gift in person. How miraculous it must be to have such command over the natural world. More than even their most advanced science.

"But the study of botany can be almost as amazing. If you decide to join me, I'll be in the flower bed tomorrow at 9 a.m." She pointed toward the gate. "I think your father is almost finished up with Mr. Gentry. He'll be wanting to settle in, no doubt."

Terra nodded. "A room all to myself, he said."

"Indeed. Well, I hope to see you around the grounds. Good luck, my dear."

Terra gave her a rare smile and rushed over to rejoin her father, who was lifting their luggage.

ANA WOKE, feeling confused and tired. She had slept for eight hours. Yet, she felt as if she had never been asleep at all. Her dream had been incredibly vivid. She felt as if she had actually been the girl, Terra.

Even now, as she lay in bed staring up at her own ceiling, she found herself wondering what had happened to the fragile girl. Had she settled into her new home? Had she decided to meet the lady of the house to plant flowers?

Then, Ana's eyes fell on the porcelain flower on her bedside table. The same one that had been in the girl's hair. Had her subconscious concocted this wild dream all to try and explain this mystery?

9

BACK TO CLASS

As Ana brushed her teeth, she considered her two pressing problems. Her arm was scabbed from road rash and a little swollen. Unlike her bruised side, it was visible, which meant she would have to hide it. Her second problem was the unread message blinking on her infotab.

After a moment's hesitation, she opened it. It was as she had feared. Another note from M.B.

Dear Anabella,

You almost looked the part yesterday. I was, of course, watching. And what a terribly close call. It's a good thing that man wasn't the best marksman.

Thinking of you,
M.B.

. . .

ANA SET THE INFOTAB ASIDE. How was this possible? How was she getting through all the academy's protections? Had someone been in her bedroom while she was sleeping to manually upload it? The thought gave her the creeps.

Still, there was no time to dwell on it. Breakfast would only be served for another half an hour. She took a quick shower and let the cold water run over her arm, hoping it would reduce the swelling.

Then, she toweled dry and prepared herself to head down to the dining hall. It was a warm summer day, but Ana pulled on her lightweight cardigan anyway. It was a little unusual, but it would be fine. She'd just hurry in for a quick breakfast. No one would notice her.

Ana was wrong. As she entered the dining room, the loud hum of morning conversation fell to silence. Why were they all staring at her?

Then, it hit her. They had all watched the challenge. They had seen everything—her tears, her song, and all of her private moments with Adam. Color rose to her cheeks. How could she have not seen this coming? Of course, she had been too busy worrying about Adam and her teammates and stewing over Madame Bali's betrayal.

She considered leaving but decided against it. She'd have to face this eventually. Besides, it seemed unfair to make Adam do this alone. She scanned the room and found him at their usual table. There was only one empty chair left. To her surprise, the rest were filled by Rockwells.

Whispers and muffled conversation began to rise. Then, someone let out a loud cat call. She looked around for the perpetrator and saw it was coming from her table. Ivan Rockwell. No surprises there.

Adam and Holden waved her over, and she hurried to take the seat between them.

"Did they do that to you too?" she asked Adam.

He held his chin high, and if he was embarrassed, Ana couldn't tell. "It's no big deal."

He grabbed her left hand in his and placed it on the table. This attracted the attention of their new tablemates. Their round table sat eight. Ordinarily, it was Ana, Holden, Adam, and sometimes Ophelia. Today, every seat was taken, and Ophelia had returned to sit with her family.

By sitting with her, Adam and Holden had broken a long-held academy tradition. Families ate together at meals. Ana had no family. Yet, she had never been alone. She now realized that they had silently paid the price for this all year long. All of their friends and family had refused to eat with them. But they had never mentioned it. Not even once.

Her heart swelled with gratitude for the sacrifice they had made for her. She also found herself a little worried. What else had they given up for her?

She had to assume the table had only filled back up because of the engagement.

An athletic girl waved from across the table. "Hi, I'm Isadora. But you can call me Dizzy. I was in the challenge too."

"That's right. Didn't you break your arm? How is it healing?"

Dizzy smiled, seemingly pleased that Ana had remembered her. "It's completely better. Thanks for asking. Congrats on your engagement, by the way!"

Ana blushed. "Um, thank you." She still felt awkward about the whole thing. It was like her private life had been put on display for the entire school. She liked Adam, and he liked her. But the whole thing felt rushed and unfinished. She and Adam hadn't even been on a real date. They hadn't said, "I love you."

The engagement was to protect her and the people she cared

about. The promise she and Adam had made to each other was just a maybe, not a someday.

Dizzy didn't notice Ana's hesitation. "Can I see your ring?"

Ana held out her hand, and soon the whole table was peering over to look at it.

"Adam has good taste," Ja said.

For the first time since the dome, Ana forced herself to look at Ja. In many ways, he appeared the same—the same familiar dark skin and deep brown eyes. His discipline remained too—his marksmanship, his attention to detail, his steady, hard work—that was all still there. But something was missing. That spark he had when he was with Xan, when the two of them were goofing off.

Ana felt guilt run through her like a blade. It had been her adviser who had interfered with the game. Xan had been collateral damage. She wondered if Ja blamed her too.

But his smile was genuine.

Ivan ruined the moment. "Who cares about the ring? What happened in all that time you were alone together?"

Dizzy and the other girl at their table squawked indignantly.

"Shut up, Ivan," Adam muttered.

"I'm just saying, you gotta try out the merchandise before you make a purchase."

Adam's eyes turned to ice. "Leave."

"What? You've got to be kidding. Learn to take a joke."

"Learn to tell better jokes."

Ivan pulled his chair back from the table. "Whatever. I was leaving anyway. You know, you're a real buzzkill like this."

After he left, the table returned to normal conversation.

The Rockwell adviser, a curt no-nonsense woman with a gymnast's shoulders, stopped by to hand out class schedules. The other Rockwells all tore theirs open and began scanning them at once.

Dizzy groaned. "Not double math. Can't I take something

else?"

"You know it's your weakest subject," the adviser stated. "Rockwells never back down from a challenge."

To Ana's surprise, the Rockwell adviser handed Ana a schedule too. "I look forward to working with you more closely this year," she said.

Ana didn't have time to reply before the adviser had moved on to the next table.

Ana opened her schedule and quickly scanned its contents. It was as she expected, with one notable exception. Speech and Debate had been removed and replaced with Advanced Combat Strategy.

"What's Advanced Combat Strategy?" she wondered aloud.

Adam and Holden both looked up from their schedules and shared a worried expression.

"He didn't," Holden muttered under his breath.

Adam snatched the schedule out of her hands. He glanced at it with sharp eyes. "He did."

Holden groaned.

"What?" Ana insisted. "What is it? And how can it be a lab?"

"It's a combat course," Holden explained. "Usually, only Rockwells sign up for these advanced levels. It's a controlled environment but still a little dangerous."

"Look at the instructor," Adam growled. He held it forward, and they all peered at it.

The name read Commander B. Rockwell.

A little line creased Holden's forehead. "Not Bold."

"What's so bad about him?" Ana asked.

"Nothing. He's a great guy. But a risk-taker."

"Now, I wish we had trained on Earth, instead of watching so much television and eating all that junk food," Adam lamented.

"You guys have got to be overreacting."

"Maybe," Adam said.

10

COMBAT

The following day, Ana and the Rockwells made their way to Intergalactic Combat. Their class was held in a separate facility, just beyond the Rockwell training fields. The walk was long. They were nearly on the periphery of the academy grounds. Ana slowed her pace as the facility loomed in the distance. The training center was a large, black geodesic dome. Its triangular panels reflected in the sunlight.

"Is this it?" she asked. "It looks like the death star."

"The what?"

"Never mind."

"Each triangular panel serves as a photoelectric power source for the interior," Holden explained.

"It's not always blacked out like this," Ja added. "Most of the time it's clear."

They stepped inside with a faint popping sound of pressure. The room was empty, sterile even, with white slick floors and ceilings. There were no desks or chairs. Ana had to guess the room was as large as a football field.

Ana recognized a lot of familiar faces. Most of them were Rockwells. As she looked through the crowd, someone slammed into her back, sending her staggering forward. She righted herself in time to see a smug Delphi walking past her.

She glared at his retreating figure. What a jerk.

"I can't believe they let him in this class," Ja said, drawing her attention away.

Shay joined them. "Hey. Glad you guys are in here too."

"Of course we're in here. The question is what are you doing here?" Adam asked.

"Harsh. You afraid to have me as an opponent?"

"Hardly," Adam scoffed.

"What *are* you doing here?" Ana asked.

"You told me the challenge would be like an advertisement for my skills. Turns out you were right. Bold invited me personally. So, here I am. What are you doing here?"

"The General signed me up."

"That checks. Well, I think it'll be a good time. Let's show these meatheads what's up."

This time it was Holden's turn to be indignant. "Hey!"

Shay elbowed him. "Just kidding."

A few minutes later, Commander Bold Rockwell arrived. "Come in! Gather around," he shouted. He gave them a few more minutes and then locked the doors with a click. "Today, we will be assessing your personal combat scores. This will help me to best form groups based on strengths and weaknesses. I will be calling you one by one and connecting you to the neural net."

A few students looked nervous.

"Don't worry; I've already gotten permission from all of your guardians."

Ana grimaced. She remembered Adam's video game that used neural net. It had been a fun, albeit silly, game with monkey ninjas. But she remembered how the first time she played there had been actual physical pain when she was hit.

Adam had laughed and said the technology was used for Rockwell training. That had been a low setting.

"Usually, you'll go straight to the locker room to change into your uniforms, but today we don't have the time. I am passing around goggles." He held up a large metal bucket and passed it to the girl in front of him. "Please take a pair and put them on. The rest of the class will not be able to watch your assessment. We wouldn't want any of you improving your technique by copying those ahead of you. So, when I call your name, step through the barrier. Does everyone have a pair of goggles?"

Ana and the rest of the class nodded.

"Excellent. Secure them now. If you remove your goggles during the assessment or try to watch your classmates' assessments, you will be ranked bottom of the class. No exceptions. I hate cheaters."

Bold called them forward in alphabetical order. Out of thirty-two students, only five weren't Rockwells which put Ana near the top of the list. Thankfully, there was one Arkwright.

"Jem Arkwright," he called.

The boy stepped forward, and a veil appeared in the center of the room, almost as if it were a wall splitting the dome in half.

After several minutes, Jem returned looking a bit drunk. He staggered on shaky feet through the crowd of students to grab his school bag. Then, he made his way to the classroom door. He said nothing, and they asked nothing. Nobody wanted to be ranked last.

As expected, Ana was next.

"Good luck," Adam whispered.

She couldn't see the instructor but assumed he was beyond the veil. She pulled her goggles down, just a for a moment. The barrier shimmered like strings of computer code, flashing past at a rate her eyes could barely perceive. She felt if she stared for long, she might go cross-eyed. Instead, she secured her goggles and stepped through.

Commander Bold was waiting for her. "Anabella Halt?"

"Yes, sir."

"Welcome. I'd say you're a sheep amongst wolves, but I saw you in the challenge. With hard work, I think you'll be able to hold your own. Pay attention in this class. It might save your life one day."

He looked down at his infotab.

"Sir?" she asked. "I was wondering who signed my permission slip."

"That would be the General himself. Now, this assessment has only one objective. Collect the key."

She had no idea what that meant, but she nodded anyway. "Yes, sir."

"And remember, Ana, strategy means playing to your strengths, even if you have to change the game." He winked. "Good luck to you."

The room faded to darkness.

ANA WAS IN A DAMP, dark place. Above her, she heard the clang of a heavy footfall on thick metal. She smelled the strong scent of decay and mold. Where was she? Underground? She shifted slightly and felt something rough to the touch. Corroded metal.

Her eyes began to adjust to the lighting. She stepped forward cautiously. Her boot splashed in a small puddle of water.

She was standing in the underbelly of a city. Maybe a sewer or electrical area? Concrete and dirty metal surrounded her. A metal ladder led to what appeared to be a grate.

Where did it lead? Probably a city. Maybe a road?

It was a Rockwell test, so if she went up, she would probably have to fight whoever footsteps she had heard. A fight she was almost guaranteed to lose. At least down here, she was concealed. Perhaps she could walk down here until she reached the next opening.

However, hiding in this dank place wouldn't win her the key. She would have to go up eventually. She wandered down the city's utility corridor, searching for the next opening.

She heard the sounds of clicking metal in the darkness behind her and increased her pace. What was that?

She continued forward.

A woman with a metal arm waited in the darkness. Her arm glinted under the dim overhead lighting, dirty titanium with frayed wiring exposed at the inner elbow. A cybernetic red eye cut through the darkness as she turned to face Ana.

The Seven did not like mods. Ana bet this would be an especially disturbing sight for them. Not that Ana was thrilled about meeting anyone that hung out alone in the sewer. Other than the dank setting and dim light.

A table was set before the woman.

What was that stupid saying the Rockwells repeated? "Fortune favors the bold." She was meant to approach. No Rockwell would hide in the shadows.

Ana couldn't afford to go rogue...yet. She didn't know where she was or what she was looking for. Surely, it would be an actual metal key. And even if it were, how would she distinguish it from any other key.

"Want to play a game?" the woman asked. She waved her hand, and three cups appeared on the table.

Ana couldn't tell if it was an impressive sleight of hand, technology, or magic. She couldn't rule out any of the three in Bellaton. Ana had a feeling she knew exactly what was coming, but she asked, "What kind of game?" She wanted to buy time to study the table and the woman.

"It's simple, Lady Halt." She plucked a metal coin as if from the air itself. It shone with filtered binary light like the veil.

Ana suspected at once. "The key?"

The woman smiled and flicked her wrist. The key disappeared once more. "Yes. Will you play?"

"For the key?"

She chuckled, and it sounded like a static echo. "Not for the key itself but information."

Ana considered. "Maybe you're a distraction. I could find the key myself."

"Perhaps, but the city is large and unfriendly." She smiled, displaying a mixture of metal and ivory teeth that fascinated and frightened Ana.

"I suppose you want me to follow the cup. Pretty boring, don't you think?"

The woman raised an eyebrow.

"I mean, they've been doing that trick on Earth for decades. How about something different?"

"If you're so familiar, why not run the game yourself? If you win, I will tell you what you need to know. If you lose, well, the rats are awfully hungry. It's not often young flesh, so edible, enters our domain."

Ana heard the skittering once more and spotted hundreds of beady red eyes, staring from the dark corners of the room. She now knew what the sound had been. Tiny metal feet. Rats. Cybernetic rats. The kind that feasted on human flesh. It was a guess, of course. But one she didn't want to confirm.

"Are you sure I couldn't make you a nice meal instead? You know, I used to work in a diner. I could whip up some sandwiches or burgers. You name it."

The woman smiled again. "That is no good, little earth girl. For, I have no human stomach anymore." She pulled at the corner of her shirt and displayed her entire right side had been replaced with a metallic alloy. "However, I can always use a little spare iron. I've heard humans have quite a reliable source that can be extracted oh so easily… straight from the vein."

Ana suddenly felt a gnawing sense of worry. Perhaps she had been wrong not to be more afraid of this woman.

"Now, shall we play or not?"

Ana tried to hide her fear. "I'll play but on one condition."

"I'll bite." She smiled, and Ana saw the metal teeth once more and thought how strong they must be.

This was a game she could not afford to lose. "You have to cover your red eye. It hardly seems fair to play a human game with such an advantage. For all I know, you can see straight through the cups."

She shrugged and pulled a scrap of fabric from her shirt, fashioning a rough eye patch. "I can win with or without an additional advantage. Does this meet your specifications?"

"That's fine. But I'll need something to place under the cups."

The coin flickered back and forth between her metal fingers before she dropped it in Ana's open palm.

Ana had never expected it could be this easy. She smiled and closed her finger around the coin. "It looks like I win."

"But we haven't played yet."

"Ah, but I already achieved my objective. The key."

"Do you think it will be so simple to walk away from my table?" Her eye gleamed. "You will never leave this tunnel with that key. Return it now and lose honorably."

Ana reached forward as if she might acquiesce. Then, she knocked the metal table into the woman and started running. The woman pursued her. Ana was only now realizing the game wasn't ending. Maybe the key had to go in a door. She hadn't planned for that.

Peering through the darkness, she spotted a large metal wheel. It was the only option. She only hoped she was right. She ran toward it and into the shadows, where a pack of rats waited. Some scattered at her sudden, violent movement, but several managed to cling their sharp metal teeth into her legs and bootlaces. She cried out but didn't stop. She reached her hands, plunging them further into the darkness until she felt the enormous metal wheel. She turned it ever so slightly leftward, and to her relief, she heard water begin to overflow in the distance.

"Water corrodes iron," she said with a smirk.

The rats, hearing the water, loosed their teeth and retreated up the walls and back into the crevices.

Ana ran back toward the metal stairs. She needed to get into the city. Maybe, there she would find a door. The woman was closing in. Ana reached for the first rung of the metal ladder and tried to pull herself up. She wasn't strong enough, and her feet kicked at the dirty wall for leverage. With effort, she pulled herself upward until her feet reached the metal bar. The whoosh of water had reached her part of the tunnel.

But the cyborg was undeterred. She clutched at Ana's leg, trying to pull her back into the depths below. Water, now several feet deep, flooded past the cyborg. But her legs were strong enough to withstand the current. Ana wouldn't be so lucky.

With one wet kick from her boot, the cyborg's grasp slipped. Ana made it up another rung and through the sewer grate.

But to her surprise, there was no city above. Instead, the scene faded, and she was lying on the white floor, panting to catch her breath.

Bold stared at her, lying on the floor. Then, he started laughing. "No one has ever done that before."

"What do you mean?" she said, clutching her side and standing.

"Most Rockwells go straight up into the city. Those who encounter the woman usually try to kill her on sight. No one tries to bargain with her, especially not trick her."

"I mean, don't get me wrong. You got bitten a dozen times by metal teeth and risked drowning, so your score won't be the best, but what entertainment."

She scowled. "I got the key, didn't I?"

He straightened. "Yes, you did. Now, grab your things and head to your next class. No lingering and not a word about your assessment. You'll get your scores tomorrow."

"Yes, sir."

THE FOLLOWING DAY, the class gathered to receive their combat scores. Ana found a spot on the gymnasium floor next to Adam and sunk down beside him. They were so close that their knees touched, and she felt a little flutter rise up in her chest.

He smiled up at her. "Nervous?"

For a moment, she thought he was talking about their legs touching. Then, she blushed, realizing he meant the combat scores. "I just want to see how I did."

He nodded, looking tenser. "Me too. My dad will see these scores."

"I'm sure you have the best score in the class."

Ja sat down next to them. "Don't count on it."

Adam chuckled. "We'll see."

A few moments later, Shay and Holden had joined them too.

"How do you think you did?" Ana whispered to Shay. She was, after all, the only other outsider in their group.

She frowned. "Not as well as I wanted to. A sniper got me from a rooftop when I was going after some equipment. What about you?"

"I got the key, but it was a really close call. I'm sure they'll dock points for it."

Commander Bold Rockwell entered the room and took his spot at the front. He rubbed his hands together with anticipation. "Alright! We are going to start giving out combat scores. Your name will be projected. We'll see a few clips from your sim journey. Then, a score will be displayed. Afterward, you'll be sorted into your platoons."

The lights in the room dimmed, and a holographic projection the size of an entire wall formed in front of them. Bold stepped to the side to watch at an angle.

The image of the city street appeared before them, and Shay blinked into existence in the middle of the street. She whipped her head around, her dark hair falling in her eyes. She tucked a strand behind her ear and moved into the shadow of a nearby skyscraper.

Ana nodded approvingly. That seemed wise. It would reduce her visibility to any enemies. She slunk on that way for another block or two until she saw an abandoned drone. Her eyes caught on it, and she ran across the street toward it.

A sharpshooter caught her, and she fell.

The class let out a collective sigh of disappointment, and Bold paused the feed. "What did Shay do wrong?"

"She walked into a trap!" someone shouted.

There was a small amount of laughter.

"Hands please. And can anyone be more specific?"

A few hands went up. Bold nodded at Dizzy.

"She was so excited about the drone that she didn't stop to think before acting. She walked right into the open without looking for enemy combatants."

"Correct. A good soldier must always have awareness of his or her surroundings. Now, what did Shay do right?"

"She stuck to the shadows!"

"She took a moment to take in her surroundings."

They watched several more clips from other students' journeys. When they reached Adam's clip, it was like watching an action movie. Adam found a dropped weapon cache and hijacked a helicopter. The same one that had sent several other students running down alleys.

Ana was sure his score would be excellent.

Ana soon realized not everyone had faced the cyborg. Most of the students stayed above ground where different obstacles appeared, including a gunslinging super soldier and a drone strike. There were also numerous ways to collect a key.

One of the only other students to stay underground was the Arkwright. He had also opted to stay safely ensconced in the subterranean lair. However, he had identified a geological fault in the tunnels. He used this to crumble a section of the infrastructure, which took out the cyborg hag but also crushed his leg in the process.

As the clips continued, Ana realized she was indeed the only person who had talked to the cyborg. When her highlight reel began to play, most of the students crinkled their faces in confusion.

"What the hell is she doing talking to it?" Ivan asked.

"Is she trying to gamble with it?" another student said.

Bold paused the feed. "Now, what did Ana do wrong?"

Hands shot up all over the room.

Ana felt indignant.

"Yes, Ivan?"

"She went underground."

Bold nodded and pointed at another hand. Ana turned and heard Delphi sneer, "She was stupid enough to talk to a cyborg."

Ana gritted her teeth.

To her surprise, Adam's hand shot up.

Bold nodded at him.

"She lacked the proper advance knowledge to make the best tactical decision."

In his own way, Adam was trying to defend her.

"True. And what information was she lacking?"

Dizzy answered. "The subterranean portions of the city are crawling with cyborgs and dissidents. They're dark, damp, and dirty. Retreat is often difficult because you're enclosed."

Bold nodded. "Exactly. Now, what did she do right? Let's not forget she got the key."

"Sheer dumb luck," Ivan called out, laughing.

Ana glared at him. He didn't seem to care.

Shay raised her hand. "She was able to outsmart the cyborg and escape, using her intuition and the objects around her."

"Very good. Never underestimate your intuition. Also, it's our objective to always see you appropriately armed in defense situations, but challenges may arise. It's important to be aware of the assets around you. In this instance, water."

THE CLASS ENDED, and Adam looped his arm through hers with a smile playing at the corner of his lips. "You tricked a cyborg in a street game. Why am I not surprised?"

"I didn't realize she was so dangerous."

"Apparently. It was kind of an unfair disadvantage, actually. Every other student knew that cybers often live in the subterranean areas of the cities."

11

THE COUNCIL RETURNS

Bold Rockwell shouted, "Get dressed and report back for team assignments. Don't just stand there. Move, move, move!"

The other students began to jog toward the locker rooms. Ana followed the girl ahead of her and through a door with a pop. The room was small with a wall of sleek cube-shaped lockers. Each had a number glowing in red on the front.

Most of the Rockwells already knew their numbers. Ana had to consult a scrolling marquee to find hers—H32303. The lock was biometric. She held her hand in front of it, and it sprang open with a hiss of air. Inside was a formfitting jumpsuit. It was lightweight and didn't seem thick enough to protect her from any physical harm.

She waited until the locker room was clear before taking off her cardigan. The scrapes on her arm were still healing. She stripped and pulled the jumpsuit on. The fabric was extremely flexible but as strong as metal.

Ana hustled to catch back up with the rest of her classmates.

In the main room, Bold was pacing in front of the class.

"From now on, I want you in uniform by 8:15 and awaiting instruction."

Ana took the first available seat on the ground, not wanting to draw Bold's ire.

"Yes, sir," the students echoed in unison, except for Ana who came in a second too late.

"Excellent. Now then, for teams. When I call your name, join your teammates and wait quietly for instructions."

"Ana, Adam, Shay, Ja, Holden."

"Hey! No fair!" shouted someone from the crowd. "That team is stacked. They worked together in the challenge."

"Maybe so. Maybe no. Battle isn't always fair. You must adjust your strategy accordingly."

Bold finished calling out the teams. Then, he said, "Find a quiet spot and select a team lead. You have ten minutes."

There was a flurry of movement as everyone scrambled to find their groups. Ana saw Holden and Adam in the back of the classroom and hurried toward them. She couldn't be happier about her assignment.

When they had all gathered, Holden said, "It should be Adam. His scores are the highest."

Adam's chest puffed up, and his lips parted. But then, he clamped them shut again. After a pause, he said, "I appreciate it, but you did lead Shay and Ana in the challenge."

Shay rolled her eyes. "Adam, you want it, and it's being handed to you. Take it. And let's move on to the good stuff."

Ja snorted in laughter and clapped Shay on the back. "Good to be on your side, Noble."

Adam gave Holden one more glance before nodding and smiling. "Okay. I accept your nomination."

"Looks like we've got a few extra minutes," Holden said. "Should we do a quick SWOT analysis?"

"What's a SWOT?" Ana asked.

"Strengths, weaknesses, opportunities, and threats," Adam recited.

"I'm in," Ja said. "Start with threats?"

Adam nodded. "Okay. Shay lacks any physical combat training. She has zero technique which is a huge liability."

"What a sweet talker," Shay grumbled.

"You know we love you, girl, but you don't want to be the first to get blasted in every exercise, now do you? You're way too competitive for that. Same for you, Ana," Ja said.

Adam frowned.

Ja turned to him. "And there's your weak spot, brother."

Adam's cheeks turned red, and he clenched his jaw a little tighter.

"And *this* is why Bold put us together. We might be some of the best—" Holden looked like a plated fish in a restaurant, unmoving and eyes staring nowhere and everywhere.

"Holden?" Shay said, waving a hand in front of his face. "Comm to Holden. Do you read me?"

Holden blinked. "Uh, sorry. Adam, just make sure you watch her, especially if we're outdoors."

"What? I thought you just said it was a distraction," Shay protested.

Adam looked at him with concern. "Did you—"

Holden cut him off. "Just do it, okay?"

They didn't have much time to dwell on Holden's words or the rest of the team's SWOT analysis.

Bold was addressing the class again. "Today, we will be leaving the sim behind to work on your physical skill set. It's great to have strategy and timing, but it won't carry your rucksack. It won't outrun your enemy. Only physical training will do those things."

"You're all suited up. These suits, while lightweight, repel water and fire. They're also tough and durable. In the right conditions, they are impervious to ordinary blades. In short, they'll help keep you safe. Now, I want you to do your best out there. But injuries happen. I understand that. And so do your guardians. That's why they signed your forms. But any student caught intentionally injuring another will be removed from this class, given failing marks, and recommended for a disciplinary mark on his or her service record. Got it?"

"Yes, sir," the class replied.

"Good. For this first game, there will be no environmental obstacles. You will be armed only with a simple laser gun. When your team is called, pick one up from the buckets at the corner of the room. If you shoot someone, they will freeze. Last team standing wins."

When I call your team leader's name, step inside the red lines. The rest of you get to the bleachers and take some notes."

What bleachers? Ana thought.

Then, Bold tapped his watch, and bleachers began to slide out from the recesses of the wall, and lines appeared around the room. A red one traveled the entire length of the geodesic dome leaving only a walk path and the bleachers. Within that were a few more zones that had little meaning to her.

"Isadora Rockwell versus Helmer Rockwell."

Ana saw Dizzy stand with a scowl. From the look on her face, she didn't like being called by her given name. She had never met Helmer before. He was two years older with eyes like a wolf.

The first two teams stepped inside the red perimeter. Then, the environment began to transform. The plain gymnasium-style floor stretched and swelled, forming hills and physical obstacles. Then, to her surprise, the center of the room no longer looked like a part of their classroom at all. A warm, arid wind blew across her face. Sand was everywhere. The hills and obstacles were now dunes. The skyline was a light orange of filtered sand and sunlight.

"How did he do that?" she whispered.

"Do what?" Adam asked.

"The dunes. The air. Is any of it real?"

"Oh. The floor really moved. You saw that. And the hand-to-hand combat will be real. But the dunes themselves are an illusion. The suits have built-in tech like we used from the test simulation."

Ana could see it from the outside like she was looking through glass. This must have been how the spectators at the challenge felt. She shivered, realizing again just how on display all of her conversations and private moments had been.

Another tap on his watch, and bright strips of light ran down each team's uniforms to identify them. Dizzy's team was yellow, and Helmer's was electric green. The two leaders stepped forward to shake hands.

Then, they stepped apart, and a buzzer sounded.

Helmer wasted no time. Immediately, he struck forward and slammed his shoulder into Dizzy's chest. She stumbled, and Helmer reached to his side to draw his weapon.

Ana winced. Dizzy was going to be so embarrassed. To be taken out of the game in under a minute.

But Dizzy had other plans. She did not fall. Instead, she lunged, placing her foot behind Helmer's left leg. In one swift move, she hooked her arm around his knee, forcing his body weight to his right leg. Helmer grunted, struggled for balance, and toppled into the sand. Dizzy drew her gun and shot him.

It was then that Ana knew she was in real trouble.

Adam whispered to Shay and Ana, "Do you see how Dizzy used Helmer's weight against him?"

"Yeah, but I don't know how to do that!"

"I can show both of you, but for today, stay as far away from other opponents as possible. Run, camouflage, whatever you need to do."

The first game was over in five minutes. Ana wasn't prepared for this sort of fight. She had no combat training, and here she was in an advanced class. No wonder Holden and Adam had made such a fuss at the breakfast table.

Ana just hoped whoever took her down was as skilled as Dizzy. The only thing Helmer bruised was his pride.

"Next up! Quilla Rockwell versus Ivan Rockwell."

The former teams unfroze and moved back to the bleachers with a mix of regret and relief. The new teams entered. Their suits turning neon pink and purple respectively.

The next match started. One of the players had claimed the top of the dune and was picking off anyone who tried to come up.

Ana thought this looked like a viable strategy, and she nudged Shay who nodded.

Then, at the base of the dune, a lean boy slipped out of a headlock. He tried to run up the dune, slipped, and fell. He slammed face first into the sand, then rolled several feet down the dune. He didn't pick himself up.

Ana grimaced.

Bold's voice fell over the classroom. "Freeze."

All of the players stood still.

The boy stirred and, clutching his jaw, managed to stand. There was blood in his teeth and dripping down his lip. Tears streaked down his face. He was too panicked to be embarrassed or to try to turn away from the crowd.

Bold trekked across the sandy dunes to get a good look at the boy's face and mouth. "Rowan," he called to another boy standing nearby. "Get him down to the nurse's office."

"Yes sir!" Rowan shouted. He pulled the crying boy's arm around his shoulder and half-carried him away.

Ana was positively vibrating with anxiety now. "You said a lot of people get hurt in this class?"

"Just stick close to me. You made it through the challenge, this is nothing," Adam assured her.

But this wasn't anything like the challenge. It was fast paced.

The space was limited. Enemies were everywhere. Games were quick and nobody held punches.

There was also the little matter of Ana's injured arm. Even if she knew how to do Dizzy's move, she might break her arm in the effort.

Then, Bold called the next team with a glint of amusement in his eye. "Adam Rockwell versus Delphi DuBois."

Ana stood. Her pulse pounded in her ears. Of all the teams, did it have to be Delphi? He definitely wouldn't let her off easy if he caught her.

Adam cracked his knuckles and gave a very slight smile. "Good."

Holden put a steadying arm on her shoulder and pushed her forward. "You can do this."

Ana and the rest of the team moved into the outer perimeter while Adam moved forward to shake Delphi's hand.

Their hands clasped, and it looked more like an arm wrestling match than a handshake.

Ana saw Delphi whisper something, but she couldn't make out the words. Adam looked as if he was trying to crush all the bones in Delphi's hand.

Adam released his hand and stepped back, looking murderous. Delphi sneered in return.

The buzzer sounded.

Ana expected Delphi to go straight for Adam, but instead, he bolted backward. Two others closed in on Adam. He shot the first, but the second caught him by surprise, freezing him instantly.

Ana forced herself to look away. She needed to stay focused. She needed to find a spot to run or hide. Should she try for the top of the dune?

There was no time. Delphi was moving in on her. She ran in the only direction available, sending wild shots behind her and hoping for luck. She had none.

And now she was out of room. She'd reached the perimeter. The only way out was to rush out and catch him by surprise.

Why wasn't he shooting her? She had nowhere to go.

He was an arm's length away now. He lifted his gun and knocked hers out of her hands before she could pull the trigger.

"Winner of the challenge," he said in a mocking tone.

Ana tried to kick him in the shin.

He caught her leg in mid-air, and she fell back against the sand. Bright pain flashed. Just as Delphi was about to shoot her, the simulation froze. Bold Rockwell called out Ana's name. "Ms. Halt, you have a visitor."

Breathing hard, Delphi stared at her as if considering whether he should just kick her in the face now. But there were too many eyes on them. Reluctantly, he remained still.

He did not, however, move back to give her space. In order to get past him, she was forced to brush his body.

"Next time," he whispered.

She shivered and hurried out of the game area. As she crossed the red line, the match resumed.

The woman standing beside Commander Bold Rockwell was immaculate with gray hair and rubies that dripped from her ears like droplets of blood. Ana recognized her as Lady Jacobs from her visit to the capital, Samuel's grandmother.

"I was wondering, my dear, if you might take a stroll with me."

Ana's eyes widened in surprise, but she recovered quickly. "It would be my pleasure."

While Ana was wary of everyone on the council, Lady Jacobs had been an advocate during the Winter Ball. She had suggested they give Ana time to demonstrate her powers. Which Ana had done, at least for those who hadn't watched the video in freeze-frame over and over. She hoped Lady Jacobs was not as meticulous as General Rockwell.

About halfway down the corridor, Ana blurted out, "What

are you doing here? I mean, it's a pleasure to see you, of course, I'm just surprised to see you so far from the capital."

"You weren't expecting us? Why, we've talked with all of your teammates, the opposing team, and the students on the environmental planning committee. The only one we haven't spoken to is you. We thought you'd prefer to talk to us here rather than journey all the way to the capital."

"Is the entire council here?"

Lady Jacobs started down the marble staircase. "Oh, no, no, no. Only DuBois and I are here in the flesh. The council was adamant that a representative be present. I offered to take on the task. I thought, perhaps, I might also visit my grandson."

Ana was suddenly filled with anxiety for Samuel. He had only just been released from prison, a place where his family had put him. Was his grandmother here to return him? Thinking of it, she squared her shoulders and clenched her jaw. "What do you want with him?"

"I was hoping to see him and patch things up."

"If you cared so much about his welfare, why didn't you get him out of prison? You're the head of your family, aren't you? Don't they listen to you?"

"Oh, I gave up trying to control my children long ago. Samuel is their son, and these are their mistakes to make."

"It's not like they let him eat too much candy. They held him in solitary confinement for months and removed his eye mod."

"I wasn't aware of the eye mod." She frowned. "Well, that's certainly no way to win him back."

A low growl escaped Ana's lips before she could stop herself. "He will never come back to you."

"My, it seems you have grown quite attached to him."

Ana waited for the fallout.

Instead, a soft smile graced Lady Jacobs's face, and she let out a small chuckle. "I'm actually very pleased. You see, Ana, it's difficult for people of our standing to find true devotion, especially outside of the family. And, while my relationship with my grandson could certainly be better, I do admire him. He's brilliant, although rash. If he were to apply himself, I believe he could one day claim the family council seat."

Before Ana could properly react, they had reached their destination—a room just down from the Headmistress's office. Lady Jacobs opened the door. Inside, the council was already waiting at a large board room table. There were five of them plus a woman Ana didn't recognize. Only Ana, Lady Jacobs, and Councilman DuBois were physically present. The rest of the council were attending virtually in holographic form.

She looked down the line of them. DuBois sparkled with his usual charisma, rushing forward to incline his head and greet her. Despite his act of welcome, Ana suspected he really wanted to be here in person, so he could use his gift. She had a feeling it wouldn't work if he were virtually present.

Behind him, she saw Sir Arkwright and Lady Fleur sitting next to one another at the long table. Ana was grateful Arkwright was attending virtually. The last time she had seen him, he had attempted to cut her with his knife in order to test her healing abilities. Beside him, Lady Fleur looked impatient. Today, she wore an emerald dress and a circlet of white blossoms atop her golden hair. She would have looked beautiful if it weren't for her malicious eyes.

In the next seat, there was the unfamiliar woman—mousy in appearance and tight-lipped. And finally, at the very end of the table, Sir Noble. His holographic projection was so good, she could almost swear he was really here. He looked jumpy.

Lady Jacobs moved to take a seat beside him.

Ana noticed there was one notable absence—General Rockwell. Why wasn't he here? While she'd usually prefer to avoid him, this seemed like a time where his presence could be helpful. Last time, he'd been the one to stop Arkwright from using his knife.

She shifted on her feet uncomfortably. DuBois closed the door behind her, and she was alone with the council— two in the flesh and three digitally. She didn't like her odds, five to one. But, at least this time, she didn't have an assassin spy standing behind her pretending to be her supporter.

Councilman DuBois joined the rest of the council at the table. "We've been waiting to talk to you for two months. You've been...difficult to locate."

The rest of the council gave signs of agreement.

"I'm sorry for the inconvenience. How can I help you?"

"We've come to talk to you about the challenge. Just as a formality, of course," DuBois added.

"Of course," she echoed.

"As you know, we've talked to all the rest of your teammates, and you're the only one outstanding."

"Well, I'd be happy to answer any questions. Although, I think you know more than I do at this point. For instance, I know Madame Bali posed as my adviser and tried to kill me in the dome, but I don't know who hired her, how she died, or even who she really was. Maybe you could enlighten me about those things."

"Of course. Of course. All in good time. But first, let's start at the beginning. We'll need to gather the preliminary details. We've brought along a third-party arbiter to aid us in this process." He gestured toward the mousy woman. Her expression remained unchanged. "So, shall we proceed?"

"Aye, get on with it," Arkwright said.

The woman nodded. "Please state your name for the record."

"Anabella Halt."

"And what is your relationship to the Seven?"

Ana tried to answer the question with as much authority as she could muster. "I am Anabella Halt, heir to the Halt family council seat, daughter of the southern province, monarch of the island."

The interviewer nodded. "Thank you. Now, where were you during the challenge?"

"I was in the dome."

"And how did you come to be there?"

"I was a member of a challenge team." She hoped they wouldn't pry into the nonexistent love triangle between herself, Adam, and Holden. A love triangle that had been more about the boys than her. She didn't want to answer any questions that might give away Holden's secret. That he had the family gift. Something he wasn't ready to tell anyone.

"And why were you, a Halt, participating in a Rockwell challenge?" she asked, peering over her sharp glasses.

"Because I felt I could assist Holden, and we're friends."

Lady Fleur interrupted. "Interesting that you would choose Holden Rockwell's team when you appeared to be quite intimate with Adam Rockwell."

At the word intimate, Ana's ears turned pink. "Is there a question?" she demanded.

Lady Fleur met her eyes. "Yes. Why did you join Holden Rockwell's team instead of Adam Rockwell's team?"

It was none of her business what Adam and Holden's friendship was like, and it was *certainly* none of her business what Ana and Adam's relationship was like. She decided to go with a diplomatic answer.

If General Rockwell were here, she felt he would agree. She could just hear his voice now. "That's Rockwell business," he would have boomed.

Ana tried to channel him. "The challenge is a Rockwell family tradition. It doesn't serve to divide the family or to pick favorites. Its purpose is to drive excellence, challenge young Rockwells, and establish future hierarchies for command positions. As far as I can see, there was no wrong choice to make. I'm sure the General would agree."

Several council members nodded. They couldn't question

this answer without invoking General Rockwell's wrath when he heard the recording at some later date.

The arbiter cleared her throat. "If it's acceptable to the council, I'll continue."

"Yes. Please excuse my interruption," Lady Fleur said.

"Not to worry," Arkwright said. "It was an excellent observation."

The arbiter picked back up with her list of questions. "What skill did you bring to the team?"

Ana looked at her, and continuing to channel General Rockwell, she stared at the woman as if she were a bug. "What an insulting question? What skill do you think I brought? I'm a healer. A valuable skillset."

"Of course, I'm just reading the questions as written."

"I'd be interested to know who wrote them."

The woman did not answer. Instead, she moved on. "Spending so much time in the dome must be a very bonding experience."

Ana nodded.

"Would you say the people on your team were all trustworthy?"

"100%."

"If you had to rate them from most to least trustworthy, how would you order them?"

Ana was getting angry now. They had pulled her from class to interrogate her, not about Madame Bali but about her teammates. She glared at the arbiter. "I wouldn't."

"Excuse me?"

"I wouldn't rank them."

"But the question—"

"Is not going to be answered."

The council watched with interest but remained silent.

The arbiter moved on. "Did you have any knowledge of who was on the planning committee?"

"No. I didn't know anything about them. They didn't tell us, so we wouldn't be able to cheat."

"Ah, but it's clear that you did have help," Arkwright interrupted. "After all, you knew information about the dome before your arrival on Obsidian."

"Yes, we could see you had maps," Lady Jacobs agreed.

"We did, but not because we knew who was on the committee. Shay Noble has extraordinary technical skills, just like the rest of her family." She inclined her head at the holographic projection of Councilmen Noble. "She was able to secure the information for us."

Sir Noble let a small bit of pride creep into his expression.

"Just to be clear. She wasn't breaking the rules. There was no rule saying you couldn't hack into the system if you were able to."

"Yes, but it was somewhat implied, wasn't it?" Arkwright said.

DuBois interrupted, "As you all know, in a contract of law, implied does not count. If it's not spelled out explicitly, then they were just being clever."

Ana nodded. "Exactly! We wanted to gain the upper hand. By military rank and stats, the best students had already been selected. So, we decided to try something different. Something that might give us a chance at winning."

"Well, you seem to have accomplished that. Shall we return to the arbiter's questions?" DuBois asked.

The council fell silent.

"Is it true your team was able to alter the dome to protect your flag?"

Ana nodded.

"And this was also thanks to Shay Noble?"

"Yes. She's very gifted with technology."

"I should say so. It's never been done in the hundreds of years the game has been played."

"She's a prodigy."

"Perhaps," Lady Fleur muttered. There was a glint in her eye.

"Are you accusing a Noble of misconduct?" Councilman Noble said, straightening himself.

"Are Nobles above such suspicion?"

"Leave it to a household such as your own to cast aspersions on the honorable."

"See here, Noble. How would you feel if your next shipment of titanium was delayed?"

The argument continued for several minutes, in which Ana became dreadfully bored. Shipping arrangements and proprietary technology and legalities and logistics.

Finally, DuBois intervened. "Gentlemen, gentlemen, there's no need to get into such a disagreement."

Arkwright crossed his arms over his chest.

Ana realized that at some point during this disturbance Lady Jacobs had left the room unnoticed. Ana felt a stab of worry. Maybe, she was in their dorm right now. What would she do to him? What did she really want with Samuel?

"DuBois!" Lady Fleur hissed. "Are you attempting to use your gift again?"

Noble looked jumpier than ever.

"Yes," Lady Fleur insisted. "I can almost feel the most noxious wave of amity rolling over me. Luckily, it has little effect from so far away. If you were to try such a thing with me in the room, I would wrap you in the jun-jun vine and see how your precious voice fares when your vocal cords have been melted by acid."

That settled it. Lady Fleur was the most terrifying of the lot. Although, Arkwright still remained a close second. As Ana looked at the council members all arguing, she wondered if she could slip out of the room and follow Lady Jacobs. She took one step backward. And then another.

She had actually reached her hand for the doorknob when it

opened, sending her stumbling forward and into a heap on the ground.

General Rockwell stormed into the room and barked, "What is the meaning of this?"

"Why, Councilman Rockwell, what a pleasure," DuBois said, stepping forward and reaching out a hand.

Rockwell knocked his hand aside as if DuBois was nothing more than a mosquito. He stepped further into the room. "How dare you call a council session without me?"

"This is hardly a council session. And you were informed. Check your mail."

"A message sent five minutes prior to a meeting is not an invitation. You obviously didn't want me to be present. I find it impossible to believe you all dropped your schedules for this with no prior knowledge. And two of you just *happened* to be in town."

"Believe what you want," Arkwright said. "It doesn't matter to us."

He finally noticed Ana, still sprawled on the floor. "Ana, what are you doing down there? Which one of them did this to you?"

He didn't give her a chance to answer. Instead, he reached down a strong arm and jerked her to her feet. "Stand behind me," he instructed.

Then, he turned his attention back on the rest of the council. "No one speaks to a Rockwell without my knowledge."

"She's not a Rockwell," Noble pointed out.

"That's right," said Lady Fleur. "She is a Halt and, more importantly, a key witness to the events in the dome."

General Rockwell grabbed Ana's left hand and held it in the air. "Do you see this ring? Does a betrothal mean nothing to you?"

"We were unaware," Lady Fleur replied haughtily. "Seeing as how we were not invited to any occasion to celebrate."

Ana snorted. Were they really offended they hadn't been invited to an engagement party?

"None has been planned yet. We want adequate time to make sure the festivities are worthy of such a magnificent union."

Ana fought the urge to laugh. How could these people be running an entire planet and other colonies too? They could hardly get along and fought over disagreements as petty as engagement announcements.

But she could see the true motivation was unrelated to the engagement party. They had wanted to get Ana alone to pump her for information about the Rockwells and her relationship with them. They were worried about the power dynamic of the council and how it might be shifting.

"Of course. Of course," DuBois agreed. "But even still, you understand we must get at the heart of this matter."

"Fine. Send your questions to my office. I will have Anabella deposed and make the recordings available to you. Anything additional?"

"But we're already here," DuBois pointed out. "We may as well complete what we've started."

Rockwell leaned down in DuBois's face and growled, "I said anything additional?"

"No, I suppose not."

"Then, this meeting of yours is over. Get out of my sight."

Ana was reconsidering Sir Arkwright's rank as the second most frightening member of the council. Maybe, the honor belonged to the General.

"Ana," he said, turning toward her. "Never answer questions without me present. Understood?"

"Yes, sir."

"Very well. How's your combat class coming along? How did you score in the assessment?"

"Middle of the pack."

He rubbed a hand along his chin. "Hmm, better than expected. But not good enough. Keep at it."

"Yes, sir. Would it be okay if I return to my room now? I have a lot of schoolwork."

He waved a hand. "Dismissed."

ANA HURRIED BACK up the stairs and straight to her dorm. When she got there, Samuel was sitting alone in the living room, looking calm and collected.

"Did you see your grandmother?" she panted, trying to catch her breath.

He looked up from the projection he had been studying. "That all depends on how you define see."

"What is that supposed to mean?"

"She came in, but we didn't talk. More importantly, how did your meeting with the council go?"

He was deflecting, but Ana wasn't going to let him change the subject that easily. "You didn't talk to each other? How is that possible?"

He sighed and turned off the projection. "Simple. I hid."

"You hid? Like you ducked under a bed or something?"

A small amount of color rose to his cheeks. "Well, I wouldn't put it exactly like that, but—"

"Why didn't you talk to her?"

"Why were you so worried I would?"

"Well, based on the rest of your family..."

"It's not like that. I just didn't want to talk to the old shark."

"Shark? What does that mean?"

"It means the Jacobs family selects their council member based on wealth. My grandmother is the wealthiest member of the Jacobs family, and believe me, that's saying something. She didn't get there by being a doddering old woman."

"That's right. I forgot about that. The Rockwells choose the best soldier."

He nodded. "Every family has their own manner for choosing their council person. Seats don't change hands very often. In the Jacobs family, the richest member holds the council seat. If the markets go really wild, the member can change seats on a weekly basis. It's happened before. It's not the best for government. During one run during the 40s, they started appointing on a monthly basis using averages."

"Samuel, I'm not sure how to say this, but your family scares me."

"And Lizzie Borden kinda disliked her parents. And the Joker had a little problem with law and order."

Ana rolled her eyes.

His face grew serious. "If they didn't scare you, you'd be an idiot."

12
THE WAKE

Classes were relentless. They were only a couple of weeks into the school year, but more and more work just kept coming. This weekend was Xan's memorial. She'd missed his funeral while she was on Earth, but a memorial had been organized to give students a chance to pay their respects.

The memorial was held at sunset on the Rockwell training fields. Ana walked with her arm looped through Adam's until they reached rows and rows of chairs, overlooking a podium. It looked as though every student in the Academy had turned up and then some. It was ordinary. Too ordinary. There was nothing ordinary about a teenager dying. Nothing ordinary about celebrating Xan's life when it had only just begun.

It reminded Ana of another day. A cold, rainy Wednesday in November. Just two years prior. She remembered the familiar faces of classmates and neighbors, downturned and lined with pity. She remembered the way the wooden church pew had dug into her back. How it felt like she deserved that and every other misery life could throw at her.

She could feel the weight of that day even now. Especially now.

As they reached the back row of chairs, they slowed to a stop. Their teammates from the Challenge were waiting. Finally, they were all reunited—Ana, Adam, Holden, Shay, Ophelia, Baylan, and even Ja. They all piled onto Ja, giving him a group bear hug. When they finally let him go, Ja said in a low voice, "Well, I better get up front. I'm sitting with Xan's family."

"Of course," Adam said. "We'll be right behind you."

The front block of seating was filled entirely by Rockwells. Adam held out his hand for Ana to join him, but she shook her head. She hadn't known Xan for very long. Only a few days in the dome, though the time had seemed much longer. Either way, she didn't think it was right for her to sit with the family.

She elected to sit with Ophelia, Baylan, and Shay instead. They picked the back row. Shay filed down the row first, and Ana followed, taking the chair next to her.

"Hey, Shay. It's really good to see you. I'm sorry I never got a chance to visit after the hab. Well, you know..." she trailed off.

Shay shifted in her seat. "It's fine."

Ana could tell something was wrong. Shay had lost all of her ordinary bravado, and she wasn't looking Ana in the face. She looked uncomfortable. Really uncomfortable. Ana thought she knew why.

"Listen, if you're mad at me, I completely understand."

Shay jerked her head back. "Mad? Why would I be mad?"

"Well, my adviser and all that."

"It's fine, Halt. Really. You're not the one that's responsible."

Ana nodded but didn't say anything more. Instead, she looked around at the crowd that had formed. Most of the school had turned out, including the odious Delphi DuBois. He was standing in the corner of the room next to his brother. His eyes were black and angry. She hated him, and she wasn't alone in that feeling. He was attracting quite a few dirty looks and a chorus of muttering. When Holden and Ja had said he was unpopular, that had been an understatement.

As the ceremony began, Ana felt a heavy blanket of sadness wrap around her. It seemed the sadness of funerals compounded. Today, she carried not just the weight of Xan's death but also her mother's. What would happen when she turned fifty and carried even more? She dragged her foot on the gravel. Would she be able to carry the weight, or would it crush her into the stone? Would she even see fifty?

Someone stepped up to the podium to say a few words. It was unlike any funeral Ana had attended—more military and less comforting than those she was used to. But the sense of ritual and formality gave it a familiar feel.

As the sun set overhead, men and women dressed in full military regalia filed onto each side of the chairs, forming two neat lines. They lifted large rifles to their shoulder that gleamed with unfamiliar silver metal. And then, to her horror, they pulled their triggers. But instead of bullets, bright, fiery light erupted from the ends of the guns, flying high into the air and above the heads of the mourners. The lights crossed in the sky and rained down stars among the mourners. Ana couldn't help but reach out a hand like a child reaching for a soap bubble. This was just as ephemeral—a fitting metaphor for life itself.

The officiator said one final phrase. Ana suspected it was one they said at all Bellatonian funerals. "May he return to the stars."

The crowd of mourners repeated the words.

Tears slipped down her cheeks, and she hastily wiped them away. What right did she have to cry? When she had been a part of what happened? It had been her adviser who had tampered with the safeties.

Adam and Holden stayed behind with the rest of the family. There were private Rockwell family rituals that came at the end of the service. Ones that Ana wouldn't be able to participate in until her marriage into the Rockwell family was complete.

Instead, she trudged back up to the dorms with Ophelia.

"Are you going to be okay?" Ophelia asked when they reached her door.

Ana was taken aback. Did she look that upset? "Sure. Of course. I'm fine," she said quickly.

Ophelia gave her a small, knowing smile. "Okay, let me know if you want to bring Petrie over later."

Ana walked down the remainder of the hallway until the walls turned to sandstone with shells, and she reached the guard and her large wooden door. He nodded at her and stepped backward a respectful distance.

She had only one thought. That whoever had done this to Xan. Whoever had hurt his family. Whoever had taken the sparkle from Ja's eyes. That person should pay. And she was going to find out who they were if it was the last thing she did.

Ana had been sloppy last year. She had gotten too swept up in the academy and Bellaton that she had lost sight of why she was here. She had attended classes, made friends, and attended a ball.

This year, she couldn't make the same mistakes. She needed to find Madame Bali or her employer. They had spied on her. Lied to her. Tried to kill her.

But worse they had come after her friends. Imprisoned Samuel. Hurt Adam. Killed Xan.

Only one person would die this year… Madame Bali or the one who hired her.

INSIDE HER DORM, Ana found Samuel lounging in the living room, reading.

He looked up from his paperback, a rare sight these days. "How was the memorial?"

Ana knew how she was supposed to answer the question, but she always wondered why people asked this. She supposed it was just an opening. A chance to say things that needed to be said.

"Okay," she answered. "There's going to be a party down by the shore to honor Xan. I'm just here to change clothes."

Samuel nodded and returned to reading. He had barely stopped since he had gotten out of the simulation. Sometimes, his hands shook as if he were worried someone would rip the book from his grasp. But she didn't mention it. He would talk when he was ready.

In her room, Ana slipped off her black pumps and long dark dress. She changed into a comfortable pair of jeans and a flowy top. She washed her face with cold water in the sink, hoping that the red, puffy quality of her eyes would disappear. She wanted to be strong for the Rockwells. They had known Xan much longer than she had.

She let the emotional remnants of the memorial wash away in the sink, swirling along with her tear-streaked black mascara.

Fifteen minutes later, she heard a knock at the front door and called out, "Just a minute!"

She hurried out of her room, one earring still in her hand. When she reached the living room, the main door was already open. Adam and Samuel were standing with their faces inches apart. Their eyes were locked in mutual loathing. Their body language was tense. Adam's shoulders were squared back, and Samuel's jaw was tightened. It looked like either could explode at any moment.

Ana hurried to intervene. Why hadn't she anticipated this? Samuel had disapproved of Adam from the first day they had met, calling him a "baby monster" and warning Ana to choose a different friend. One not affiliated with the military family. No doubt his feelings had only intensified after what had happened at the capital during the winter ball.

He and Ana still hadn't discussed the dome or her engagement. So, he didn't understand what could have brought them back together.

Despite that, Samuel stepped out of her way, looking at her with a warning spark in his eyes.

"We're just headed to Xan's wake," she said, hoping to pacify him.

He nodded stiffly.

"Come on, Adam," she said, pulling at his arm. It was locked by his side, his hand forming a fist.

He didn't budge.

"We don't want to be late," she added.

Adam relented and allowed himself to be dragged forward.

"Bye," Ana called as the door closed behind them. She looped her arm through Adam's, hoping her touch would somehow prevent the argument she knew was coming.

The dynamite had been lit, and no matter how hard she tried, she wasn't going to be able to extinguish it. So, she resigned herself to waiting for the boom.

They walked in silence all the way down the hallway, down the stairs, through the foyer, and into the courtyard before Adam spoke. Finally, he grumbled, "So, want to tell me what that banker is doing sprawled on your couch? The guard said he's been there for days."

"Samuel? He's my adviser. He's going to be—" She stopped and narrowed her eyes. "Wait a minute. You talked to the guard?"

Adam shrugged.

Ana disentangled her arm from his and stabbed an accusatory finger at his chest. "I can't believe it. I knew your dad was going to spy on me." She paused for a beat. "But I didn't realize you were going to do it too."

Adam glared at her. "Is it really spying if your other boyfriend comes in through the front door?"

"He's my adviser."

"Nothing more?"

She hesitated. Of course, Samuel was more. He was her best friend. She looked forward to seeing him at the end of classes. They watched stupid cartoons together and let cereal bowls pile up in the kitchen. He had saved her life once.

"I'm not even going to dignify that with an answer," she said, crossing her arms over her chest. "Isn't it enough that I was spied on all last year? Now, my boyfriend is going to do it too?"

"It sounds like you need to choose between your boyfriends."

"He's my adviser," Ana shouted in frustration.

"You know we could find you another adviser. A better one.

Someone who could protect you, unlike that skeletal money-grubber."

"Samuel is not a money-grubber. He's not like the rest of his family."

Slow realization crossed Adam's face. "And I am."

Ana said nothing. She knew she had hurt him, but she was too angry to care.

She quickened her pace, so she wouldn't have to walk beside him. They made their way across the grounds in silence.

When they topped the academy's crumbling wall, Ana got a good view of the beach ahead. On the dark night sky, Xan's uniform number and rank shone in bright golden letters. She felt something clutch in her throat. She said nothing to Adam but allowed him to walk beside her again.

As their feet hit the sand, Ana saw dozens of students lounging around a bonfire and more filling their cups at a nearby table. The sound of crashing waves and chatter filled her ears.

Last year, Ana would have been worried about getting caught. After all, this wake was no school-sanctioned event, especially not the drinks. But this year, she was unconcerned. Ana had proven herself the heir to the Halt family council seat and gotten engaged to a Rockwell. Well, for now anyway, she thought, daring to glance over at Adam.

Wordlessly, Ana left Adam with his friends and walked closer to the bonfire. The stories were all about Xan, and she sat for a while to listen. There were countless stories about Xan getting in trouble. None of which surprised her. After all, Xan had plunged into the challenge headfirst, whooping and full of excitement. Even though, he knew how dangerous it would be.

A younger Rockwell, maybe thirteen, told a story about how Xan had helped her when she was struggling during drill practice. It turned out he had helped a lot of people.

Ana thought back to the story Holden had told her during

the challenge. Ja had been running away from home when he first met Xan. Xan joined him, and when they got caught, Xan had taken the blame. The two had been friends ever since.

She smiled and listened as more stories were shared. Some in quiet, reverent tones. Some with shaky voices and tears. Some with laughter and fond remembrance.

Eventually, someone noticed her.

A recent graduate with broad shoulders and a short, efficient buzz-cut looked at Ana across the crackling flames. He narrowed his eyes. "You're not a Rockwell."

Dizzy interrupted on Ana's behalf. "She will be soon! Look at her hand!"

The graduate eyed it and understanding flickered across his face. "You're Anabella Halt."

More heads swiveled toward her.

She nodded.

"So, you were with Xan when he died?"

She started to speak, but her voice came out in a rasp. She took a swig from her cup and tried again. "We were on the same team, but I wasn't on the excursion where he died."

"Still, you know what his final days were like. Can't you tell us something?"

His harsh features couldn't hide the sadness in his eyes, and Ana couldn't deny him. She swallowed her guilt and sadness. "I didn't know Xan for very long. Although I wish I had after hearing all of your stories. We met through the challenge. Holden and I wanted Xan on our team because he had good Rockwell records, but" — her lip curved upward— "he also liked to break the rules."

The graduate snorted and a little bit of punch dribbled down his chin. He swiped a hand at it.

Dizzy chimed in, "Understatement of the year! He 'borrowed' his dad's jet once. Just wanted to fly it around. Of course, when he landed it back in the garage bay, his dad was waiting."

They all laughed.

The graduate urged Ana to continue.

"Well, when Xan came to our first practice, I could see how good he was. He didn't break Ja's sharpshooting record for accuracy, but he was close. Fast too. And always making everyone around him laugh."

"It was the same in the challenge. He was whooping when we entered the dome and the first to suggest patrolling in pairs. He set up the hab. Made a ton of jokes. He was in high spirits the whole time. He was really in his element."

When she finished, the conversation moved easily to the next story. After an hour, she excused herself to refill her cup.

She spotted Baylan, towering over the refreshment table. She moved to stand beside him. "Hey, Bay. Whatcha drinking?"

"Just the house punch. Learned my lesson last year."

It was just this time last year that Ana had met Baylan at a party. Well, met may have been too strong of a word. She had seen Baylan fall off of a twenty-foot cliff. The one just to the left of where they stood now. He had been severely injured but made a miraculous recovery.

"That was a scary night, and I didn't even know you yet."

She poured herself a cup of the house punch— something electric green with fruit she didn't recognize. A few others queued up, and they moved to give them space.

She took a sip. It was strong, but the flavor was good, tart but sweet like a kiwi.

"Actually, there's something I've been wondering about that night."

"Shoot," he said, his hands in his pockets as they walked across the beach and away from the crowd.

"Were you pushed? There were rumors."

He considered. "Not exactly. I didn't understand it at the time, but it was Delphi. He and Zane followed me up there.

Delphi gave me a little encouragement, if you know what I mean."

Ana knew all too well what he meant. "I can't believe he hasn't been expelled," she fumed, kicking at the sand. "Why didn't you tell somebody?"

"I wasn't really sure what had happened until I saw the dome footage. Then, I knew. Besides, he would have just weaseled out of it anyway. It would just be my word versus his, and I was off-campus after hours and under the influence."

"At least, the other students seem to know what's up. He's become a real pariah this year."

"Oh yeah? How *is* the school year going?"

"Same as always," she hedged. "I heard you graduated while I was on Earth. Sorry I missed it."

"You didn't miss much. It seemed wrong to throw some blowout party after everything that had just happened."

"You deserve a party though."

"Just getting out of here is enough for me. My family finally stopped blocking my graduation. Turns out my dad was impressed with my work during the challenge. He got me an assignment on another planet, working on a geological study."

"Wow, Baylan," Ana said. "You deserve it. Really."

"Thank you. I couldn't have done it without you."

"I didn't do anything," Ana said. *Except for cause an enormous mess and get Xan killed.*

HOLDEN, Ivan, and Adam, dragging behind, joined them.

Ivan clearly had enjoyed his fill of the green punch. He had a pleasant, dreamy expression on his face, and his pupils were dilated. He clapped a hand on Ana's arm and began to shake her hand. "Sorry I was a jerk at breakfast. Welcome to the family, Ana."

"Thanks," she said through gritted teeth.

Baylan's eyes trailed down to her ring finger. "Wow, Ana, you really buried the lead. You and Adam, huh?"

Ana tried to smile. If they were alone, Baylan might be one of the few people she could actually talk to about Adam. Not about her bargain, of course, but about their fight. About her uncertainty. They had spent a lot of time together one-on-one during the challenge, and she knew he would have her back.

Instead, she made polite conversation and tried to pretend she wasn't fighting with Adam...again. After a few minutes, she excused herself to go get another drink.

She eyed the drink table and spotted a glass bowl of shiny black powder. She couldn't believe someone had brought Lights Out to a wake. Lights Out was a street drug derived from a neurotoxin. Even in this diluted form, it was *still* dangerous. The last thing the Rockwell family needed was a kid getting blinded.

She was getting hungry, and the meat at the end of the table looked past its prime.

She scooped up more green punch. This time going for more of the fruit. She picked out a few pieces and started eating them.

A few minutes later, Holden joined her, leaning against the table and running a hand through his dark blonde hair. "Careful," he warned. "That fruit is strong."

She paused in mid-bite. "Really? How strong?"

Holden peered into her cup and realized there was no drink in it, just fruit. "How much have you eaten?"

"Well, this cup was filled when I started. I was hungry," she added a little defensively.

"That fruit is alcoholic, even when it's not in punch."

"Oh." Ana's stomach sunk.

"Wait here. I'll get you some water."

By the time he returned, she was beginning to feel the effects of the fruit. He handed her the cup of water, looking at her with growing concern. "Drink this," he instructed. "I'll get Adam."

She had a few sips of the water. Her eyes felt heavy, and her tongue felt loose. "Don't bother."

"You guys fighting again?"

She couldn't be bothered to lie. Not to Holden. "Are we that obvious?"

"To me. Wait here. I'm getting Adam."

She pouted in the general direction of his turned back.

Adam returned with Holden seconds later. He took one look at Ana and asked, "What's going on with her?"

"She ate the fruit."

A wave of vertigo came over Ana, she felt bad. Really bad. Like the planet was violently spinning, and she might be flung off at any moment.

Adam tried to support her, so they could make the trek back to the school, but she pushed him off. "I don't need your help."

"Don't be stupid. You can't just walk off by yourself."

"Oh no? Watch me." She made it a few steps before swaying dangerously.

Adam and Ana made it a dignified distance from the beach. Then, he reached down and scooped her up in his arms.

"Put me down," she demanded.

"You'll just trip and hurt yourself. It's my fault you ate the damn fruit."

Ana stopped struggling and rested her head on his chest. The rhythmic rise and fall of his heartbeat made her sleepy. Soon, she could hardly keep her eyes open.

She woke as they reached her door.

The guard hurried toward them. "Sir! Is the lady okay?"

"She's fine," Adam grunted. "Just get the door please."

The guard held Ana's hand against the door, unsealing the lock. Then, turned the knob and allowed them to pass.

"Ana!" Samuel whined. "You've been gone for—" He stopped when he saw Ana bleary-eyed in Adam's arms. His whine turned to a growl. "What did you do to her?"

Fire sparked in Adam's eyes. "I didn't do anything. She drank too much."

Ana hit Adam in the chest with a balled-up fist. "Did not. Put me down."

"Can you stand?"

She glared up at him.

He set her down.

"Bad, bad fruit," she muttered.

"She ate the fruit in the punch," Adam explained.

Samuel wrapped an arm around her waist and led her to the couch. He called over his shoulder to Adam, "Get her friend, the Fleur girl. Tell her to bring bindi root."

Adam eyed Samuel with distrust. "And leave you alone with her?"

"I live here," Samuel pointed out. "Are you going to help or not?"

Adam left.

Samuel settled her gently on the couch in a sitting position. "Did he give you the fruit?"

"No. I ditched him at the party."

"That's the first sensible thing you've said all evening."

Ana felt her eyelids were impossibly heavy. Too heavy to keep open.

"Ana, Ana." Samuel shook her awake. "You can't go to sleep right now."

"But I'm tired," she whined.

He gazed down at her. "What if I make you a coffee?"

He started to pull back, but she grabbed his collar. "You have pretty eyes. Even now. They're different. But I still like them. So many colors. Maybe I'll paint them."

He stepped back and cleared his throat. "I'll just get that coffee."

Before Samuel could finish the coffee, Adam returned with Ophelia and the bindi root.

She chopped it, taking care to squeeze it with the edge of her knife to release the juices. Then, she swept the root and juices into the bottom of a mug. She poured hot water over the top. "It'll need to steep five minutes," she instructed.

"Thank you," Samuel said.

"Yeah," Adam grunted.

Ophelia gave a small smile. "Ana is lucky to have two boys who care about her so much."

Adam and Samuel glared at one another. Ophelia didn't seem to notice.

Five minutes later, she woke Ana gently from her slumped position on the couch.

Ana groaned.

Ophelia said, "Hey, I have a nice tea for you. It will help you feel better."

Ana accepted the mug with shaky hands. Ophelia steadied it and helped Ana bring it to her lips.

After a few sips, Ana felt the world begin to steady a little. "Thank you, Oh-feel-ee-yah," she said, drawing out the syllables. "You're a good friend. I never expected to have so many good friends." She smiled blearily up at Ophelia.

MEANWHILE, in the kitchen, Samuel and Adam were alone.

Samuel was leaning against the refrigerator with his arms crossed over his chest. "What sort of a guy brings his date home like this? I warned her about Rockwells."

From across the kitchen island, Adam scowled. "And what? You think you're better? Because you walked away? You know blood is forever. You know there is no walking away. Look at Ana. Her mom left Bellaton. Look where Ana is now. Are you lying to her or yourself, banker?"

"Why, you arrogant little prick. You have no idea what Ana's mom went through to keep her safe."

"I know it didn't work."

"Some boyfriend you are," Samuel growled.

"I think you mean fiancé, and I'd say I'm doing just fine."

Samuel paused. "Fiancé?"

"What did you think that ring on her finger was doing? Just catching the sunlight?"

Samuel turned on Adam and strode into the living room. Ana was gently snoring with her face leaned against the back of the sofa. Sure enough, a ring sparkled on her left hand. Samuel's eyes widened in surprise. How could he have failed to notice this? How could he have been so blind?

Adam smiled at his crestfallen expression.

WHEN ANA WOKE, it was still dark outside. The only light came from a single brass lantern in the hallway, casting shadows against the living room's sandstone walls. Ana was curled up on the couch. Someone had covered her with a blanket, and her feet were tucked against something warm—Samuel.

He was sitting on the opposite end of the couch, staring at the wall. For once, there was no book to distract him. She saw worry etched into his unguarded expression. It didn't look as if he had slept.

She studied him for a moment longer before stifling a yawn.

He heard it and turned to look at her. "You're awake."

"Mhmm," she mumbled. She sat up.

"How are you feeling?"

She vaguely remembered getting up earlier and vomiting. Someone had pulled her hair back and helped her wash her face. Probably Ophelia. But, to her surprise, the nausea had passed. In fact, other than being tired, she felt pretty good. She would have to thank Ophelia later. Whatever had been in that tea had been miraculous.

"Embarrassed. This is the second time I've made a fool—" She stopped talking and blushed. The last thing she wanted to do was remind him of that night at the capital, when she had so brazenly pressed her mouth to his, ignoring the consequences. She hurried to move her feet from his warmth. "I'm going to get some water. Do you want anything?"

"Wait," he grabbed her arm before she could slip away. "Please."

She settled back on the couch next to him, a faint blush dusting her cheeks. She pulled a blanket over her lap to warm her bare legs.

To her surprise, he reached for her hand, lifting it gently into his lap and examining the soft skin on the underside. He brushed his fingers across her palm, sending an unexpected shiver down her spine. Then, reluctantly, he turned her hand over and looked at the ring there.

He gave her a sad smile. "When were you going to tell me you're engaged?"

Ana's heart dropped. He knew. Had he noticed the ring while she was sleeping? Or had Adam said something? Why hadn't she told him sooner? Why was she so bad at this?

He was still waiting for her answer.

"I, well, I'm not. Not really."

He gazed into her eyes. Something he had never done before, despite the many hours and days they had spent together. It felt as if he was searching for the answers her lips were unwilling to give. The intensity made her nervous. Like he would discover all of her secrets. A part of her wanted to pull away, while another part longed to move closer.

He said his next words in a soft, low voice. "That Rockwell says you are engaged, and I'd say your hand agrees with him."

"Sorry," she murmured, dropping her eyes to their hands, which were still joined together. Her ring shining traitorously up at her.

"Why would you say yes to him? That night in the capital, before I was arrested, you wanted nothing to do with him. He lied to you. He used you. Now, you're engaged to him. Is there something I'm missing here, Ana?"

She didn't answer. She couldn't tell him that she had bartered her hand in marriage for his freedom. He wouldn't allow it.

He waited for her to say something.

"I don't know," she whispered.

"Do you love him?"

"I-I'm not sure. Maybe."

Samuel released her hand and stood up. After a pause that ripped Ana apart, he said, "If you're in love, if you're getting married, those are things you should share with the people around you. I thought, at the least, we were friends."

"Samuel," she moaned. She didn't know what else to say. What could she say? It had been weeks, and she had said nothing. "I wanted to protect you."

He turned and gave her one last fleeting glance. "No, Ana. You wanted to protect yourself."

13
COLD SHOULDER

When Ana woke, the dormitory was quiet. She opened her door and tiptoed down the hallway. When she peeked into the living room, she expected to see Samuel crashed out on the couch and hear the holovision blaring. It was how she started most days. He would mutter a "good morning" and drag himself to his bedroom.

Instead, she found an empty couch, a clean kitchen, and a silent holovision. All that remained were the lingering ghosts of yesterday— communal sorrow from Xan's memorial, Adam's jealousy and distrust, Samuel's pain at her betrayal, and her own crushing guilt.

Things weren't any better outside of the dormitory.

At breakfast, Ana and Adam didn't speak to each other. They sat at opposite sides of the table in stony silence. Ja, Holden, and Ivan sat in between them.

Ana had a cup of coffee and two pieces of toast. "Can someone pass the butter?"

The butter was sitting inches in front of Adam's left hand. He didn't move to help or even acknowledge her request.

After a moment, Holden frowned and reached over to pass it to Ana.

"Thanks," she muttered.

From behind his mountain of food, Ivan chuckled. "Trouble in paradise, huh?"

"Drop it," Adam growled. He downed his glass of green liquid and slammed it on the tabletop. Then, he stood and left without another word.

An awkward silence passed over the table.

"So, what's up, goldilocks?" Ivan said in a singsong voice. "This Rockwell not quite right? You tried baby bear," he looked at Holden. "And brother bear." Ana assumed he meant Adam. "You ready for papa bear?" He raised a suggestive eyebrow.

Ana grimaced. "Not in a million years."

Ja and Holden glared at Ivan.

He raised a hand in surrender. "Whoa, calm down. I was just trying to lighten the mood."

"Well, it's not working," Holden said. His ears were bright red, and his hand was balled into a fist. He looked like he wanted to punch Ivan.

Ana put her hand on top of his fist. "It's fine. Really."

Ivan smirked but said nothing.

"I should go," Ana said. "Sorry about this." She stood, taking her piece of toast with her and leaving the dining hall.

OPHELIA CAUGHT up with Ana outside of the dining room.

"Thanks for last night. You know, for the tonic and holding my hair when I was sick."

"I'm glad you're feeling better, but I'm not the one who held your hair."

Ana blushed. She remembered a soothing hand on her back, and someone pulling her hair back. Someone had helped her. "Did, um, Adam leave with you?"

"A little before, actually. He and Samuel were talking, and he left right after. He looked"—she searched for the word—"triumphant."

That must have been when Adam told Samuel about the engagement. So, it must have been Samuel who held her hair back. He had helped her even after he knew she had kept secrets. If it was possible, she felt even worse.

Reading her expression, Ophelia said, "Is everything okay?"

Ana launched into a brief version of the story.

Ophelia listened. When Ana was finished, she said, "Adam should have known Samuel would live in your dormitory. It's tradition. At least one adviser always stays in the dormitory."

"Exactly!"

The tiniest frown crossed Ophelia's brow. "But why didn't you tell Samuel about your engagement?"

The tiny flicker of righteous indignation was snuffed out. "Well, you know it's not exactly real."

"You could have told him that."

"He'd just gotten out of this terrible prison, Ophelia. He still flinches when he has to go out into the sunshine. It didn't seem like a great time to tell him I agreed to a political marriage."

"Are you sure that's the reason?"

"What other reason is there?"

Ophelia shrugged. "Well then, it should all be okay. You'll apologize to Samuel and tell him you're worried about his health. And you know Adam. He'll forgive you, too."

UNFORTUNATELY, Adam had not forgiven Ana by the time she arrived in Combat Class. She was the last one in her group to come up from the locker rooms. When she approached, Adam turned his back to her, feigning interest at the beginning of class.

Shay shot a quizzical glance at Ana and mouthed, "What's with him?"

Ana shook her head, indicating she couldn't talk about it now. It wouldn't have mattered anyway. Class began right away.

The room was subdivided today to allow for more concurrent matches. It also meant Commander Rockwell's attention was divided too. As a result, the games were a little dirtier today. Ana had already seen a few grudges play out. So, she wasn't at all happy when their third match was against Delphi.

Things were… not going well for her team today.

After a second drill went awry, Commander Rockwell called out, "Having a personal conflict, are we? Well, I don't care. If your team loses this next match, so be it."

Adam was determined not to lose. Instead, he tried to rack up enough points to carry the entire team, while still pretending Ana didn't exist. He moved on the offense, taking big risks for big rewards. Shay followed him to provide backup, muttering "dumbass" under her breath.

Holden, for his part, was trying to get some points in too, but he kept having to step in to help Adam.

Meanwhile, it was all Ana could do to stay out of Delphi's eye line. They kept running into each other, and she was sure it was on purpose.

She looked up and saw two opponents about to drop down from above Adam. She started to call out, but Holden rushed in from the side.

In her moment of distraction, someone body-checked her into the wall with a sickening thud. Her left side took the brunt of the injury. Her wrist radiated white, hot pain. For a moment, she saw black and orbs. She slid down the wall into a sitting position, taking deep breaths. She could not pass out. She could not pass out.

She was attracting some attention now. Holden was looking right at her. She wondered if he had been trying to watch out for her and Adam at the same time or if he had seen a flash of a vision. Ja looked over, too, and spotted Delphi's smirk. His eyes flashed. In seconds, he had Delphi in a chokehold. "You think hurting people is funny?"

Delphi wheezed out a reply that Ana couldn't hear. Ja clearly didn't like it. He looked like he had tightened his grip.

Commander Bold broke up the fight and went to check on Ana. He lifted her wrist gingerly. "Fractured or broken," he declared. "To the infirmary."

"But sir, I don't need—"

He laughed. "I almost forgot. I guess you don't, do you? Well, take the rest of the day off and go heal that wrist. I'll expect you back tomorrow."

She nodded and stumbled to her feet.

From the safety of the hallway, she took a good look at her wrist. She could already see the color rising. "Fractured or broken," he had said.

She wasn't sure whether to cry or kick something.

ANA HEADED STRAIGHT BACK to her dorm.

As usual, the guard was standing at attention just outside the door. "Good morning," he said, inclining his head to her. If he wondered why she wasn't in class, he didn't ask.

She tried her best to smile at him, but her mind was elsewhere.

Would the guard report her arrival time to Adam? Would he want to know she had come back straight after class? She felt anger rising in her chest. He had been spying on her, and now, he was the one who was acting wronged.

If he hadn't been so childish today, distracting the entire team, she wouldn't have been alone and defenseless. She wouldn't have been body checked into the wall. Her arm wouldn't be… like this.

She pushed her anger down and tiptoed through the front door, hoping to avoid Samuel. She wasn't ready to talk to him yet. What could she say? "Oh, yes, hi Samuel. I am engaged. I bartered my hand in marriage for your freedom. Isn't that lovely? Let's do lunch."

He would never let that stand. And what choice did that leave Ana? More lies?

The lights were still out, and the scent of coffee was not in the air. He was probably still sleeping.

She entered her own room and shut the door securely behind her. She crawled into her bed and blasted her wrist with the cryocanister, praying it would help and that Command Bold had been wrong in his medical assessment. Could fractures heal on their own?

A THUNDEROUS KNOCK on the front door woke her. Ana started to push herself into a sitting position but stopped. Her wrist was throbbing. She remembered her injury and looked down at her wrist and forearm—swollen and bruised.

With care, she rose from her bed and pulled on a cardigan to conceal her arm. She ambled to the front door. The lights were all out, and it was dark outside. How long had she slept? Shadows from the light of the moons danced across the walls. As she crossed the living room, the ornate brass lanterns lit automatically.

Samuel still wasn't here, and she was beginning to worry. Where was he?

And who was at the door? Ana was surprised anyone would

come by at this hour. Could it be Adam? Maybe he wanted to apologize, after all.

She cracked the door open and found herself eye to eye with a familiar old woman. "What are you doing here?" Ana sputtered.

Ms. K with two floral suitcases. She pushed past Ana and dropped them onto the finished concrete. The suitcases expelled a large quantity of dust. "Well, this imploded faster than I expected."

"Huh?"

She waggled her eyebrows. "You and Samuel."

"What's that supposed to mean? We're just friends."

"Sure," Ms. K snorted. "So were Bonnie and Clyde. Now, which room is mine?"

"Room?" Ana echoed. "You're- you're moving in?"

"You think I'd leave you kids alone? Ha!"

"What about my brothers?"

"Taken care of." She wandered toward the hall of bedrooms.

Ana trailed behind, feeling helpless to stop her. "Are you going to be my adviser?"

"Not in so many words."

"What does that mean?"

Ms. K stopped at the first door, crinkled her nose at the musty air, and closed it. "Look, Samuel is a good kid. He's smart. He can take care of himself. But he's got a lot of baggage." She considered Ana for a moment. "Guess you're not all that different, are you? Anyway, I don't know what you did to him, doll, but he needed to clear his head. So, here I am." Ms. K started to open the next door.

"That one's mine," Ana said.

"Better skip a few doors then. I'm a snorer."

They continued down the long hallway.

"So, you're engaged to a Rockwell?"

Ana nodded. Had Samuel told her, or had she just learned through her intelligence network?

"He's a looker; I'll give you that much."

Ana felt color rush to her cheeks.

"You sure you want to marry him? Being a Rockwell means a lot of things. None of 'em good." She put her hand on the next doorknob and started to turn it.

"Wait-" Ana said.

It was too late.

Ms. K opened the door.

It was Samuel's room. As the door opened, her curiosity was piqued. She had never actually been in his room before. The familiar smell of books and tobacco hit her like a tidal wave. There was a hand-carved wooden bed, low to the ground, with a simple white sheet pulled neatly over the top.

The wooden side table was covered in books. A small reading lamp had been left on. An ashtray, partially filled, sat on the windowsill. The window, partially cracked, let in the moonlight and a warm breeze.

Suddenly, Ana felt a wave of homesickness. "Do you think he'll come back?"

"He's staying with some friends."

Friends. Did Samuel have friends? Ana had never really given it much thought. In fact, she had never really considered what his life was like when he wasn't with her. He had been so secretive when they first met.

How well did she really know Samuel? She had visited his loft above the bakery a couple of times, but no one had ever been there. But he was in hiding then, so maybe that wasn't an accurate picture.

She knew he liked to read. She knew he was incredibly smart and good at almost every subject, that he could see numbers and strategies in his head in a way that was unique. She knew he had a slew of bad habits. He smoked and stayed up too late. He rarely cleaned up and ate too much takeout. He was anti-social.

On the other hand, he had a strength of will she greatly admired. He had once been a Jacobs. Yet, he'd had the courage to choose another path. Though he still had a great deal of wealth, it meant very little to him. The only time he ever spent it was on other people, like Ana.

He was always looking out for her. He had watched over her after her mother's death. He had been the one to save her from the car accident. He had helped her escape to Bellaton and told her all the things she needed to know.

He'd safeguarded and delivered the letter from her mom. He knew its secrets, but he had never once pushed her to open it. He had always given her space. He had always protected her.

Now it was her turn to protect him. But she felt like she was already failing.

"Oops, ocupado," Ms. K said, shutting the door.

She skipped another door and finally decided on the room seven doors from Ana. "Well, kid, this'll do me," she said, slamming her suitcases down. She unzipped one and pulled out a long expanse of black plastic. "Do me a favor and run this in front of the door."

Ana accepted the plastic strip tentatively. "What does it do?" She'd seen enough of Ms. K's handiwork to be suspicious.

"Blow off the leg of anybody who comes in the damn door."

"What?" Ana shouted.

"Just kidding. Alarm sensor. Calm down, kid. Go get some sleep. You have classes in the morning."

14
RESEARCH & DREAMS

Ana took Ms. K's advice and went straight to bed. She didn't think she'd be able to fall asleep. Her wrist was in so much pain. But two painkillers later, and she was out.

Once more, Terra was winding through the elaborate gardens of the Fleur Estate. She searched the horizon for the lady of the house, feeling unsure of herself. She'd been debating whether or not to meet her all morning.

Lady Fleur had invited her to learn how to plant flowers. Had she been sincere, or was she just being polite? Finally, she decided there was no harm in stopping by. If Lady Fleur had been sincere, it would be rude not to show up.

She spotted her in the distance. She was here. Just as she had promised. She was wearing all white and an enormous sun hat. She kneeled on a small towel, and her hands dug into the soil. Terra had known she would be here, but it was still surprising to see a lady of her standing with dirty hands.

Lady Fleur looked up and waved at her.

Terra waved back enthusiastically, a bright smile pulling across her face. She immediately felt she must look very childish. A small blush bronzed her cheeks.

Lady Fleur wiped the sweat from her brow. "Good morning, Terra," she said as she approached. "How do you like your new home?"

"Oh, the cottage is wonderful. Father and I are very comfortable. Thank you."

Lady Fleur smiled. "It must be difficult for you, moving to a new place and making new friends. What do you think of your new classmates?"

Terra bit her lip and answered in a breath, "I'm not sure I'll ever fit in here. I'm not fancy. I'm not anything special."

"Hmm," Lady Fleur said, considering Terra's words. "What do you think of these bulbs?" she asked, pointing to a patch of vivid blue blossoms in the center of the garden.

"They're lovely," Terra answered, a bit confused at the change of subject.

"Did you know they're not native to this region?"

Terra shook her head.

"They were originally grown exclusively in the Southern Province. A gift from an old friend," she added. "But even though they don't originate here, look how they thrive. They add to the subtle color from the white lace and the green velvet. Don't you think?"

Terra nodded.

"The trick is to bloom where you're planted. You see?"

Terra felt uncertain.

"Even if you are different, you may be a beautiful compliment to those around you."

Ana woke with a start. This dream was just as vivid as the first. She stretched and yawned. Still tired.

Bloom where you're planted, huh? Ana was currently planted in the middle of a huge mess. Her left arm was just as bruised and swollen as it had been last night. She covered up with a cardigan and went to find Ms. Kandinsky.

After some light begging, Ms. K agreed to message the main office that Ana would be out of class for the rest of the week on Halt family business. To her credit, she didn't ask why or lecture her about the importance of schoolwork. She was either uninclined or simply too busy from the constant calls coming in on her infotab.

Ana returned to her room and thought about her dream. It had left her feeling somewhat encouraged and more than a little curious. The details of the garden had seemed so real. She wondered if it was a real place. Maybe she had seen a photo somewhere.

She took out her colored pencils and started sketching. She started with the lines of the house in the distance. She couldn't remember them all, but in her mind's eye, she saw a large white monolith with balconies. She left the details vague and empty.

Next, she drew the outline of the tall, squared shrubberies that obscured the brick wall that surrounded the interior gardens. She tried to remember when she—Terra—had been standing beside it, talking to Lady Fleur for the first time.

She moved into the garden. Down the center, leading to the back patio, there was a straight walkway, enveloped by a trellis and shaded by dark green vines. This was easier. She could still see the labyrinth of pebbled walking paths that separated up sections of the garden.

She started on the details of the flower bed she had just dreamed about. She could still remember all the details. She pulled out a blue-colored pencil and drew the vibrant blue flowers, giving it dark shading on the underside of the petals. Then she branched into the small white flowers that surrounded it. What had Lady Fleur called them again? White lace? She added the soft, velvet-like green plants, too.

After an hour, she frowned. She wasn't satisfied with the drawing at all. She was missing so many details, and the overall look was off, somehow.

. . .

Last weekend, Ana spent all of her time with Ophelia. She volunteered at the Dock Street Animal Rescue, stayed up late watching Holovision with the Fleur girls, and helped Ophelia with her botany project in the greenhouse. She was also eating all of her meals with Ophelia. She was worried she was wearing out her welcome, not with Ophelia but with the other Flour girls.

So, this weekend, she decided it was time to do some digging. She had already searched Madame Bali's name on her infotab, of course. But she hadn't tried the school's archives.

She made her way to the study center. It was nothing like a library. Physical books were largely out of print in Bellaton. The ones that existed were antiques. All available information was online.

The study center had viewing rooms, where you could step into a scene in three dimensions, similar to how General Rockwell had viewed the footage of the challenge. She had tried it out herself for astronomy class. It felt like walking among the stars.

There were also information pods. To Ana's eye, they looked like oversized black eggs. You stepped inside and closed the door. There was a comfortable leather chair at an ergonomic incline. Once the pod was closed, it was totally soundproof.

Inside, you could call up whatever information you wanted by voice command. There were hand controls, too. One on each armrest.

Ana took her seat and shut the pod door, not wanting to be overheard. As she did so, the lights dimmed, and a pleasant projection of stars filled the space in front of her. It had saved her last settings she supposed. Clever.

"Hey there," greeted a disembodied voice with a warm Southern accent.

Ana still found it a little unsettling. At home, the A.I. sounded like A.I. The pronunciation was good, but the inflection and tone were missing something. The human element. But not this A.I. It sounded like a real person. Even stranger, the dialect sounded like a caricature of her hometown on Earth.

She tried to ignore the weirdness.

"I'm looking for any records or information on Madame Bali."

The A.I. replied, "I'd be happy to help, hun. Can you spell that first name for me?"

Ana was taken aback. "Oh, uh, yeah. Serena, I think. S-e-r-e-n-a."

Writing appeared, wrapping ever so slightly around the shape of the egg, like a panorama.

Serena Bali

Born March 3, 1981

Parents – Jaq Bali (living) and Mina Lisand (deceased 2009)

Last Registered Location: Southern Province

Occupation: Botanist, Royal Accreditation

So, according to the records, Madame Bali was a real person, and more importantly, she was alive.

Beneath the given text, the words "see more" flashed.

"See more, please."

There was a slight pause, and the biography disappeared. It was replaced with the fiery, glowing symbol of the council and the word "RESTRICTED."

"Fine," she grumbled. "Please pull up the record for Jaq Bali."

The record appeared on the screen.

Jaq Bali

Born February 22nd, 1947

> Parents – Jacques Bali (deceased 1977) and Christina (deceased 1981)
>
> Last Registered Location: Southerly Province
>
> Occupation: Horticulturist

"See more, please."

This time, the computer obliged.

> Despite no formal education, Jaq Bali is known for his academic paper and discovery of the Jazberra Fruit. The rind, when aged and ground, provides the basis for excellent fertilizer. The scientific properties can be reviewed in this paper.

Ana frowned. While it was noteworthy that Jaq had achieved enough fame to gain the council's attention, she wasn't particularly interested in fertilizer compounds. "No thanks," she said aloud.

Ana racked her brain. What conclusions, if any, could she draw from this new information? Madame Bali was a real person, and she was alive. Did that mean the fake Madame Bali knew the real one? It seemed likely. Who would take the alias of a living person if they didn't know them? It would be an odd choice.

So, if fake Madame Bali and real Madame Bali knew each other, what was their relationship? Were they friends? Maybe, even family?

"Computer, is there a photo of Jaq Bali?"

The computer flashed up a series of photos of a lean man with dark, curly hair. In the one front and center, he squatted in the middle of a large expanse of dirt. He was smiling at the camera, a smudge of dirt under his left eye.

He didn't look like her Madame Bali. Their hair color was

similar, but that was where the similarities stopped. Her skin tone was deeper than his—a warm, light brown, and while her hair was dark brown, it was coarse and straight. Their faces were different, too. And not only in shape. His face was warm, happy, and sundrenched. Hers had been distant and reserved.

But what about her mother?

"Computer, please pull up a photo of his wife."

Significantly fewer photos appeared. Jaq was in one. It looked like perhaps it had come from an article related to his discovery. The other appeared to have been taken as a hospital admittance. She bore no resemblance to her Madame Bali at all —fair skin tanned in the sun and wavy sand-colored hair.

So, maybe not family? But they could still be friends or acquaintances, even. Then, it hit her. Did that mean fake Madame Bali was from the Island too?

She decided to see if there was any information on Serena Bali's mother, Mina Lisand. It made for dry reading. She yawned. Her poor night of sleep made it easy to nod off in the peaceful study pod.

The words blurred together, and Ana blinked longer and slower until her eyes closed. But her sleep wasn't restful. Not even for a moment. The lights went dim, and then they began to rise. And once again, she was in the body of a girl named Terra. And they were of one heart and mind. Ana faded out of existence, and Terra became the center.

Terra smiled as she sunk a bulb into the ground. Today, she and Lady Fleur were splitting bulbs and replanting them into a new arrangement. Terra kept her head down and focused on her work, wanting to make sure she didn't damage any flowers.

However, her head snapped around when she heard a sharp,

unnatural intake of breath. Next to her, Lady Fleur's eyes had rolled back, and all Terra could see were the whites of her eyes.

Terra dropped her spade. "Lady Fleur? Are you okay?"

Lady Fleur closed her eyes and took a deep breath. She placed her hands on the earth to steady herself. "Perfectly fine, my dear. Just a spell of dizziness. These things are quite normal with age."

Relieved, Terra nodded and returned to her planting. Her heart still beating a little faster than ordinary.

After a moment, she looked back over to ask where the next plant should go and saw Lady Fleur slumped over. Her eyes were moving wildly.

"Lady Fleur!" she squeaked in terror.

There was no reply.

Terra scrambled to her side. She reached out a hand to steady her, afraid Lady Fleur might start thrashing. The soil from her hands stained the Lady's petal pink top. Was she about to have a seizure?

As Terra looked down, she saw another woman lying in Lady Fleur's place. In her mind, the garden soil was replaced with dirty black asphalt. A young woman in her thirties lay unmoving, her mouth slightly ajar. Her last words hanging on her lips.

No! Terra shook herself. This was different. This was happening now. She needed to get up. She needed to get help.

But suddenly, Lady Fleur's eyes settled. Her breathing returned to normal. She let her eyes close for a long moment and then sat up.

"Don't worry. I'll go get help," Terra told her.

Lady Fleur looked a little pale but otherwise okay. "That won't be necessary. They already know." She looked at Terra. "Please don't cry. I'm really very sorry I frightened you."

Terra swiped at her cheeks. She hadn't realized she was crying. "It's okay. What do you mean they already know?"

Lady Fleur sighed. "I suppose it will be impossible to keep the secret much longer. Now that you and your father are living on the grounds. Most of the staff know. You see, Mr. Fleur once had many rivals."

Terra nodded, listening intently. She needed to understand what had just happened. She needed to know Lady Fleur would be okay.

"One of them slipped poison into our food. A neurotoxin called Elysium. You may know it by its diluted street form—Lights Out." Her features tensed, and a scowl creased her forehead. "The thought that people could take a drug that has ruined my family for fun. It's—it's difficult." She paused for a moment. "It's a deadly compound at the right concentration. My daughter was still small, and at her body weight, the concentration killed her." She said with a swell of emotion. These were old wounds. "My husband and I, however, live on."

ANA WOKE, wishing she could go back to sleep. She wanted to know more about what had happened and the poison. She wanted to know what would become of the Fleurs. She was almost certain Lady Fleur was lying. She felt sorry for Terra. She understood the loss of a mother. It looked like now Terra would lose Lady Fleur too.

Ana stretched, preparing to leave the pod. But the screen changed. The biographical information for the Balis disappeared.

Instead, a video began to play. It was a video of a modern loft. No, it was Ophelia's aunt's loft! And then, Ana entered the frame. She was staggering forward with an unsteady gait, a tight purple dress clinging to her curves.

Oh no. A spike of fear shot through her body.

Sure enough, the video version of herself looked from side to side to see if she was alone. Then she opened the door to the greenhouse. The recording followed her. Finally, they reached the fateful moment. Ana leaned over the Stargazer Lily and plucked a petal. Looking around once more, she shoved the stolen petal into her pocket.

They had it all. On video. The very thing that could ruin her.

The video ended, and words began to appear before her.

You're not the only one who can dig.
- M.B.

Ana stared at the screen until the words faded away. Mutely, she stood. Someone was still watching her. Closely.

Now, more than ever, Ana was determined to find answers. She wouldn't be blackmailed by some invisible person. The dead didn't walk, and they didn't write stupid notes. Someone was messing with her, and she'd had enough.

15
GHOSTS & GALLANTRY

On Saturday morning, Ana woke around noon. She made her way into the kitchen to pour a cup of coffee. The stove was on, and something black and viscous, like tar or motor oil, was bubbling on the stove. The smell burned her nostrils.

In the living room, she could hear Ms. Kandinsky yelling into her infotab, "Listen. If it was easy, anyone could do it!"

Ana sighed. So far, Ms. Kandinsky was proving to be an awful roommate. She was as paranoid as Samuel but with more violent tendencies. She rose with the sun and spent most of the morning talking loudly into her infotab. The kitchen had become a makeshift laboratory.

Worst of all, Ana's romantic, bohemian dormitory had begun a disturbing transformation. An oversized doily now covered the rich wood of her coffee table, and a mauve and country blue floral afghan adorned the back of her low velvet couch. The side table was barely visible beneath a layer of tchotchkes. In short, the dorm was starting to resemble Ms. Kandinsky's apartment.

Ms. Kandinsky herself was restless. She didn't like being confined to the dorm, preferring to work in the field.

The only one who was really happy about the new arrangement was Petrie. He had taken an immense liking to Ms. K and was often found sleeping in her lap. Ana suspected she was feeding him scraps. She eyed his belly, which was growing closer and closer to the floor.

Careful to avoid the boiling tar and its fumes, Ana made a pot of coffee. She flagged Ms. K's attention and held up her cup, silently asking if she wanted some. Ms. K nodded and continued to yell into her infotab.

As Ms. Kandinsky finished her call, Ana drank her coffee and milled around the living room, taking in the latest changes. She found something new almost every day.

Today, it was the curio cabinet—the one that had been empty since Ana moved in. It had been left abandoned and dusty. Now, the glass sparkled, and inside the shelves were packed with porcelain figurines of angels, shepherds, and sheep.

She sighed. It looked like something a grandmother might collect.

However, as she looked closer, she realized these were no ordinary angel figurines. There were no chubby cheeks or eyes transcendentally uplifted to the heavens. Instead, their eyes radiated a fierce power. Even more unexpected, the angels had weapons.

What she had mistaken for a shepherd's crook was, in fact, an AK-47. Another had a golden sash... of grenades. The one she thought was holding out a dove of peace actually held a ball of flame.

Ana stared at them in horror.

At some point during this new and disturbing discovery, Ms. Kandinsky had ended her call and walked over to join Ana. "Can't take your eyes off them, can you?" she asked, mistaking Ana's anguish for awe.

Ana paused, attempting to gather the right words. "I just… never imagined… angels would have so many weapons."

"Why do you think every time one appears, they have to say, 'Fear Not!' It's because they're strapped!"

Ana decided it was time to extract herself from this conversation. "Um, sure. Let me just get your coffee."

She set her empty cup in the sink while Ms. K sat down with an exaggerated groan. Petrie immediately slunk over and crawled into her lap. He circled twice before curling up in a ball, purring traitorously.

Ana handed Ms. K her coffee cup.

She accepted it. "Thanks, doll. I'm pooped. I've been talking to field agents all morning."

"Everything okay?" Ana asked.

"Nothing for you to worry about. You wouldn't believe the coddling I give these do-nothings. I oughta—" She eyed her pot of tar with a wicked gleam in her eye.

"Well, I can't hang around anyway. I'm going to meet Shay."

She made a move to leave, but Ms. K called out, "Don't forget the backstory."

"I know. I know." Ana sighed and repeated, "You're Lola Applebottom, and you're from the island. You've been called in to advise on protocol. Your grandmother was a healer."

"And?"

Ana sighed. "And you're senile."

Ms. Kandinsky nodded, and an alarm went off on her infotab. Another call.

Ana waved and made her exit.

It was a Saturday, so Ana knew exactly where to find Shay. She stepped into an abandoned classroom with blacked-out windows and the hum of technology. At the sight of an outsider, kids scrambled.

Shay turned, "Oh, it's just you. Grab a chair."

She gestured for everybody else to chill. There were roughly twenty kids, mostly Nobles, all splayed out to compete in a video game tournament. Unlike the Rockwells, these kids were changing the program and hacking the specials, so the game was constantly evolving.

Ana pulled up a chair and watched for a while.

After a moment, Shay smirked and pressed a key. Every player's screen turned into a pixelated mess, except for hers, of course. A chorus of swearing and controller slamming commenced.

She took the opportunity to glance over at Ana. "Halt!" Shay said. "You look like crap."

"Thanks," Ana said.

"Did Adam do something else? You want me to hack into his info tab, look for embarrassing pictures or unsavory search history?"

Ana laughed. "Thanks for the offer, but I think I'll pass."

"You know I could do it."

"I know. But actually, I do need a favor."

"Name it."

"What's the price?"

"Free if you just spit it out."

Ana smiled. "I want files on Madame Bali. They're restricted."

Shay didn't look up from her game. The screen was rapidly normalizing, and twenty avatars were after her now. "Like by the school?"

"Like by the council," Ana whispered.

Shay set her controller down. "You want me to hack a council clearance level?"

"You're telling me you can't do it?"

Shay lowered her voice and looked around to see if anyone was paying them any attention. The ones closest to them were focused on their pixelated game screens. "Oh, I can do it. But damn, Ana, that's an ask."

"I know. I wouldn't ask if it wasn't important."

"But why? Why are you still looking into her? It could be dangerous."

"Not looking is even more dangerous. Whoever hired her is still out there. This is the only way I can get the upper hand."

Shay nodded. "Okay. It might take me a little bit of time. It's not that I can't crack it, but it'll take time to do it without anyone noticing."

"Let me know if I can help."

Shay snorted, returning to her usual demeanor. "Start by taking a coding class."

"Fair," Ana agreed.

When Ana returned to her dorm, she stretched out on the couch. Even though it was still only late afternoon, she felt exhausted. It was as if she hadn't slept in weeks. She stretched the ugly afghan out over her legs.

Ana's eyes began to blink longer and slower between each blink, but she didn't rest. Not even for a moment. The lights went dim, and then they began to rise. And once again, she was in the body of a girl named Terra. And they were of one heart and mind. Ana faded out of existence and Terra became the center.

Mrs. Fleur was having one of her bad days, and Terra was alone in the garden today. It felt like there was a weight on her heart.

The secret was out. A long time ago. Mr. and Mrs. Fleur would die. Just like their daughter. They had all ingested the poison, and in the end, it would claim each of their lives.

Terra pushed these hopeless feelings down. Instead, she decided to think about how lovely these flowers would be. Once she was done with her work here, she would take a cutting to Mrs. Fleur's bedroom. Something to cheer her up while she recovered.

In these early stages of the disease, Mrs. Fleur had occasional episodes, but there was a great distance between them. Mr. Fleur, on the other hand, had seen his last light of day and was now in total and complete darkness. He would never regain his vision and soon the seizures would take him. But not today.

When Terra was finished, her neck was sore from bending over the bed, but she was full of pride, knowing the tulips would be beautiful.

ANA WOKE FEELING groggy and dragged herself into the kitchen to make coffee. She didn't care that it was eight o'clock at night. She ran her hands under the cool water of the kitchen sink. When she was done, she checked her fingers, looking to see if she'd gotten all the dirt from under her fingernails. Then, she remembered, it had only been a dream. Her hands weren't dirty at all.

She laughed at herself and started the kettle.

Just as she poured her cup and settled back onto the couch, she heard the door open. She leaned around the corner and spotted Samuel creeping through the door like a teenager sneaking out to a rock concert.

He froze when he heard Ana call out, "You're back!"

She leaped from the couch to give him a hug.

He took a small step backward and patted her on the head. "Hello, Ana."

She frowned. As always, his expression hid everything— his secrets, his insecurities, and his heart. It had always been this way. There was still so much about him that she didn't know. "Where have you been?" she asked.

He yawned, feigning disinterest. "Engagement gifts. Such trouble. What to buy? You see, I wanted to purchase you something from the Sears Catalog, but then I remembered that catalogs hadn't been printed on Bellaton in more than one hundred years. So, to answer your question, I've been reviving the dying print industry single-handedly. You can see why it took me so long. But never fear; as a baron of industry, my venture has been successful. You can expect your throwing stars and submachine gun in 5-7 business days. Also, a Gideon Bible."

So, he was still mad. She decided to play along, hoping he might soften. "I've always preferred a shotgun. I like the way it kicks back, makes me feel like I could take on a zombie horde."

"Sorry, no exchanges," he said grimly. "I'm afraid the return shipping wouldn't be worth the money. Perhaps your fiancé can use it."

Ah, there it was. The sticking point. "Listen, Samuel; I'm really sorry. I should have told you straight away."

He held up a hand. "There's no need. You don't owe me anything."

"But I do. You saved my life. And we're friends. I was really worried when you were away. When you got back, you looked" —she stopped herself from saying the word fragile— "you looked tired. I didn't want to worry you."

"Should I be worried? Do you not want to marry him?"

"Yes. I mean, maybe. I'm just not sure," she said quickly.

He squinted the way he did when he looked at complicated math equations. "But why? Why would you agree if you're not sure?"

"Can we just drop it? I'm not marrying Adam right now. We are just dating. And I am perfectly capable of handling him and his dad."

Ms. K entered the room and saw Samuel standing in the kitchen. She swooped in and planted an enormous, wet kiss on his cheek, which he accepted with minimal wincing. "Thank God you're back. I didn't think I'd make it another day in this shoebox."

Things were awkward between Ana and Samuel over the next few days. Samuel hadn't abandoned her, but he now treated her with polite, distant courtesy. He inquired about her classes. He helped her with a few practice problems. Mostly, he silently read and watched.

Ms. Kandinsky had decided to hang around a little longer, though she now disappeared for days on end.

IT WAS WELL AFTER MIDNIGHT, and Ana was sleeping. The eerie creak of her bedroom door woke her. She rolled over, blinking. Was it morning already? She expected to see Madame Bali with her infotab. Then, she remembered Madame Bali was gone, dead.

She rolled over to face the door. No one was there.

"Hello?" she called softly.

There was no reply.

She looked around in the darkness. It wasn't morning yet.

It must have been someone down the hall. Maybe Samuel was doing his night owl thing, or Petrie was chasing a mouse. She closed her eyes.

Then, she heard the sound of rustling cloth.

She shot up in bed, clutching the covers to her chest and peering around in the darkness.

In the corner of the room, a figure stood stock still and shrouded in darkness. She sucked in her breath. Dark hair, knotted tightly on her head, and impeccable posture. It was Madame Bali. But it wasn't. Her olive skin was sallow. Her posture wasn't quite right either. Her eyes were filled with hate. More than when she had fired the arrow.

Ana locked eyes with her for what felt like a solid minute.

It couldn't be. It was a shadow. A nightmare. She just needed to wake up. She closed her eyes for a long moment and took several deep breaths. Then, she opened her eyes again.

The shadow was gone.

Ana tried to tell herself it was only a bad dream. Her imagination had gotten the best of her. However, she still couldn't go back to sleep. She didn't dare shut her eyes.

What if she woke up, and Madame Bali was hovering over her?

Madame Bali was dead.

Ghosts don't exist.

She repeated the words in her mind. Then, with her remaining courage, she wrapped her blanket around her shoulders, crawled out of bed, and hurried to escape her room. She went down the hall and straight to the living room. The holovision was still on.

Maybe, this was the sound she had heard. She started to sit on the couch.

"Ow," the couch moaned.

Ana jumped.

Samuel rose with a floral afghan wrapped around his shoulder. "Hey, whatcha doing up?" His voice was low and rumbly from sleep. He looked at her and noticed the fear in her eyes. He scooted to make room for her.

"Sorry I woke you," she said.

"It's no big deal. Is everything okay?

Ana considered telling him about what she had seen. Then, she decided against it.

"Thought I heard something," she said.

He rubbed one of his eyes and yawned. "Probably the holovision. Sorry. Bad habit."

"It's okay." She knew she should go back to her room now, but she couldn't face it. Not yet. She was still too shaken.

"Wanna watch something?" he asked.

"I'm not bothering you?"

"I don't mind being bothered. Besides, it's not like I have classes tomorrow. I can sleep until dinner." He started flipping through the catalog. "What are you in the mood for?"

"Anything but horror."

He looked at her again. "Ask me no questions, and I'll tell you no lies, huh?"

"What?"

"Oh, nothing."

16

DELPHI'S DEFEAT

Ana paced outside of the combat classroom. She had arrived early. After last night, she didn't feel like eating breakfast. She still felt on edge.

She saw Holden coming up the hall and waved.

"You're here early," he greeted.

"You, too."

"I wanted to get in a little extra practice."

"Without Adam," she added with a knowing smile.

"He's been a little distracted lately. You might know something about that." He raised an eyebrow.

Before he could ask any more questions about Adam, she asked, "Wanna warm-up together?"

"Sure."

They headed into the classroom and found a spot in the corner of the room. Ana sat on a mat and attempted to reach her toes. She felt the stretch in her trapezoid muscles. They must be sore from tensing or maybe from sleeping on the couch.

Samuel had been gone when Ana woke. He was probably in his room, sleeping the day away as promised.

Holden joined her on the mat.

They worked in companionable silence for a few minutes.

"Hey Holden, are you always awake when you have your visions? Or do they, I don't know, sometimes come while you're sleeping?"

He considered. "I'm such a deep sleeper that I really don't know."

She smiled, thinking of their time in the challenge when she could hear his snoring from across the hab.

"If I have, I don't remember."

"Are your visions always of the future? Do you ever see the past?"

"So far, everything I've seen is in the future. There aren't a ton of Rockwells with the gift that are alive, and because I haven't gone public, I can't exactly ask any of them."

"Oh," she mumbled. "That makes sense."

There was a lull in the conversation, and she stretched with her good arm toward her toes, careful not to jar the broken one. It wasn't throbbing anymore, but it was stiff and swollen. Holden lowered his head and leaned to stretch his hamstrings.

"Holden," she said again. This time, her voice was almost a whisper.

"Yeah?"

"What about, um, the dead? Have you ever seen them?"

Holden stopped what he was doing and looked right at her. His eyes scanning her. "Ana, what's this about? Are you having nightmares?"

Her cheeks turned red.

"Oh, um, it's nothing like that. I'm just curious. You and Ophelia are the only other people I know who have the gift."

"You'd tell me if something was bothering you?"

She nodded, not meeting his eyes.

He didn't believe her. It was written all over his face. "You don't have to do everything by yourself. Just ask if you need help. Okay?"

He looked so earnest that she couldn't tell him no. "Okay," she lied.

He nodded, and they finished their warm-up while making small talk about his drill practice and her artwork. They didn't talk about Adam or the gift anymore.

"GOOD NEWS, class. You've all reached the average threshold."

There were moans and groans in the class. After weeks and weeks of hard training and combat matches and simulations, Bold scored them "average." He continued, "As a reward, we'll be conducting our next match at an undisclosed location. So, you're suited up. Let's ship out."

Most of the class seemed pretty excited about the prospect of leaving the academy and training on a new course. This game wouldn't be broken into one versus one. Due to time constraints and the size of the terrain, it would be team-based. The game was over when every member of one team had been eliminated.

When Ana stepped out of the transportation jet, her jaw dropped. She was standing in the very same cityscape that had been used in the simulation from their first day of class.

Bold laughed. "Recognize the place?"

The students broke out in conversation over this new development. Some celebrated. Others complained. A few skipped straight to strategizing.

Bold held up a hand. "Quiet. We need to make the most of our time here. You have your suits, you have your weapons, and you know the rules. Game starts in..." He tapped his watch and the number five appeared in red glowing text in the sky. A countdown.

Adam yelled, "Come on. We need to get further away from the pack. This will be a bloodbath."

They sprinted behind him further into the city.

After her last adventure into the subterranean levels of the simulation, Ana was pleased they were staying topside this time. There were six teams of five—all within a mile of one another.

When they heard the buzzer go off, they turned down an alley. A few minutes later, they stopped to catch their breath.

"If we can break for a minute, I can build a tracking device. It'll light up red whenever someone from another team comes within a quarter-mile."

"How long?" Adam asked.

"How long will it take you to remove the magnetic resonator from that hovercar?"

"Three minutes," Holden said, shattering the window with the blunt end of his weapon.

When the tracker was up and running, it lit up almost immediately.

"Shit," Adam hissed.

"Time to move," Ja said. "Get me to a rooftop, and I can hit any target on the street."

LESS THAN AN HOUR LATER, the game had tightened up. There were only two teams remaining, and they were vying for the same prize—a military-grade chopper with artillery. It could end the game in minutes.

Three guys were closing in on Adam. He scanned until he found their locations. Two on the rooftop. One behind a building. All waiting for him—an ambush. But why three on one?

Where was their fourth man? He had seen them lose their fifth. Had they lost the fourth too?

Adam signaled to their own sharpshooter, Ja. Trusting in his teammate, he stepped into plain view in the center of the empty street. He was the perfect target. Silently, Ja fired two shots, and the rooftop snipers were out of the game.

The one on street level Adam took care of.

But the game didn't end. Where was the fifth?

Holden jogged out to Adam's side. "Delphi is after Ana. We need to get two streets over. Fast."

"Someone could get there a lot faster with the grappler," she said in a singsong voice, holding out a teched-out grappling hook. She'd been trying to convince them to try it for weeks, but no one wanted to lose the points.

"Fine," Adam relented. "I'll do it."

Shay looked smugly satisfied as he soared through the air.

ANA WAS CORNERED. She had run an entire block, only to turn on a dead-end street. She shot at Delphi, but he had some tech upgrade that was deflecting most of her shots.

She looked back at him and tripped over a piece of garbage on the street, landing hard on the asphalt. He closed the distance between them and loomed over her. He had grown taller and broader since the challenge, though only months had passed. A growth spurt.

She couldn't beat him in hand-to-hand combat. They were not matched in skill or size. Ana had less than a year of lessons. He had years, if not a lifetime.

She could have outrun him. That's why he had cornered her.

He put one boot on top of her arm, just above her wrist, and let it rest there, applying just enough pressure to pin it. She could feel gravel pushing into her skin, leaving behind a rough pattern. After several weeks, the swelling in her wrist had gone down, but it still hadn't healed. If he pushed any harder, the pain would be excruciating.

"It's unfair how quickly you heal."

Ana's eyes widened. He wouldn't really do this. They weren't in a simulation.

"In fact, what does it even matter if I accidentally step on it? I could push it down until it—" he made a clicking sound in the back of his throat and smiled malevolently.

She felt vomit rise in the back of her throat.

"Hey, loser," a voice called out.

Ana tore her eyes from Delphi and saw Adam striding down the alley toward them.

Delphi grinned. "Two for one."

Adam didn't return it. Instead, he waited until Delphi thought he was winning, then shot the grappling hook into the air. As he did so, a nearly invisible noose tightened around Delphi's foot, and he flew through the air, like a rabbit caught in a farmer's snare.

He dangled, upside down, five feet off the ground.

Adam smirked up at him.

Delphi looked positively rabid, dangling, red-faced, and shouting.

Adam held out a hand and pulled Ana to her feet. She gave him a high five. "Would you like to do the honors?"

"It would be my pleasure," she said with a curtsy. Then, she shot Delphi in the head. Of course, he didn't die. But he did freeze, which meant they didn't have to hear his obscenities anymore.

A canon sounded, signaling the end of the match and a win.

Bold came around the corner with a trail of students behind him. He shook Adam and Ana's hands. "Well done. And to the end with the full team. Very impressive."

Delphi stifled a moan from above.

"Don't worry, Mr. DuBois," called Bold, a smile playing on his lips. "I'll get you down." Bold pointed his weapon at the cording. He hit the minuscule target with no trouble whatsoever. The cord snapped, and Delphi hit the pavement with a loud thud. "Oops," said Bold. "I guess I should have turned on an artificial gravity device before I did that. Ah well, you're not hurt, are you?"

Delphi grunted and picked himself up with a grimace.

Bold didn't wait for an answer. "Excellent. Ana, Adam, truly excellent teamwork. Now, let's all get back to the academy before you're late to your next classes."

Adam and Ana walked side by side back toward the transport.

Adam cocked his head to the side and smirked. "Not so bad, Halt."

"Not so bad yourself."

He was smiling, his green eyes fixed on her brown ones, for the first time since their argument. "I was wondering. What are you doing later?"

She shrugged. "Nothing much."

"Want to go on a date with me?"

"Sure," she replied as if they hadn't been fighting for weeks. "What did you have in mind?"

"That all depends on how many school rules you want to break." He gave her a rogue smile.

AT SEVEN O'CLOCK, Ana was putting the finishing touches on her outfit. Things had been so stressful. She was looking forward to seeing something—anything—beyond the academy's walls that didn't involve shooting or running.

Normally, she went for a comfortable pair of jeans, but Adam had told her they would go somewhere special. So, she chose an emerald green taffeta skirt that came mid-calf and a fitted black sleeveless top. Both compliments of Michael's selection.

Her dark hair had grown and was now just below her shoulders. It had been two years since she had cut it all off to support her mom during chemo. It felt weird to cut it now like her hair was some sort of marker of time. A reminder of what she had been through. What she had survived. She ran a brush through it.

She held it back and liked the effect. She looked around for something to hold it back and saw the porcelain hair clip. She hesitated and then clipped it in.

She left her room to wait in the living room. She wanted to make sure she was the one to open the door this time. Not Samuel.

She needn't have worried.

He was at the kitchen island, leaned over a graphic projection. Using his finger in place of a stylus, he was scribbling numbers and symbols. Equations, she guessed, though it was far beyond her level of knowledge. He didn't even hear her come in.

"What are you working on?" she asked.

"The portal equation."

"The one from that book you read in the simulation?"

"Yeah."

"Why do you care so much?"

"It's just… stuck in my head. I won't be able to sleep properly until I solve it."

"Hasn't it remained unsolved for over one hundred years?"

He shrugged.

At seven o'clock sharp, Adam knocked on the door. Samuel

glanced at her with an expression that clearly said, "I'm *not* getting that."

Ana ruffled his hair. "Well, I'm off. Stop to eat."

Samuel frowned and looked back down at his work.

OUTSIDE, Adam was wearing a suit and tie. If she wasn't mistaken, it was the same one from the Winter Ball. The one with the emerald tie that set off his eyes. She wondered if she had subconsciously chosen the skirt for the same reason. Green.

"You look amazing," he said, grabbing her hand and giving her a twirl.

Her skirt swirled around her legs.

"You, too. Is that the same suit from the Winter Ball?"

"Different suit. Same tie."

He led her out of the building and onto the grounds.

It had been months since they had been alone together, and she found herself unsure what to say. It felt like a lifetime since they had watched movies in bed while Ana recovered.

"Where are we going?" she asked as they stepped out the door and into the courtyard.

"It's a surprise."

"No fair." She pouted.

"Okay, how about I let you ask three questions?" he said walking backward, so he could face her.

"Where are we going?"

He laughed. "That's like wishing for more wishes. Try again."

They were close to the main gates of the academy now.

"The town?" she asked.

"Nope."

"Dinner?"

"That's part of it."

"No combat?"

"No swords. No simulations. Just us in the real world. On a date." He grinned.

"That sounds pretty good. Will they be serving food in this real world?"

"Only the best."

They reached the school gates, and to Ana's surprise, the guards allowed them to exit with no commentary.

She stared at him in awe and jerked her head back toward the guards. "How did you do that?"

"I told my dad the engagement and new coursework were making you stressed. This date has been 'officially sanctioned,'" he said using air quotes.

Just outside the gates, a two-seater aircraft waited. The door was already open. There was no pilot inside. Adam stepped inside and offered his hand, palm out. She grabbed it, returning his smile.

"I hope you don't mind me flying?"

"I let Holden fly me in the vacuum of space, so I guess it's only fair you get your shot, too." She laughed.

"I'm a way better driver. You'll see. Besides, we're not going far."

The door closed automatically behind them.

Adam fastened his harness and reached over to help Ana with hers. His hand brushed her side. He gave her a small smile.

Then, he clicked the harness in place and put his hands on the panels in front of him. They took off silently into the darkening sky. She stared out the window and watched the ground drift away.

"You okay?" he asked.

"Yeah, I'm fine. I've never done anything like this before. I've only been up in the air those times we took the Rockwell jet."

"I get it. Those things are so plush, you barely know you're in the air. You don't get a view like this."

She nodded. The entire expanse around her was mostly

made of dark, tinted glass. On the outside, you couldn't see in, but from the inside, you could see everything. There wasn't much to see outside of the academy and its little seaside town. Just small dots of light below. The academy was intentionally isolated for the students' safety.

After about twenty minutes, she saw lights not below but ahead. A giant, floating barge the size of a cruise ship hung in the air.

"Whoa! What is that?"

"Our dinner reservation."

They pulled into an open bay, and it sealed behind them. Adam helped her out of her seat and onto the metallic floor.

An open doorway turned green, and a man in a coat and tails arrived.

"Rockwell, reservation for two?" he inquired.

Adam nodded.

The man inclined his head and said, "Right this way, please."

The meal was lavish, and the view was even better. They talked about what an idiot Delphi was, how much better Ana was doing in combat class, and Adam's upcoming test in math. They talked about everything…except their argument.

When they landed back on the academy grounds several hours later, Adam held out a hand to help her out of the jet. Their eyes met.

"It was my fault," they both said at once.

"I didn't mean to spy on you," he blurted out. "The guard just kept on giving me reports. I should have tried harder to stop him. I didn't take it seriously enough. And I shouldn't have lost my temper and accused you of anything."

"I'm sorry, too. I should have been the one to tell you."

He wrapped his arms around her. His breath was hot on her neck and then her ear. He whispered, "I don't want to share you, Ana. Not with him. Not with my family either."

A shiver ran down her spine. He tilted her head upward and brushed his lips across hers, and she melted into it.

When they reached her dorm, he said, “Come run with me again. It’ll be fun. And it’s great for stress.”

“Ah but then you’ll be stressed. As you’ll recall, I won our last footrace.”

He laughed. “So, I’ll see you at 7 AM?”

“Yeah, you’ll see me.”

17
SHATTERED

"Whoa! Look who is back for the morning run," Ja said. "Thought you were getting lazy on us, Halt."

"I guess we'll see who comes in first," she said with a grin.

He laughed. "I don't know if you're as fast as you were last time. I might have caught up to you."

"Doubt it."

She was pretty sure Adam would pass her, but she thought she could keep pace with Ja and Holden.

Ana went to take a shower after returning from a long day's run. As steam flooded the shower, she half expected to see a message appear in the steamy glass like some cheesy slasher movie. But there was nothing there.

However, ever since she had received the fourth note in the library, she hadn't slept well.

One of the notes had come through on her infotab. Could it have left a trace? Maybe she should ask Shay about this, too. But that would mean revealing a lot. Besides, she only had one as an example. Shouldn't she wait until she at least had two to show her?

Then, she caught herself. What was she thinking? Was she expecting another note? Was that what she had reconciled herself to?

Last Spring, Lady Fleur had given Terra a gift for her fourteenth birthday— a beautiful porcelain watering can. It was dainty, hand-crafted, and thoroughly impractical. Painted with beautiful flowers in pink, ivory, and green. It was one of her favorite things.

Like the watering can, Terra also felt dainty and fragile and maybe even a little impractical. Her father was a large man and a hard worker. What he needed wasn't a daughter but a son. Someone who could do more than grow beautiful flowers. He needed a helper.

Instead, he had hired a laborer. A squat, broad-shouldered man named George. He was strong as an ox.

She kept herself busy, tidying their cottage and making it as much like a home as she could. She had planted herbs in the windowsill for cooking and flowers by their front door. She liked to water them with the porcelain water can, even though it required her to refill it three separate times.

Her father always said things were to be used and enjoyed, not kept in pristine packages to look at. Things broke. That was a part of life. It didn't mean you should be scared to use them.

Terra always felt his words meant more. Things broke. Like her mother. Like hearts. But sometimes they could be mended.

After her mother's murder, it felt like Terra had been dropped from a great height. Her handle had been broken and a large fissure ran from down the side.

It was only many years later that she felt those parts had been repaired, glued back together. She was not perfect, but she could hold water once more.

Today, her father had gone into the city to pick up some supplies for the spring planting. As always, he would begin by giving the yard a thorough compost and overseeding to ensure a plush, green lawn.

Terra tried to hide the anxiety she always felt when he left the walled grounds. She didn't want him to know that her heart still fluttered when she thought of it.

Instead, she was determined to focus her efforts on tidying the cottage and making a hearty dinner for his return.

She turned on the holovision. Another murder in the city. The food shortage was sending people into a panic. When people were afraid, they were dangerous. She cut the holo off and took several soothing breaths. It would be fine. Her father had been to and from the city many times.

She opened the windows and let the fresh air run through the cottage. She stripped the bedding from her father's bed and then her own, picking up some trousers and work boots along the way. She dropped the work boots in the entry and took the clothes to the laundry.

Most of the fabric had been designed to be odor resistant and stain proof, the sorts of garments that one needed to wash every two weeks or more. However, for a laborer and outdoorsman, they needed more frequent attention. Terra wanted her father to look well. Not like a widower. It was hard enough to be a widower without looking like one. She started the load.

Then, she washed and peeled several blood-red potatoes, a Bellatonian staple in this region. They had a slightly acrid taste that gave them a spicy kick when prepared with the right spices. Perfect for a stew base.

The first herbs were poking through the dirt in their window boxes. She grabbed her beautiful pitcher and headed out to water them.

On her second refill, she noticed her father's helper, George, at the gate. He was bent over, clutching his knees. He had a gash across his cheek that was still bleeding, and his arm was red with road rash.

With the watering can still in hand, she ran toward the gate. What was wrong with George, and where was her father?

The thought echoed in her mind with each footfall.

Where is he?

Where is he?

She crossed the grass and reached George. He looked even worse up close. He was still bent over, and his breathing was coming in gasps. Yet, her father was nowhere to be seen.

This time, she said the words out loud, "Where is he?"

The groundsman pulled himself together enough to look up at her. His eyes were still wide with shock.

Terra felt the familiar clutch in her throat. She knew. She knew that look on George's face. She had seen it before. Something terrible had happened.

"Is he- is he okay?"

She couldn't bring herself to ask the question she really wanted to ask. The question she feared the most.

The groundsman shook his head. "I'm sorry."

She dropped the porcelain watering can. It shattered into a million pieces against the hard stone. Along with what remained of her battered heart.

Sometimes things break.

But they don't always mend.

Ana felt someone shaking her awake, and she looked up from the coffee table where she had fallen asleep doing her homework. Her breathing was erratic, and she struggled to catch her breath. Tears were shining on her cheeks.

Samuel crouched next to her, and concern lit his features. In a surprisingly tender gesture, he reached out and wiped one of the tears from her cheek. "What's wrong?"

It took her a moment to pull herself together, to remember that she was not Terra. She was not in the garden. She was Ana, and her father wasn't dead...probably.

Samuel rested a hand on her back, while she struggled to

resume normal breathing. "Ana? Can I get you anything? A cup of tea?"

She nodded, jerking her head wildly.

He got up and walked to the kitchen and began brewing the tea, while she dabbed at her eyes with a leftover napkin and tried to compose herself.

When he returned with the tea, he placed the china cup in front of her and oriented its handle leftward. "I made it how you like. With too much sugar and cream."

She nodded.

"Were you dreaming about your mother?" he asked quietly.

"No," Ana said.

Samuel's face hardened a little. "About… the challenge?" he asked, almost as if he was afraid of the answer.

She shook her head again. "It was nothing. Just a bad dream. Nothing to worry about. I'm fine, really." If she said it enough, maybe she would believe it. She had to admit, these no longer felt like dreams.

He looked at her unbelieving but nodded. "You know you can tell me anything, right?"

She punched him in the shoulder. "Of course, I do. But there's nothing to tell. In fact, I'm really embarrassed. It was just a bad dream."

He nodded. "Well, why don't I stay up and keep you company anyway? It's not like I'm going to bed anytime soon. Why don't we put on some cartoons? Something stupid."

She nodded.

When Ana had calmed down, she went to the bathroom to brush her hair and wash her face. As she brushed her dark hair, she thought of Terra. She had been a teenager this time. Almost Ana's age. There was something oddly familiar about her. She just couldn't quite think what. It was almost as if they had met before.

18

DELPHI'S REVENGE

The dreams came every night now.

Ana was tired all the time. She was falling asleep in class. Her eyes had dark circles underneath. She knew she should say something. She knew she should try to stop them. But the truth was she didn't want to. She was deeply invested in Terra's story now. It was like watching a movie, and she wanted to know how it ended. No, it was more than that. She wasn't watching. She was acting.

She felt haunted.

She shook away such superstitious nonsense. It was just a dream. It was normal to dream. Why shouldn't she find out what happened? It was just her brain, designing an entertaining story for her. Nothing more.

And if they sometimes made her cry, well, that was normal too. Dreams were supposed to be cathartic.

She yawned over her chemistry experiment. Her solution had turned blue, and now, she was just waiting on the rest of the class to catch up. She propped her chin in her hand.

When Ana woke, she had the most unpleasant sensation that someone was watching her. She sat up, wiping some drool from her lip. Everyone was gone. Class must have let out while she was sleeping. But why hadn't anyone woken her?

She heard a chair scrape against the marble floor. She whipped her head around and saw Delphi getting out of the chair behind her.

Her eyes widened in fear. She was alone with Delphi—the one person in the world she most wanted to keep her distance from.

He smirked. "Look who's finally awake. You must not be getting your beauty rest. Too busy with Adam Rockwell, trying to look like a hero."

She stood. "Leave me alone, Delphi."

He moved quickly to step in front of her. "Not so fast. We're talking."

"With you, talking is dangerous."

He smiled as if she had just complimented him. "You didn't seem worried about how dangerous I am the other day. Usually, worried people are cautious. They don't lure their enemies into traps and string them up in front of their class. They don't humiliate them." His voice shook, betraying a hidden current of rage.

"I didn't pick that fight; you did." She tried to move around him, but he stepped to the side and blocked her path.

"Don't play the victim, Ana. You're the one who came here. You're the one who entered our world. You could have stayed home, but you wanted power, a council seat, a crown. You're just another imposter trying to usurp a council seat you don't deserve. And, in the end, they all meet the same fate." He drew a finger across his neck. "I'd be doing the council a favor by killing you."

Adrenaline pounded in her veins, and everything in her told her it was time to run. She didn't care if she lost face. She just wanted out of this classroom. Now.

She made a quick move to his left, hoping to get around him and make a break for the door. He grabbed her right elbow and pulled her back in front of him. He grasped her shoulders with an iron grip.

"Let go of me!" she shouted.

"No," he whispered. "I don't think I will."

All her instincts were screaming at her to try and step back, but she ignored them. Instead, she listened to her Rockwell training. She stepped forward and thrust her weight at him. It worked. She knocked him off balance. He staggered back a step. It was enough. She was around him, and the door was just ahead.

"Stop," he said in a soft, dangerous voice.

And to her absolute horror, her body obeyed. She wanted to move. She wanted to run. She needed to fight through this. She needed to get far away.

"Don't move."

She felt like she had been paralyzed. In the challenge, he had used persuasion to make her walk toward the edge of the cliff. This wasn't persuasion; it was crushing power. She felt helpless beneath it. She struggled and finally with great effort lifted her left foot an inch off the ground.

Delphi's sharp gaze caught it. "No. You're not going anywhere."

"The class will be back soon," she said, finding her voice in her terror.

"They are all in the courtyard now. Everyone but us." Then, his eyes gleamed. "Walk to the window and see for yourself."

She followed his instruction like a magnet seeking iron. She crossed the room in seconds and stood at the window.

The chemistry class was, indeed, below. They were standing in front of the fountain, pouring in their solutions one by one. The fountain began to change colors, first dark and murky, then electric green, before finally settling on a soothing shade of sea foam green. Bubbles rose from the fountain, and water burst upward, creating a breathtaking display.

But Ana didn't have time to watch.

Delphi was behind her now. He was so close she could feel his hot breath on the back of her neck. He leaned forward and let one arm graze her side as he reached for the window latch. He pushed it open.

She stared out. What was he doing? What could he possibly want?

"Climb into the window."

"What?" she shouted. "No way!"

"Now," he hissed.

Though her legs were shaking, her feet moved to obey. She crawled up onto the window ledge and hovered in a crouching position, clutching the edges of the window with all her might. She was vaguely aware of pain in her wrist.

She wondered if she screamed for help if anyone would hear her. And if they did, could they reach her in time?

Before she could act, Delphi changed tactics. His voice became honey. Using every ounce of persuasion he possessed, he said, "Relax, Ana. Let your feet dangle. It's a beautiful day."

She did as she was told. He was right. It really was a beautiful day. The leaves were beginning to change in the trees, and the sky was clear. She could feel the sun on her face, and she wasn't afraid. In the distance, a flock of birds passed over the academy. She felt almost as if she could fly.

And then, Delphi suggested it. "I bet you could fly, if you tried."

"Maybe so," she murmured.

"The Halt family has many abilities. Some are said to be able to do all sorts of amazing things. I don't see any reason why you couldn't fly. Have you ever tried?"

Ana thought about it. She hadn't ever tried! How did she know? She hadn't tried. And what a beautiful day to do it. A beautiful day to fly for the first time.

She shifted her weight ever so slightly forward.

"Try hanging by your arms first," Delphi suggested. "Just put one hand on each side of the windowsill and lower yourself down."

Ana turned so her feet were hanging outside of the window, and her knees were on the ledge. She was facing inward, looking Delphi straight in the eyes. They glinted like burning embers.

"Now," he commanded.

She wrapped her arms around the ledge.

"That's it. Hold onto the ledge and hang your legs over the side. It's the first step. Then you'll know if you can do it."

It all made sense.

As she moved, a part of Ana's brain was aware of the shouts and screams from her classmates below, but she felt disconnected from it.

She could feel her feet dangling against the stone, thirty feet in the air. She could feel the wind whistle between her legs, ruffling her skirt. She wondered if this was what the tingle of wings felt like.

She could hear his laughter and smell his breath as he leaned over to assess her progress. "Good. Now, let go."

Just as Ana was about to do so, she heard a loud shout and a thud.

Something in her wakened, and she realized what she was doing. But it was too late. She was already slipping. She couldn't maintain this grip.

Inside, she heard the sounds of a scuffle. "Help!" she cried.

"Hold on," Samuel shouted.

She tried, but her injured wrist couldn't support her body weight. It hadn't finished healing. There was something terribly wrong with it. What was left of its strength snapped like a twig. Only one hand held her. She could feel her arm beginning to shake. She wouldn't be able to hold on. Just as her fingers slipped, Samuel grabbed her forearm. She was screaming, and he was pulling her in the window.

Delphi was slumped on the floor, unconscious. Whatever Samuel had done to him, it hadn't been kind. Ana lay crumpled on the floor, catching her breath, blinking her eyes trying to figure out what had happened. Samuel wrapped his arms around her and said, "You're okay. You're going to be okay."

The first of the class began to spill in the door. Adam's green eyes fell on her in her crumpled heap with Samuel's arms locked around her. His eyes were worried, then they shifted from fear to a spark of annoyance. He rushed over, pushing Samuel out of the way. "Ana, are you okay? We saw you coming out of the window. What were you thinking?"

"It wasn't me," her voice shook. "It was Delphi. He- he made me—"

Adam understood at once. He took in Delphi, lying in a heap next to one of the lab tables. "I'll kill him."

"Would it solve anything?"

"We won't know if we don't try..." he grumbled. Then, he looked at Ana, scanning her from head to toe. "But what happened to your arm? Did he—wait a minute—isn't that the one you—"

Her eyes were as wide as saucers and filled with fear. "Please. Don't say anything else."

Adam stopped.

Kids were beginning to file into the classroom now.

"We need to get her out of here," Samuel said to Adam. "Ana, can you walk?"

She nodded.

Adam put an arm around her to steady her, careful to avoid her broken wrist.

"Let's go. You too, I guess," he said to Adam.

The three of them hurried out of the classroom, pushing past a startled group of students.

Back in the dorm, Samuel handed Ana a cryocanister. "Go rest and ice your wrist."

"Where are you going?" she asked.

"To get something for your wrist."

"From the infirmary?"

"Of course not. I'll steal it from the greenhouses."

"But won't they still find out?"

"Ana, there are eyes everywhere on this campus. Trust me, they already know." Samuel turned toward Adam. "You, come with me."

Adam was so surprised that, to Ana's shock, he followed.

FIFTEEN MINUTES LATER, Samuel returned alone. He handed her a salve. "Spread it on the swollen area. It'll mend the bone, but it won't set it properly. That means you might not have a good range of motion, but the pain should stop."

She accepted the jar and spread the clear liquid on her injured arm, wincing in pain at every light touch. "Thank you."

"Pack your stuff."

"Where are we going?"

"You'll see soon enough. Let me know the moment the council contacts you."

"But what about you? You're leaving again?"

"To prepare."

"Don't you have questions about what happened?"

"Hundreds, but I know enough to protect you. Your wrist is broken, which means you can't heal. After the challenge, you made a grand speech declaring your powers and attempting to free me. Thanks for that, by the way."

"You watched that?"

He looked at her like she was crazy. "Ana, it's the first thing I did when I got out. Well, second, I ate a sandwich and smoked a cigarette first."

"Oh, I—"

"No need for that. I figured you didn't want to talk about it, so I left it alone. And if I'm being honest, I didn't want to talk about it either."

"Samuel."

"By naming yourself successor on a false pretense, you committed an act of treason. I'm not sure what the council will do next, but they would be within rights to execute you. Also, I'm assuming somehow Adam and his dad fit into this scheme." He thought for a minute. "Well, maybe not Adam. Just his dad then? Anyway, rest while you can."

ADAM AND ANA walked side by side in silence. The warm ocean breeze blowing in the space between them. Ana didn't reach out to grasp Adam's hand. She wasn't sure what he was thinking. Was he angry? Was he hurt? She honestly had no idea.

As they continued down the moonlit path, Ana couldn't help but think something was wrong. They were a couple. They were sneaking out after hours together. They should be laughing, smiling, kissing.

Instead, they moved in stony silence. Adam's jaw was tense, but his face betrayed nothing. She couldn't read him.

Was he going to break up with her?

Finally, they reached the wall, where she had found him looking at the stars one year earlier. Now, he was looking at his boots. His brow was furrowed.

Instead of scaling the wall, he sat down with his back pressed to it. As she moved to do the same, he put out a gentle hand to guide her down beside him, making sure her injured arm didn't move or bump the wall in the process.

Finally, he broke the silence. "You could have told me, you know."

"I wanted—"

"—to protect me, right?"

Surprised, Ana only managed to nod.

Adam's jaw tightened once more, and this time she could read the frustration on his face. "Why don't you let me protect you every once in a while?"

She put a hand on his chest, over the spot where the arrow had pierced him. Even though she couldn't see the mark through his shirt, she knew the blue dot was just beneath. "You've given me too much help already."

"That wasn't your fault. Besides, you healed me. Although, I'm a little fuzzy on how."

"A plant," she muttered. "Holden had a vision that I would be shot with an arrow. So, I stole a few petals from a healing plant when I was staying with Ophelia and her aunt at the capital. I hid it from the cameras."

He let out a breath. "So, it's true. You really can't heal. I knew it was, but I guess I was hoping somehow I was wrong."

She bit her lip. "I tried. Really hard. I just...can't."

"I used to wish every day that I would be the one with the Rockwell family gift. That I would have visions. But that's not how the gift works."

"Yeah, but no one will kill you for it."

They lapsed into silence. He broke it after a moment. "There's more, isn't there?"

"More what?" she asked, anxiety rising in the pit of her stomach.

"Secrets."

"I'm the one who put the hot sauce in Ivan's cereal. No regrets."

"Be serious. The council won't ignore this." He brushed his hand gently against her injured arm. "Is there more?"

She looked down at her lap, letting her hair hide her face. She nodded. If she didn't tell him now and he found out, their relationship would be over. But if she really told him everything, their relationship might be over anyway. "I'm not sure where to start."

She was stalling.

He knew it too. He moved to sit in front of her so that their knees were touching. He took her uninjured hand. "Just tell me."

Ana decided to start in safe territory. The notes. "I think Madame Bali might be alive."

"What?" Clearly, whatever he was expecting, it wasn't this. He dropped her hand in surprise.

She winced. "I got the first note at your house."

"My house! Why didn't you say something?"

"Well, we had just had that fight about the maid."

"She was probably the one who planted it. But you said first? How many have there been?"

"Um, maybe four or so."

"Four!"

"Sorry, do you still want to know the rest?"

He did. Adam wasn't satisfied until Ana had recited each and every single note she had received.

"Is this why you've been falling asleep in class and looking so tired all the time?"

"Well, actually, that's another thing. I've been having these dreams about the same girl every night."

"Those creepy notes would be enough to give anyone nightmares," he muttered. "There's another thing that's bothering me. My dad isn't one to miss details."

"Oh." Ana had hoped this wouldn't come up. "Um, yeah, he did notice. He was re-watching video recordings at the manor. I accidentally saw him when I was getting a glass of water. It was late. He noticed me watching from the hall."

Adam let out a low groan as if he had been kicked in the stomach. "He blackmailed you into the engagement."

"There was another video, too." She covered her face with her hands. "While we were on Earth, Samuel was in a simulation prison. They were torturing him. He couldn't sleep or eat. He was alone, and it was my fault. I had to fix it. Your dad gave me a way."

The silence was terrible. Ana peeked through her fingers at him. His cheeks looked splotchy and red and though he didn't blink, there were tears in his eyes.

"Adam," she gasped, reaching for his hand. "I'm sorry. I should have told you. I should have trusted you."

He pushed her hand away and stood, brushing at his eyes. "It was all for him."

"It's not like that. I swear. You know I like you."

"Like isn't enough. Not anymore." His voice shook. "I have to go. I can't do this now."

She clutched at the back of his shirt, but he pulled it easily from her grasp. He wouldn't let her see his face. Instead, he scaled the wall and dropped over the side.

She couldn't climb with her wrist like this. She couldn't follow him.

A MESSAGE CAME through on her infotab. The council hadn't even bothered to grace her with their presence. Instead, they sent a pre-recorded message. The polished voice of Councilman Dubois said, "Anabella Halt, you have been summoned before the council. You must appear at once."

Well, she thought. They didn't mince words, did they?

Get to the capital now. Pretty straightforward. What would she do when she got there? Was this why Samuel told her to pack her bags?

She had to assume they heard about the window incident. Were they calling to see if she was okay? Were they calling to talk about Delphi and how he would be expelled from school? She doubted it.

Or had more members of the council, like General Rockwell, watched the footage from the challenge? Had they learned her secret like Samuel had predicted? Had they realized that none of the cameras showed her hands as she leaned over Adam before his miraculous healing? Or worse had they somehow found footage that actually showed the petal?

Perhaps they were just putting two and two together. Ana had only healed once. And it hadn't been captured on video. The only witness had been partially unconscious.

Now rumors were flying about how she had fallen out of a window. At least two people had seen her injury firsthand—Lydia and Delphi. There were probably others who were suspicious. Students who had tried to shake her hand, hug her, hand her a heavy book, or compete with her in combat class.

Or perhaps the council had their own cameras rigged up throughout the school. They might have seen for themselves. The only room she was sure was clean was her dorm. That didn't extend to classrooms, and Ana had exhibited some unusual behavior.

What did she do now? She couldn't ignore them. That was a surefire way to get picked up by one of those black helicopters like the one that came for Samuel months ago. Unlike him, she might not be lucky enough to walk away. Who would bargain for her life? Would Adam? Was it even fair to hope for that?

Of course, the other ugly option was that she could go. If she went, she couldn't heal. Surely, they would ask her to display her healing abilities. Surely, they would ask why her arm was injured. These two things were inevitable.

That only left her with two options— run or hide. She wasn't sure either was truly viable. None of the options were good.

Samuel looked over her shoulder. "What's that?"

She handed the infotab to him wordlessly.

He played the video. His face was neutral but pale.

"It's what we expected," she said.

"Don't worry. I have a plan. We'll just have to put it into motion faster than expected."

"You don't expect me to go, do you?"

"Of course not. We're going to the one place they can't follow—the island. Finish packing and meet me at the dock in one hour. Sooner if you can manage it."

19
FAREWELL & SET SAIL

Packing was difficult. There seemed to be an unexpected flood of visitors, starting with Ms. Kandinsky who had been away in the field for several weeks.

"A boat ride? Count me out," she said, sitting heavily on the edge of Ana's bed.

Ana grabbed several hangers of clothes and tossed them onto the bed. "Oh, do you get seasick?"

"Something like that."

"You're really not coming?" Ana asked. "Can't you just whip up some Dramamine in the lab?"

"I don't do water. Everyone's got limitations kid. Don't push it."

"Sorry," Ana muttered.

Ms. Kandinsky patted her on the head. "Don't worry about it. You're gonna be just fine. Besides, you're going to need someone here. Once they realize you're gone, all hell is gonna break loose."

After Ms. Kandinsky's departure, Ana began packing in earnest. She crammed clothes into her bag, tossed her infotab on top, and started zipping.

There was a faint knock on the door. Adam stood there, his hair bedraggled and his clothes uncharacteristically ruffled.

"Hi," she breathed. "Do you, um, want to come in?"

"Is it just you?"

"He's out making preparations."

Adam nodded and crossed the threshold.

"I'm so sorry. I feel so bad—" she started.

He held up a hand to stop her. "My dad manipulated you, the same way he manipulated me last year. He wanted an engagement. He never cared about your feelings or mine."

Relief flooded her body. He understood.

He continued. "You're not the kind of person who can look at someone suffering and turn away. Not even a stranger like that maid. So, I can't be mad at you for wanting to free Samuel. I mean, I am mad, but I'm trying not to be." He clenched his hand into a fist at his side. "But why didn't you tell me? You should have told me."

"I know. I'm sorry." She reached for his hand, and he pulled away.

"I don't know what Samuel is to you. For that matter, I don't know what I am to you. And I want to know. I want to have the time to figure it out with you. Like a normal couple. You know, without the fake engagement. But I know about the message from the council, and I know where you're going."

She hesitated for a moment before saying, "Maybe you could come with me."

He shook his head. "I have to stay. Someone has to misdirect the council. They'll be expecting a jet with you on it. I can fly to the capital. They won't know you're gone until it's too late."

She pulled back from him. "You don't have to do that. This isn't your mess to clean up."

He shrugged. "It's fine. I want to do it."

"Won't the council be furious?"

"Probably. But my dad started this. Let him get us out of it."

Ana sighed. "You know from here things are only going to get more complicated."

"How so?" he asked.

"Someone is trying to pick off my family line. I'm the last one standing. It's probably someone from the Seven."

"So what?" he said fiercely. "We'll eliminate every single one of them."

"What if they're council members?"

He paused. "It would be more difficult, but it's been done before. Their family could choose a successor."

She gazed up at him sadly. "What if it's a Rockwell?"

A storm passed over his features. "I don't know. There isn't- you haven't-"

"No. Not yet. But it could be. Adam, this world, this government, the Seven— they're all you've ever known. You've got a place here. One day, gift or no gift, you'll be on that council."

"You can be too."

"That's the difference," she said a little sadly. "I don't want to be. I don't want that future."

He frowned. "Then, what *do* you want?"

"I don't know yet."

"Then how can you be sure?"

"I'm sure."

He wrapped his arms around her, tighter than usual as if holding onto something that was already slipping away. She rested her head against his chest and listened to his heartbeat. Then, he pulled back and bonked her affectionately on the head. "Safe travels, Halt."

"Safe travels," she whispered.

ANA REACHED the dock half an hour later with a large duffel bag tossed over one shoulder. It had begun to drizzle, and her hair was sticking to her neck and face. She wondered if she looked as dejected as she felt.

Samuel was dressed in dark galoshes and a long raincoat. With his long hair and day-old stubble, he looked like he could be a member of a deep-sea fishing crew. He waved as she approached.

Trying to at least pretend things were okay, she called out, "Ahoy matey!"

He rolled his eyes. "The crew are loading up the last of the cargo. We'll be ready in fifteen minutes. Your—Adam—is doing us a real favor."

Sure enough, the crew hurried to and fro, loading cargo onto the large boat ahead. To her surprise, it appeared to be styled after a Spanish galleon.

"This seems like a lot of stuff."

"I had originally intended for you to return to the Isle this summer. I never thought we'd need to get underway now. The currents are even more dangerous this time of year. As such, we shall require additional provisions."

Ana raised an eyebrow. "And I see you found the best boat in the fleet."

"Do I detect snark?"

"Uh, yeah. It looks ancient. Like 1700s pirate style."

He smiled. "Trust me. It'll get the job done."

"If you say so."

He left her then to talk with some of the crew, regarding final preparations, and she wandered down the dock to get a better look at the ship.

To her surprise, someone was waiting for her behind a stack of crates. Shay. She was wearing the earrings she had crafted from Ana's old cell phone— bright green and silver. The electronic components looked like little freeways dangling from her ears.

As Ana grew closer, she noticed Shay's unusual body language. She was biting her nails, and her eyes were flicking around nervously. Her hair, usually black and silky, looked greasy as if she had been running her fingers through it.

Shay didn't say hello. Instead, she pressed a small chip and a slip of paper into Ana's hand. "I wanted to give you this. It contains all the files you asked for, even some correspondence between Madame Bali and her handler. I just couldn't trace their origin point. Sorry."

"Don't apologize. This is amazing."

Shay didn't acknowledge the compliment. She continued on, "Now, to access these files, you'll just set the chip on top of your infotab. The files will sync automatically. Then, type the password on your slip of paper and complete the requested retina scan."

Finally! Ana had almost given up hope of reading the files about Madame Bali. Shay had come through just in the nick of time. "Thanks! Seriously, this is going to be—"

Shay's face turned dark. "Don't thank me."

"Oh, do you want me to pay you? That's no problem. I'll just borrow some money from Samuel." Ana turned to find him, but Shay grabbed her sleeve. Ana eyed her with confusion. "What is it?"

Shay's confident demeanor crumbled. "Money's not the problem. There's something I have to tell you. Something about the dome. And what happened there. It's all in the files. I should have told you sooner. But I didn't think—I didn't want you to, well—"

"Just say it," Ana said, her voice a little sharper than she had intended. A thousand scenarios ran through her mind. What did Shay know? Had she seen something in the dome?

"You're right. Sorry. Madame Bali approached me. She wanted access to the system," Shay blurted out.

Ana's mouth dropped open.

"I thought she was your adviser. I thought she wanted to check in on you, or maybe cheat for our team, you know, absolute worst-case scenario. I never thought, believe me, I never thought it was possible she wanted to hurt you."

"What did she say?"

"Not much. She told me she was worried about you. She said she wanted to be able to access the system and knew I was trying to hack it. She wanted to know how it was coming along." Shay hung her head. "The truth is there was one piece I was missing. One thing that would allow me to hack the system. Once I was in the dome. She passed that piece to me. In exchange, I gave her access to the rest."

Ana was shocked. She couldn't believe it. One of her friends, her teammates, had been the one helping Madame Bali. No, that wasn't fair. Ana had lived with Madame Bali for months. Shay hadn't known. She hadn't meant to...

Then, Ana remembered who she was talking to, and her blood turned cold. "What did you get out of it?"

From the looks of it, if Shay had felt any lower, she would have fallen through the dock and into the water below.

"She paid me. I thought it was a good business decision. She could look in on you, and I'd make some quick money. I couldn't have been more wrong. I'm so sorry. Unbelievably sorry. Xan was—" her voice broke. "He was a great person. He didn't deserve to die. And I'll never forgive myself."

The ice in Ana's veins melted. She put a hand on Shay's shoulder. "It wasn't your fault Xan died. You couldn't have known."

For a moment, the words of another echoed in her ears. "It's not your fault she died, you know." She shook them away.

"Are you going to tell my family? Are you going to tell Ja?"

Ana paused. What was she going to do?

Finally, she decided. "I'm not going to tell your family. What happened in the dome is none of their business. They weren't there. They weren't impacted. I'll keep your secret."

"And Ja?"

She shook her head. "He should hear it from you. When he's ready. When you're ready."

"You've been a good friend, Halt, and I've been a lousy one in return. If I told you this months ago, maybe some of these things wouldn't have happened."

"We can never know that."

"So, I hope you'll be safe on the island. And on your trip. And I hope when you get back, you'll still consider me your friend."

Ana gave Shay a hug. "Of course, I will. Take care of Ophelia. And talk to Ja."

Shay nodded and wiped a tear from her cheek.

Ana slipped the chip and paper into her pocket and went to find Samuel.

To her surprise, she found him standing next to Zora. "Zora!" she said, giving her a small hug. "What are you doing here?"

"Mr. Samuel decided it would be wise to bring along someone who had actually been to the island before. I'll be your guide. I'll also make sure you look gorgeous along the way."

Ana laughed. "Thank you for coming, but I'm still not wearing that emerald eyeshadow."

A slightly bent and weathered man with stringy hair approached. "Just the three of you?"

Samuel nodded.

"The captain is ready."

They followed him down the dock and up a long plank to the ship. When they reached the main deck, he said, "Welcome aboard the HMS Breeze. I'm First Mate. Name's Grimes. Now, this isn't going to be your ordinary voyage. The waters are going to be rough. Traveling this time of year is not advised. But the captain is as experienced as they come. Done it a number of times."

"We understand the risks," Samuel said, cutting him off.

He grunted. "Well then. Lemme show you to your cabins. Mind you, don't be expecting luxury."

"That's fine, Mr. Grimes. We have no such expectations."

"And you'll have to do some work too. There's no room for idle hands on a ship on a voyage such as this. It wasn't easy to get reliable hands who can keep their yaps shut."

"Also, fine. In fact, I look forward to hoisting the sails."

"You'll do none of that," Grimes snapped. "Only experienced sailors will touch the sensitive equipment."

"Of course. Just a joke," Samuel said quickly.

Grimes stared him down for a long moment. "We'll need pairs to do night watch. All you got to do is stand on deck and holler to the captain if something's not right."

"Don't you have equipment for that?" Ana asked. How antiquated was this boat? Even on Earth, there was sonar to detect things in the water ahead and tools for detecting weather fronts too. Could this ship really be lacking this basic equipment?

"What do you take us for? Oyster brains? We're brimmed to the gills with every gizmo and gadget the Nobles can produce. But nothing beats the human eye, especially as you approach *the island*," he whispered the last two words as if they were bad luck.

"I don't mind taking the first watch," Ana volunteered. She didn't like the idea of being alone in her cabin right now. She was sure her thoughts would turn to Adam or Shay. Neither were things she wanted to dwell on right now.

"I'll join her," Zora offered.

Grimes led them down a wooden staircase into the lower cabins. "A quick *orientation*," he said with a sneer. He didn't seem to have much respect for non-seafaring people. "Cabins are below deck. Mess hall is above the bow. The captain is *not* to be disturbed."

He led them in front of three doors and grunted, "These three. Doors open." Then, without further ado, he left.

"Not much of an orientation," Samuel muttered.

"Since he dislikes the mainland so much, it's less likely he will have given away our secret to informants."

Dinner consisted of grab-and-go sandwiches and an unrecognizable red fruit. The captain made a brief appearance. He was of short stature with a bright red beard. He bowed to Ana. "A real treat to have another Halt onboard my vessel. It has been many, many years. The seas can be rough this time of year, so I hope you'll remain safely below as much as possible, my lady."

ANA AND ZORA took first watch that night.

"Where will I stay when we get there?" Ana asked. "It isn't like I know anyone."

Zora laughed. "You're the daughter of the Southerly Province, remember? Any family would be honored to have you stay with them. But I was hoping you would stay with me."

"You have a house on the island?"

"Yes, a whole orchard actually. I inherited it from my grandfather when he passed away a few years ago. It has sandy soil and many fruit trees. At first, I saw it as a burden, far out from the city, but now it is home."

"I'd love to stay there."

"Then, it's settled."

Zora walked the length of the starboard side of the ship.

Ana headed for the helm.

Many hours later, leaned up against the mast, she fell asleep, looking out at the vast expanse of stars. She felt safe for the first time in a long time.

20
DANGEROUS WATERS

Later that night, Ana dragged herself back to her cabin. When her head hit the pillow, she didn't run her hands under it to look for notes. She simply closed her eyes and fell asleep.

The darkness lifted almost at once. She was Terra again. She was in a hallway, waiting in front of a large wooden door. Anxiety rose in her chest like a butterfly trapped beneath a cat's claw.

Terra passed a large, gilded mirror. She was fifteen years old now. A young lady. But her face was pale, and her eyes beady and dark. She had almost forgotten how grief and worry can change a face. It had been years since her mother died. Now, her father was gone too.

The Fleurs had been kind enough to let her stay on through the funeral with no mention of expelling her from the premises, but she knew their kindness wouldn't last. Surely, they would kick her out. A girl like her. A nobody. She stared at her reflection with newfound bitterness.

She heard the creak of the doorknob *turning and jerked to attention. Lady Fleur exited the room. Her face looked worn, tired.*

She curtsied.

"Terra, will you come in?"

Her heart hammered in her chest like a bird that might fly away. She longed to fly away too. She knew that this was the talk she had been dreading—the moment they would send her away. And she couldn't bear it.

She pulled her shoulders back and tried to hold her chin up, to make her father proud. But she wanted to cry already.

In the office, Mr. Fleur sat poised at his desk. It must be a good day, she thought. It had been weeks since he had left his bed. She noticed he was able to sit upright without a pained expression contorting his classically handsome features.

He was wearing a crisp button-down *shirt, and someone, probably Madame Fleur, had combed his hair. It was straight as a pin and slicked neatly to the sides. Most of the usual signs of his accident were hidden. For just a moment, Terra imagined what Mr. Fleur must have been like before he was poisoned. She could just imagine him, sitting in a chair like this, in front of a desk. Hard at work.*

The illusion was shattered by his eyes, of course. They were almost entirely dark. The pupils expanded. Now, a thick dark film was spreading.

The same darkness that would leave him crippled and finally dead.

Terra could feel the tears welling up in her eyes. She tried not to blink for fear their cascade would never end. How could one room of people hold so much sorrow and so much misfortune?

In spite of everything, even though they were about to send her away, she wanted desperately to stay by Mr. and Mrs. Fleur's side. She wanted to be a part of Mrs. Fleur's rare genuine smiles that broke through more and more these days. She wanted to care for Mr. Fleur through his darkest days and cry with him when the light left his eyes forever.

She knew it was improper to feel such things. She was a low-born groundsman's daughter. An employee. An orphan. A burden.

In her rising swell of misery, she had almost failed to notice the two men in neckties, sitting in hardback chairs at Mr. Fleur's side. She couldn't read them. Their faces were as straight and polished as their suits.

Mr. Fleur cocked his head, listening for her footsteps. "Terra," he said fondly. "Come on in, my dear. Sit with us. I'd like to introduce you to Mr. DuBois, my personal lawyer, and Professor Fleur of the Royal Conservatory."

Confused, Terra remembered her manners and dropped into a curtsy.

"So formal. What a polite child," noted the professor.

"Don't be scared, Terra," coaxed the lawyer. Terra felt strangely soothed. The man had a honeyed baritone voice.

Terra glanced back at Mrs. Fleur in the doorway, looking to her for reassurance. Before realizing how childlike this must look. Many years had passed since she had arrived at Fleur Estate. The nightmares came less often, but the scared, shaking little girl still lived inside her. The one who longed to hold her father's hand. The one who wanted someone, anyone to tell her things would be okay.

Mrs. Fleur nodded encouragingly, and Terra moved to take a seat at the table.

She waited as a small silence passed. The lawyer pulled out a briefcase, touched the biometric lock, and produced some papers. "Terra, we are here to discuss your future."

Terra's breath caught in her throat. "Mr. Fleur," she gasped. "Please let me stay. I know I am not as strong as my father, but I will work as many hours as it takes to make up for my weakness. I can help in the garden in addition. I won't be a burden, I swear! Just, please don't send me away."

Mr. Fleur looked taken aback.

Terra clapped a hand to her mouth in horror. She had embarrassed herself and Mr. Fleur too. And in front of Mr. Fleur's business associates. A blush crept up her neck and filled her cheeks.

Mr. Fleur chuckled. "Don't be silly. No one is sending you away. We are here to see to your future. And I hope you will accept that it lies here, with us."

"Oh," the words slipped past her lips. She couldn't say more for fear of bursting into happy tears.

"We want you to stay here, living as you always have. You'll help Mrs. Fleur in the gardens, and you can stay in your current rooms, or if you prefer, move into the main estate. It's your decision and no bother either way. But, of course, a young lady of your age needs a future. The Royal Conservatory takes on apprentices at sixteen. So, you have one year to prepare."

Terra couldn't respond. She was too shocked. It was as if she had fallen into a dream. No, she had never even allowed herself to dream of such things. A commoner like herself being allowed to attend the royal conservatory. A future in the sciences.

"There is only one question left to be answered. Do you accept?"

She finally found her voice. "Oh yes," she gushed. "A thousand times yes."

He smiled. "Very good." She noticed a tired note in *his voice. "In that case, I shall leave you in very capable hands." He turned to the two men. "Belford, Jax, I expect all the paperwork in my inbox tomorrow. Yes?"*

"Of course, sir. We will handle everything."

"Very well. Then, I bid you both a good afternoon." He stood.

Terra noticed then how his left hand clenched as he did so. It was his tell. Despite all the outward signs to the contrary—his drawn-back shoulders, his expensive, pressed dress shirt, his manicured hair and trimmed mustache, his air of leadership and professionalism—Mr. Fleur was not a well man.

This entire meeting was a highly coordinated piece of performance art. One which he was putting on almost entirely for Terra's benefit. He needed to be a man of sound mind *and body today as he called in favors and broke social norms.*

They nodded and stood politely as Mr. Fleur did so. His wife hurried over to lend him her strength. They all shook hands one last time.

"I'll be back with tea service," Mrs. Fleur said as she glided arm in arm with her husband from the room.

They had played their parts well. Mr. Fleur had appeared a powerful businessman, *too busy to stick around for something as mundane as paperwork. Mrs. Fleur had appeared the adoring wife and an excellent hostess. Only Terra knew the truth.*

Mr. Fleur would collapse in the hallway. His eyes going totally black as the blinding light came and the nerve pain shot fire up and down his body like a circuit board.

She tried to put the thought from her mind.

Mr. Dubois placed the first document in front of her. "We have a lot of paperwork to get through. Let's get started."

Terra pulled her attention back to the men at the table. Mr. Fleur had done all of this for her. It would be a poor thank you to slack on the finer details. "Just tell me what I need to do."

After an hour of explanations and signatures, the paperwork was finally complete. Terra was the legal ward of the Fleur family, and her application for the conservatory was complete.

Professor Fleur, the senior of the two men, *said, "Young lady, before we go, I must impress upon you're the magnitude of what we've done here today. There are 127 apprentices at the Royal Conservatory." He paused, and she wondered if she should say something like what a grand number or how lovely. "Can you guess how many of them are not born into the Seven families?"*

"Probably not very many," she said.

"Six. There are only six. Do you understand?"

She nodded. "Yes, sir. I will do everything in my power to make the Fleurs proud."

He snapped his briefcase shut. "Certainly. You must. It is a debt you take on but one that you will never repay."

Ana woke up from the dream with a gasp. She knew who the girl was. She knew who Terra was. Her face had been growing steadily more familiar as she aged in the dreams. In this last one,

Ana had gotten a long look in the mirror. The face reflecting back had been unmistakable.

The girl in her dreams was Madame Bali.

The girl Ana had been dreaming of and rooting for was the same woman who had tried to kill her. How had she overlooked it? It was so obvious. Her tan skin, her dark hair, her rigid posture, her formal speech. Ana had overlooked all these things because Terra had also been vulnerable and kind-hearted.

Nothing like the cold woman she had become.

Ana couldn't sleep for the rest of the night.

THE FOLLOWING DAY, Samuel was at her door. "Ana, I know you're kinda royalty, but there isn't a cook on board," he said pointedly.

"Ha. The only thing being royal has done for me is give me a list of enemies I could roll across the main deck."

"True. Does that mean you'll make something?"

"Let's just drink that rum I gave you."

"No way," he said, pulling the bottle from her grasp. "You're dangerous when you drink."

"Hey!" she said indignantly. "How was I supposed to know the fruit was going to do that?"

He narrowed his eyes. "I'm not talking about the fruit."

"Oh." She turned bright red. He was talking about the capital. The kiss.

She punched him in the arm.

"Ow."

"Serves you right. There's something weird I have to tell you."

"I like weird."

"I'm not sure you're going to like this. I've been dreaming of

Madame Bali as a child. The thing is... I think the dreams are real. I mean, I think they might be."

He considered. "What makes you think they're real?"

"The detail, the emotion. They're just not normal dreams. And I wake up so tired."

He looked at her for a long moment. "Is this what's been going on?"

"I thought they were just nightmares until today."

"What changed?"

"Well, I've been watching this young girl grow up. Her name is—was—Terra. It never even occurred to me that she could be connected to Madame Bali. But in this last dream, she was a teenager. She looked just like her. Could the dreams be real?"

"It's possible. There are ways. But I think you can forget about it for now."

"How am I supposed to forget about it?"

"The Island will block all signals and kill all mainland tech. If someone is interfering, they won't be able to do so for much longer. The dreams will stop."

To her surprise, Ana had mixed feelings about that. These dreams, if they were truly memories, were a gateway to Madame Bali. She could learn from them. Now, she'd be stuck with only Shay's hacked messages for intel.

"You two take the first watch. If you see anything out o' the ordinary, you call out to ol' Grimes. He'll be over in a flash."

Ana and Samuel's eyes met, and they exchanged an amused glance. Grimes was way over the top with his pirate routine. The captain had already let it slip at breakfast that Grimes' real name was Grimaldi and that he was a retired salesman.

Samuel offered to watch from the crow's nest. Ana suspected

he really just wanted to climb it. Sure enough, he ignored the mechanical lift and artfully pulled himself to the top with ease.

"Miss climbing in my window?" she called up.

"I never climbed in *your* window. I climbed into the dormitory window. You make me sound like some sort of pervert."

She laughed.

They fell into silence, separated by many feet now. She stood and leaned against the wooden pole, looking out at the dark roiling waters.

If she were to fall in, the boat would be gone in just minutes. She felt a chill at the nape of her neck. The sea was dangerous—a force of nature, unbeholden to the whims of man. It could not be tamed nor conquered, enticed nor wooed. It could lap at you with warm gentle waves like a kitten drinking milk, or it could crash down on you with the force of a semi, pulling you to a still, watery grave.

She sunk down and let her back rest against the mast. A large raindrop hit her bare shoulder. Then another. "I think it's going to rain," she called up to Samuel.

Large waves began to form, rocking the boat gently back and forth. The wind picked up, whipping her hair around her face. "Hey, do you think we should wake Grimes?"

Samuel made his way down from the crow's nest. "All we have to do is holler, remember?"

They both snickered.

But once Samuel made it down, the heavens let loose their fury. Water pelted them, and in mere seconds Ana's shirt was soaked through, and her hair clung to her head in damp strands.

She started forward to meet him and nearly slipped on the wet decking.

Samuel caught her, and his face was just inches from hers. "You okay?" he asked.

She could feel his warm breath on her lips, and her eyes met his. Something crackled between them, like static electricity.

Samuel set her upright and stepped backward. "I'm going to go wake Grimes."

Ana nodded, still staring.

Thunder rolled across the water, and lightning flashed in the distance. By the time Samuel had returned with Grimes, the boat was falling and rising with the waves.

A particularly big surge sent a small amount of ocean water washing across the deck.

Noticing the fear in her eyes, Samuel shouted against the wind, "Ana, why don't you go below?"

She shook her head. "I'm fine."

Grimes pointed to the sail. "If we don't get it down now, it will tear."

Samuel nodded and started climbing.

The waves were massive now, breaking across the side of the ship, sending buckets of saltwater surging from one side to the other.

Ana was afraid, but she was more afraid of returning below deck. Wouldn't she be more likely to drown there, if the boat were to flood? She thought of scenes from the movie Titanic.

No, she would stay on deck.

Samuel was gone. She watched with trepidation as he made his way up the slippery metal, climbing out over the very ocean itself. One misstep and he would be lost. She gritted her teeth.

And then small whirlpools began to form off the starboard side of the boat. It was unlike anything Ana had ever seen. Like the water going out of a bathtub.

"Hold on," Grimes yelled.

The boat dropped several feet at once in the next swell. Ana's sneaker slipped again. She grabbed the mast to steady herself. But when she looked up, she saw something wholly unexpected.

In the crow's nest was the unmistakable figure of a woman, shrouded by wind and water. How could that be? No one had been up there. No other woman was even on deck. Zora had gone to sleep hours ago.

She stepped back from the mast and squinted up through the rain. Maybe it was her imagination, but it looked as if the woman's hair were knotted on the top of her head. Just like Madame Bali's.

Ana was no longer touching the mast when the next wave struck. A surge of water gushed over the edge of the boat. Ana lost her footing and slipped. Before she could stop herself, she was being washed over the railing of the boat. She screamed—an ear-splitting sound that no one could hear over the gale-force winds. She tried to grab for the railing, but her hands were too slippery.

She was now plummeting toward the roiling, black sea. Seconds later, she plunged into the icy blackness. The shock of the cold and impact knocked the wind out of her. But she recovered after a minute.

She thrashed against the current, trying to keep her head above water. As the next wave surged, she knew her time was up. When it crashed, she would be slammed underwater.

SAMUEL JUMPED the last eight feet from the mast to the ship's floor. "Ana!" he yelled. His boots splashed through inches of water, and he peered out into the sea. It felt like his heart had completely stopped in his chest. The sick realization passed over him that if he didn't find her in the next minutes, she would be gone. Forever.

He screamed her name, hoping she would hear him and call out in return. But it was no good. She would never hear him over the winds. He called anyway, shouting until his voice was hoarse.

Her reply never came.

TERROR, unlike any Ana had ever experienced, gripped her heart. She kicked her legs and threw out her arms as hard as she could, trying desperately to swim back to the boat.

But she was no match for the raw power of the sea.

The wave sucked her under and crashed, burying her under a torrential force of water. The force knocked the air out of her lungs, and in her panic, she inhaled black water. She was desperate, alone, and afraid. She was going to die.

A bright light appeared in the darkness. Could it be "the light?"

No. The light was coming from her engagement ring. Its warm glow engulfed her, repelling the water, and forming a protective sphere around her. Through no effort of her own, she rose from the ocean as if she were inside a soap bubble. She crossed the stormy sky, moving toward the boat.

Everything went black.

SAMUEL COULDN'T BELIEVE what he was seeing. A luminescent orb surrounded Ana, and she rose from the sea, floating upward in the air as if invisible strings were guiding her. The orb grew, engulfing Samuel. Inside their bubble, the wind was still, and the rain had stopped.

Moments later, she landed on the deck with a light thud.

Samuel rushed over, losing a boot in the process. He fell to his knees beside her and pulled her into his lap. "Ana, can you hear me? Ana?"

There was no reply. She was paler than he had ever seen her, and her eyes weren't opening.

"Do something," he urged himself.

For a second, his mind was a white blank of panic.

CPR. He knew the steps. Before he moved in with Ms. K, he had lived in a homeless shelter. Once, a man outside had gone into cardiac arrest. After that, Samuel had learned. But working on a plastic manikin had not prepared him for *this*.

This was no test dummy. This was *Ana*.

He took a deep breath and walked through the steps.

1. Lay the victim flat on their back. 2. Check for breathing and pulse.

He could do that. He just needed to focus on one step at a time. He lifted Ana from his lap and lay her flat on the deck. Then, he brought his head down to listen for breathing. There was none. He could feel adrenaline ignite in his veins.

She wasn't breathing.

You need to calm down, he coached himself. You need to focus. She's not breathing. That means you need to do it for her.

3. Give the victim two breaths.

He lifted her neck and tilted her chin to open her airway. God, he hoped he was doing this right. He pinched her nose and breathed into her mouth. He saw her chest rise. Good. That was promising. He did one more rescue breath.

Now what? 4. Begin chest compressions.

He twined his hands together and slammed them into her sternum. His hands were between her breasts, but he didn't even register the impropriety. He was too afraid he would break her ribs. Too afraid he wasn't doing the compressions fast enough.

If he messed this up, how would he ever live with himself?

Foam started to come out of her mouth, and he was so startled he almost stopped.

Behind him came the calm, steady voice of the captain. "You're doing fine, son. Two more breaths now, and ignore the foam."

Samuel followed his instructions. He pressed his lips to her cold, blue ones and breathed out for one long second. Then, he did it once more.

"Good, now the compressions. Thirty. Go."

Samuel did. Thankful that, at last, someone was here to tell him what to do. Twenty more compressions in, and Ana coughed. More foam came from her mouth. She took in a rattling breath.

"There's a good lad," the captain said. "Roll her onto her side. You've done your job well." The captain draped a blanket around Ana from shoulders to feet.

She opened her eyes.

SHE SUCKED IN A RATTLING BREATH. It burned like fire in her lungs, but she tried again. Each time taking in a little more air. Samuel was clutching her now. She could feel his body shaking. "You're okay. You're okay," he kept repeating in the same desperate, hoarse whisper.

Waves continued to lash the boat mercilessly, but the sphere was growing. Soon, it engulfed the entire boat and even the waters around them. It pulsed three bright lights like the aurora borealis and expanded like a bomb. Except everything in its wake became calm. The rain stopped. The thunder and lightning were gone. The water was unnaturally, perfectly still.

Ana's ring glowed like a sun going super nova.

Somehow, the sea had been tamed.

She looked up at the rapidly lightening sky. It was as if the ring's light had chased the storm away, although she knew the winds blowing that fast had probably just passed as quickly as they came.

"You're okay," he said again. This time, his words reached her.

"I-I," her teeth were chattering. "I think so, but I'm so cold."

"This blanket will warm you, but it has to do so gradually," explained the captain. He turned to Samuel. "Don't let her remove it for an hour."

"Yes, sir. Thank you, sir," Samuel said.

She had never seen him treat an adult with so much respect. Maybe none of the ones in his life had ever earned it. She felt like she was seeing a piece of him that he had left behind long ago—the part that went with fancy parties, internships, and everything else that came with being a part of the Seven.

Samuel wrapped her tighter in the blanket.

21

STONES & MIST

The following afternoon, Ana was back on the main deck. She looked out at the water. It was dark and still. The wind, which had been so ferocious the day before, had died down to the slightest breeze, barely enough to fill the sails. She took a deep, steadying breath. It hurt.

She had bronchitis when she was eight, and she remembered coughing and coughing. Her mom had given her honey and lemon tea to soothe her throat. She wondered if they had any tea bags in the mess hall.

A few feet away, she spotted Zora and Samuel together.

"What the hell was that last night? That orb swallowed the ship," he hissed.

A knowing smiled pulled on Zora's lips. "That's no ordinary ring. That's the sea stone. It's a Halt family heirloom. I don't know how Ana found it, but it was once her grandmothers."

"My grandmother's?" Ana croaked, her voice still raspy.

"Ana!" Samuel said with a jolt of surprise. "What are you doing out of bed?"

"I wanted a cup of tea."

"Go back down, and I'll bring it to you," he offered.

"I don't want to lie in bed. Too much time to think. I'd rather hear about the ring."

"Okay then. How about tea and lunch? I'll cook." He gave her a large smile that stretched painfully across his face, but his eyes were dark and moody. His cheerful demeanor was as unnatural as those "hang in there" posters in her dentist's office back on Earth.

"I should like to see that." Zora snorted.

"Rude," he said.

The corner of Zora's lip twitched. Then, she turned to address Ana. "How are you? Did you get enough rest? You didn't wake?"

"I'm okay. My throat is sore. Wake? No. Why would I—"

Zora looked pointedly at Samuel. "Someone was so worried he couldn't stay away. He was in there on the hour, just staring at you like a great overgrown lizard."

"It's normal to check in on a patient."

"I hope I don't have to remind you you're not a doctor."

"Well, if there was one on bloody board, you can bet I'd have sent them in my stead."

"We'll be on the Island soon enough. Magdalena will see to her there."

"Who's Magdalena?" Ana interjected.

"The oldest woman on the island. I suppose you could think of her as the cultural or spiritual leader of the Southern Province. She'll be 121 this winter."

"Wow." Ana took a moment to digest this. Did this mean life spans were extended on Bellaton? It had never occurred to her to ask.

"People on the island tend to have extended lifespans," Samuel said in answer to her silent question. "Scientists think it is due to their diet, rich in seafood. Also, the amount of salt is said to be—"

Zora's lip quirked upward. "Hmmph."

"And I suppose you have a better explanation?"

"Not one you'd accept."

Ana ignored their bickering. "You said this ring once belonged to my grandmother?"

Zora nodded. "And many, many generations before her. That stone may be thousands of years old."

"But did it really pull me from the water and stop the storm? That's not possible, is it?"

"I don't know much about it, in truth. Only that every Monarch of the Southerly Province has worn it for as long as our history exists."

Ana looked at it skeptically. "It doesn't look that old."

"I'm sure the stone has been reset dozens of times."

Ana nodded. "Still, I've never seen anything like this at school."

Zora lit up. "Wait until you see the Island. The technology and the magic far surpass the mainland but in their own way. You'll see soon."

"Are we close?" Samuel asked.

"Oh yes," Zora said, inhaling a deep breath of ocean air with a look of deep pleasure on her face. "Feel how still the wind has gotten. By nightfall, we will reach the stones."

"The stones?" Ana croaked.

Samuel extended an elbow. "We'll tell you all about them in the mess hall. You need to sit and, from the sounds of it, a bowl of hot soup is in order."

On this, Zora agreed wholeheartedly. So, Ana accepted Samuel's arm, and the three of them made their way to the mess hall overlooking the bow.

Ana sat and looked up with pleading eyes. "Could I get a cup of tea, please?"

"Certainly," Samuel agreed, passing her gently onto a wooden bench. "Zora can keep you company."

"With extra lemons and honey."

A sad smile passed over Samuel's lips. "Like your mom made. Of course."

A few minutes passed and Samuel returned with a cup of piping hot tea with two lemon slices in the cup and sweet enough to give a toothache. He gave a little bow. "Tea for thee, my lady." He turned to Zora. "Soup and sandwich okay?"

She shrugged. "Anything is fine for me. Can I assist you?"

"No, I'll be fine. This is in my wheelhouse."

Samuel returned twenty minutes later with grilled cheese sandwiches made on thick, crusty sourdough bread. Accompanying this was a bowl of creamy light orange soup.

Ana squinted at it.

"Try it. It's got a similar flavor to potato."

It was delicious and salty. She sipped it and her throat felt immediately better. "This is really good."

"Surprised?" He passed Zora her bowl and sat down in front of his own.

"Well, yeah. I didn't think a Jacobs would know how to cook."

"It's something I learned on Earth."

Ana raised an eyebrow. "From who?"

"I learned it at the soup kitchen."

"You worked at the soup kitchen? Why would you—" she stopped in mid-sentence. "Oh."

"I wasn't exactly a volunteer."

"Oh," she repeated.

"It's nothing. I neither want nor need a pity party. You're the one with the sore throat. Just enjoy the soup."

Zora remained quiet throughout this exchange, blowing gently on her soup before raising the spoon to her lips. She sipped it and nodded approvingly. "Excellent."

"So, um, about the stones," Ana said, changing the subject.

Zora put her spoon down. "When you get close to the island, you always know. The instruments die. The wind dies. Then come the first stones. Tall and jutting out of the sea. And usually mist."

"Dangerous conditions," Samuel added.

"But very fortunate for the people. It is hard to conquer a lone island, far out in the waves, surrounded by mountains that do not allow ships to pass easily. An island that often has fog hanging low around its shores, where the systems on planes go haywire. And most of all a place where all who walk on its shore are weakened. Legend has it that intruders die within twenty-four hours."

They finished their food.

"Do you want to sit up on deck?" Zora asked. "I want to watch and see when the stones appear."

"No, I think I'll go back to my room, but you stay and enjoy."

Zora nodded.

Samuel followed Ana down the narrow steps to the cabins. "Are you going to sleep?" he asked.

"No, I'll probably do some reading."

"Do you mind if I join you?"

She shrugged. "Sure. But you know you don't have to worry. I'm fine. Really."

He nodded but hung by the door.

She grabbed her infotab and settled into bed, sitting cross-legged. She pulled the covers up around her like a shawl. There were no chairs in the room, and Samuel lurked in the doorway. Finally, after a long, awkward moment, he settled in on the floor with his back against the bed.

"You don't have to sit on the floor."

He waved away her comment. "You stretch out. Get some rest."

Ironically, it was Samuel who fell asleep. His head leaned back against the bed.

Ana smiled down at him. "Goodnight, Samuel," she mouthed. She wondered if he had gotten any sleep at all last night. It sounded from Zora as if he had been at her door the whole time. She had to admit she would have done the same for him.

Then, she returned her attention to her infotab.

Messages between Madame Bali and her handler. Most of them were boring. Just reports on what Ana was doing. Her comings and goings. Nothing new to her. And of course, both parties were very careful to never use their own names.

Finally, after reading a two-page essay on her poor eating habits, she found something interesting. The first message came from the address associated with Madame Bali.

Are you sure this is the only option? The girl could die.

Are you getting cold feet? Remember the aftermath of the Oceania.

That was the end of that particular chain. And nearly the end of all the messages altogether.

Whatever this was, it had been the motivation Madame Bali needed to continue her mission. What was the Oceania?

OVER THE NEXT DAYS, Ana slept, read, and drank a lot of tea. She had been surprised at how sore her arms and legs were on the second day. Meanwhile, Samuel was never very far away, fetching cups of tea, bringing soup, and doting on her like a mother bird.

Right now, he was sitting next to her bed reading. She prodded his shoulder with her toe. "Let's go up on deck. I want to see Zora."

Ana was still nervous on deck, worried that somehow another rogue storm would arrive to wash her away, but this evening was beautiful. The sun was setting in the eastern sky. They found Zora staring off the starboard side of the ship. She pointed at the horizon, and Ana gasped.

She had been expecting natural rock formations, like mountains, volcanos, or outcroppings. However, rising from the sea were massive, carved monoliths. From the lines, she guessed they had once been perfectly square, but time and water had softened their edges. Despite that, deeply grooved markings remained behind. They reminded her of the hieroglyphics on the Egyptian pyramids. The sight was breathtaking and strange.

In the shadow of so many overwhelming thoughts and worries, Ana hadn't given much thought to the island. But now that she was so close, she could feel the excitement building in her veins. She was traveling to the place where her mother, grandmother, and great grandmother had been born. And probably centuries of other relatives before them. This was her ancestral home.

The breeze was mild today, and Ana thought this was lucky. Otherwise, the boat might be damaged on the stones. "How will we pass through?" she asked.

"Slowly. Carefully," Zora said.

A DAY LATER, there was no longer enough wind to fill the sails. Their technology was useless. Everything was on the fritz. Ana had no signal on her infotab. Even without a signal, it seemed to turn off and on sporadically. The ship's instruments had armed the ship before the captain reluctantly cut all power.

They drifted helplessly through the calm waters.

Food rations consisted of protein tablets, fruit, and leftover crusty bread. No one was actually hungry, but everyone wanted to eat real meals again.

Ana spent most of her time below deck, playing games that didn't require a signal or technology. She quickly learned she was terrible at crossword puzzles.

In a moment of weakness, she agreed to a game of chess with Samuel. He had to remind her which pieces were which.

"I don't stand a chance, do I?"

He grinned.

The game was over in less than five minutes.

Ana groaned.

"Don't feel bad. I saw what you did in that first combat simulation. You could be great at chess. You just need to learn the game and traditional moves."

She shrugged. They played again and again until it was finally suppertime.

It was the third day with no wind. A thick fog had pooled around the monoliths, reducing visibility and creating an impossible dilemma. Attempting to navigate between the stones could easily damage the ship. They couldn't use advanced technology. The systems were so haywire that they had become dangerous. What if their weapons systems were self-detonated?

So, they waited.

The following day, the conditions had not changed. And they were out of bread. The captain called all hands to the main deck for a meeting. The protein tablets would sustain them, but the crew was already growing impatient.

When Ana reached the main deck, she found most of the crew were already here. The captain paced in front of the crowd, waiting for stragglers.

"I know you're all bored and miserable," the captain announced. "That's why we'll be taking a small fleet of rowboats and escorting the princess to the island directly. I'll need some volunteers from the crew."

No hands went up.

The captain began to pace. "Oh, come on! Are you all so superstitious?"

"It's not superstition; it's real," shouted a man. "The island is cursed."

"Folks just drop dead out of nowhere."

Ana had heard all of these rumors and more. The crew whispered that the mist represented the barrier between the living and the dead. That the isle itself was some sort of purgatory. The sickness was judgment.

The captain cut his eyes upward in exasperation. "Island sickness is a studied phenomenon. It's not a curse. As long as you don't step foot on the island, you have nothing to fear."

He waited. No one spoke up.

He grunted his frustration and barked out, "Whoever doesn't go is cleaning the johns for the rest of the voyage. And scraping rust off the figurehead." No hands went up. "Dangled upside down," he added.

A few hands went up.

"Fine, fine. You then. We leave in one hour. Ready six boats."

"Six?" a crewman called out incredulously.

"Yes, six. Two for our passengers and four to accompany. We leave nothing to chance in the waters of the Southerly Province. Now, steel your nerves. You'll insult the princess."

Ana wasn't insulted. In fact, she was frightened too. Frightened of leaving the safety of the larger boat. Frightened of being so close to the dark water that had almost been her tomb. And even a little frightened of the Island itself. A part of her believed the outsider sickness would strike her down too.

Samuel spent the hour leading up to the departure arguing against it. He railed against the captain, the weather hazards, and anything else he could come up with. Finally, he turned to Zora. "Let's just give it a few more days. Ana needs to rest."

"Ana is fine," Zora said. "She's had her strength back for days. This is what we came here for, remember?"

He muttered under his breath, "Traitor."

Zora ignored him and went to pack her things. Ana followed.

When she returned, the deck was bustling with activity. The crew was preparing water, protein tablets, and various equipment. Samuel seemed to be perpetually under foot, and it occurred to her he might be doing it on purpose. After all, he was keeping up a steady stream of grumbling, and so far, he had refused to lift a finger to help.

Soon, small hand-carved boats were being lowered into the water. Finally, Samuel fell silent. He crossed his arms over his chest and began to sulk.

Ana sighed and grabbed his hand to pull him away from the crowd. They ducked around a corner and out of the crew's way. "Samuel, you're the one who planned this. What's wrong? Talk to me."

He looked down at their joined hands. Ana blushed and tried to pull back her hand. He held onto it. His eyes locked on hers before drifting slowly down to her lips.

She shivered.

"My problem is—" He wrapped an arm around her back and drew her closer. His face was so close that she could feel his breath across her lips.

Her lips parted in anticipation, and her heart picked up tempo.

And then someone behind them cleared their throat.

Ana and Samuel jumped apart, disentangling themselves.

"It's time to leave," Zora said with a hint of a smile on her lips.

Ana nodded wordlessly, her face flushed. What was she doing?

Zora didn't linger, returning to the area where preparations were taking place and leaving them alone once more.

"I'm sorry," Samuel said, taking another step backward and running a hand through his hair. "I shouldn't— Just come back soon, okay?"

Normally she would have said something snarky, like, 'Thanks, Mom.' But right now she was having a hard time forming a sentence. And she was well aware of just how much Samuel was *not* family.

"Send a flare if you need me," he said.

She tried to shake her lingering thoughts of his lips and the way he had looked at her moments before. "No way. You'd get sick."

"That might just be a superstition," he said.

"Like the one that turned on the ship's weapon's system? We are *not* testing it."

He sighed, closing his eyes briefly. "Then, I'll see you when you've learned to heal."

She laughed nervously. "Yeah, when I can heal."

What if she couldn't?

ANA, Zora, and their accompaniment boarded the wooden rowboats. Each was only large enough to hold two people. They were absolute works of art, hand-carved into the shapes of animals. As Ana stepped down into hers, she saw it was in the shape of an otter-like creature. By the time they had all disembarked, there was a tiny fleet of toy-like ships floating gently in the water.

The captain stood on the bow of the ship and saluted, and some of the crew waved from their various stations. As they rowed toward the stones, Ana watched the HMS Breeze shrink into the background.

Everyone in the boats was in high spirits. Despite their reluctance to volunteer, most were adventurers at heart and excited to get out on the water. Friendly chatter spread between the boats as they rowed.

After half an hour, one of the oarsmen called out, "The Hall," and a chorus of cheers went up. The song was bawdy and loud, and everyone sang along. After the first two verses, even Ana joined the refrain.

However, all singing stopped as the first boat reached the stones. Ana could hear her rower suck in his breath and hold it. She thought of the old Earthen superstition about holding your breath while passing a graveyard.

As the first boat passed the first stone, the hieroglyphics began to glow blue. Ana held her breath now, too. Even though the stones seemed mystical and spooky, she didn't believe the island was purgatory. She did, however, believe in Bellaton's superior military technology. What if the stones were some sort of signal to command?

But nothing happened. Her boat followed the first. Then, the rest came until they were all floating amongst miles of stones. Mist wrapped its way around the boats until it was difficult to see even ten feet ahead.

Apparently, while Ana had been talking to Samuel, lots had been drawn to find the last rower. Nobody wanted to get any closer to the island than necessary. Ana wanted to laugh it off, but the mist was eerie, the water deep and dark, and the rowers silent. The only sound was the wooden oars slipping into the slick, black water.

Time passed, and the sky grew dark. Ana worried that she and her rower would be lost in the darkness. Separated from the group. In a place where no one would come for them.

Just as Ana thought they may have to spend the night in the

boat, lights flickered on the horizon. Ana heard voices lifting in unison. Just like on New Year's Day, she felt that same warm hope envelope her. But there was something more, a feeling of joy. Maybe even homecoming.

Were they singing for her?

The mist began to clear, and she could see the shadow of an island. This was the place that even the Seven couldn't wipe off the face of the planet. It hummed with a sort of energy that Ana couldn't explain. It was primal, and she felt it run through her bones. Perhaps it was the same invisible force that sickened outsiders or brought down aircraft.

The lead oarsman called, "Land!"

As they grew closer, she saw a thousand dots of light, flickering gently in the ocean breeze. Ana's rower had ceased his efforts, not wishing to get any nearer. But a warm zephyr rose up and blew them closer to the shore.

When the boat began to drag the bottom, her rower began to look panicky.

"Don't worry," she assured him. "I can wade in from here." She grabbed her duffel bag and stepped into the water. It was warm and came only to her calves. She put her hands on the carved otter's nose and pushed the boat away from the shore.

Then she made her way to the beach. When her feet touched the sand, the crowd parted. Each person was holding a candle, and Ana could make out their faces in the flickering light. She hesitated for a moment.

Then, she heard someone approach behind her. She turned to find Zora.

She took Ana's bag and nudged her forward. "Go on," she whispered. "Your people are waiting. Walk to Magdalena."

At the end of the parted crowd was an old woman with her arms held wide. She stood on the beginning of a polished walkway. It was made of similar stones to the ones she had passed in the ocean.

Ana walked through the crowd, and as she did, they sunk to their knees. She felt overwhelmed by the gesture. Their faces in the flickering firelight were smiling and hopeful. Ana had to remind herself to keep walking and not just stand and stare.

Magdalena had thick hair that fell in long gray waves around an aged and weathered face. Her body was stout, and her spine was curved. She used a cane to steady herself. Ana could tell from the deep lines on her face that she smiled often.

She spoke in a resonating tone for all to hear. "Welcome home, princess." Its cadence reminded her of Zora's. A preteen girl passed Magdalena a crown made of rose gold, shell, and pearl. In the center was a gemstone that matched the one on Ana's hand. The girl stepped back into the crowd. She reminded Ana of the girls who had helped her get ready for her very first welcome parade.

Magdalena gestured for Ana to kneel. She lowered her voice so that only those closest could hear. The words were unfamiliar, but they had a relaxing cadence. This was a tradition, an ancient one.

Then, she placed the crown atop Ana's head.

Ana rose to her feet, and the crowd raised their candles into the air and sang one last verse of the melody she had heard across the waves. Then, one by one, they blew out their candles. The crowd departed, leaving Ana, Magdalena, and Zora alone on the beach.

Just ahead, between a thick canopy of trees, was a walkway made of stones. It reminded her of the ones in the ocean—enormous and carefully hewn with etchings.

"May I call you Anabella, or would you prefer a more formal address?" the woman asked.

"Ana, please."

"Well, hello, Ana. I'm Magdalena." Her watery eyes sparkled in delight. "You are the spitting image of your mother."

"You knew my mom?"

"Oh yes. The Halt family rules the Southerly Province. Your mom grew up here. It's not just your looks. It's so much more." She paused as she looked Ana over. "You've hurt your wrist, child. Why don't you heal it?"

"I can't. I don't know how."

"It's not a matter of knowledge but of feeling."

Ana frowned. "I don't understand."

"All Halts have the power to heal themselves. It should be innate. Do you ever remember being hurt as a kid? Needing to go to the doctor for a broken arm, stitches, or a sprained ankle?"

Ana shook her head.

The old woman smiled so broadly that Ana could see a tooth missing. "Then you already know how. The question is, 'What's stopping you?'" She studied Ana.

Ana crossed her arms over her chest. "I've never healed myself. Worse still, I've never healed anyone else."

"But you can."

"But I haven't."

"Maybe it would be best to let you get some rest. You've had a long journey. You're welcome to stay with me though my lodgings are far from grand."

"That's okay," Ana said a little too quickly. "I'm staying with Zora."

"Ah, I see. Until tomorrow then."

On the long walk home, Ana's emotions rumbled like thunder before a storm. She didn't remember any sprained ankles or broken bones, but she did remember her mom's cancer. She remembered it every day.

Not every Halt was a healer.

No matter what that stupid old woman said.

22
THE SEA WITCH

The island was misty, and it rained a lot in the early afternoons. It made the plants grow like magic, reaching high into the air and wrapping around everything in sight. It also meant that Magdalena preferred to meet early in the morning.

Zora agreed to escort Ana before she started her chores on the property. They followed a sandy path through a grove of fruit trees until they reached the jungle. There, the path turned to dark, rich soil. It twisted and turned, and plants threatened to overtake it in multiple places. Finally, they found their way to the ocean.

"Will you be okay on your own from here?" Zora asked.

Ana nodded. "Of course."

"Okay. Continue on the sand for a quarter mile, and you'll see Magdalena's cottage up near a grove of trees."

"Thanks," Ana said, suppressing a yawn.

"It's no trouble."

Zora departed, and Ana took off her shoes to walk on the sandy beach. It felt good between her toes, and the sound of the ocean was calming.

Magdalena's home came into view after just a few minutes. Despite the local lore, Magdalena "the sea witch" did not live in the rocky caves. She lived beside them near a small grove of blossoming trees. Her cottage was modest and homey. The porch railing was made of driftwood, the porch itself overlooked the ocean.

As Ana made her way up the beach and toward the grove, she noticed bits of paper dangling from the limbs. She stopped to look, reaching out a hand. She pulled on a bit of string and saw there were words written on the papers. The one closest read, "I pray that my sister is well again."

Next to that one, a shriveled paper, torn nearly in half, read, "Please help me find work."

Ana's mouth dropped open. These were the prayers from the mainland, the ones they had folded into little boats on New Year's. But how was that possible?

Her eyes caught on familiar handwriting just a foot away from where she was standing. Ana had to stand on tiptoes to reach. She plucked two thick papers down from the tree. These were her prayers. These were her words.

She hadn't known what to ask for on the first, so it read simply, "I love you, Mom."

The other was more specific. "Please free Samuel."

She held each paper up, staring in disbelief. No one had seen what she had written. No one. Not even Zora.

Somehow, the prayers from the mainland really did reach the island. In the same way that the island's song reached the mainland.

Ana felt a shiver down her spine.

Maybe, just maybe, there was something worth believing in.

Magdalena found her standing by the tree. "Have you found yours yet?"

Ana nodded mutely.

"Do you mind if I see?"

To her own surprise, Ana held it out.

Magdalena read it and smiled sadly. "I'm sorry about your mother. I was always fond of her. Knew her since she was a baby. What happened to your other friend?"

Ana grinned. "He's actually on the boat. But it did come at a price."

Magdalena nodded. "Most things worth having do. Now, should we take a look at that wrist?"

Ana offered it out. "It doesn't move the way it used to."

The old woman studied it for minutes. "The aura around it is practically black," she muttered. "You've put it all there, haven't you?"

"All what?" Ana asked.

Magdalena didn't answer. Instead, she put a gentle hand on Ana's arm and began to hum gently. She moved her fingers as she did it as if she was plucking at invisible threads.

Ana felt a sudden onslaught of emotions—anger but beneath that sadness. "What are you doing?" she asked through gritted teeth.

"Healing," Magdalena replied. "Before you can heal others, Anabella Halt, you must first heal yourself."

"I don't want to heal myself. I want to—"

"I know," the old woman said, a hint of sadness in her tone. "I am sorry, but it is the only way. You have to feel the bad to feel the good. They are one and the same."

Not long after, Ana stomped back to Zora's through the jungle. *Heal yourself. Tap into your feelings. What a load of b.s.* She made so much noise she drew the attention of a nearby herd of graybeasts. One trumpeted.

"Exactly," she muttered.

After Zora went to bed, Ana studied her wrist. It was no longer crooked. It looked… normal. She tested it, flexing it from side to side. She turned it like she was opening a jar of jam. Everything worked. Whatever else she was, Magdalena was a skilled healer.

Somehow, that made Ana even angrier.

Ana returned the following day. She was feeling well-rested and less irritable than the day before. Even though the old woman, Magdalena, had been pushy, she *had* healed Ana's wrist. She wanted to help.

If Ana could learn to heal, it would change everything. She couldn't deny that. She walked the jungle path alone today, leaving Zora to water the graybeast herd. They did an excellent job of keeping pests away from the fruit trees.

Magdalena was waiting by the shore. "Good morning, Ana! How does your wrist feel today?"

Ana hung her head, feeling a little ashamed of her behavior yesterday. She hadn't even said thank you. "Much better. Thank you."

"Shall we go for a walk?"

Ana nodded.

Magdalena wasted no time in getting to the point. "So, you say you can't heal?"

"No, but I want to learn," Ana said. Then, she asked a question that had been in the back of her mind for several days now. "How is it that you can heal? Are we related?" Voicing the thought aloud gave her a brief surge of hope.

"I'm sorry, no. Most people on the island have a bit of the ability."

Ana's jaw dropped. "I thought it only passed in the Seven families."

Magdalena's lip curved up. "That's what they want to

believe, but it isn't true. All gifts originate from the Island. We are the oldest inhabitants of this planet. Two thousand years ago, there was a solar storm that impacted several planets and moons. We accepted the refugees, having lost much of our own technology in a past cataclysm. As a show of unity, our leaders married theirs, forming the Seven families and the advent of the gift."

"Are you saying everyone here has the ability to heal?"

"Most have at least a touch of the gift. Enough that we can do things together. Like at New Year's."

"The song! I was with Zora by the docks. It was the most beautiful thing I have ever heard," Ana gushed, remembering the warm feeling that had wrapped around her like a blanket.

"I'm so glad. I hoped it would reach you in particular."

"Does that mean—" She was almost scared to voice it. It was too good to be true. "Does that mean someone could take my place then?"

"I'm afraid not. The gift has always been strongest in your bloodline, and yours is the only one that would be accepted by the other families. Excuse me, my dear, but would you mind if we moved to my porch? I'm afraid the rain is moving in early this morning."

Ana nodded and let Magdalena set the pace—a slow, ambling one. By the time they reached her porch, Ana felt the first raindrop hit her face. Two low chairs fashioned from driftwood sat on the front porch.

Ana offered an arm to help Magdalena sit and then took her own seat. "You said all the gifts originate here. Why not today? Why only healing?"

"Hmm, I guess you could say we specialized. Wise men don't look to the future but focus on their present. Plants grow in their own time, especially here on the island."

"What about persuasion?"

"You've experienced it yourself. What did you think of it?"

Ana shuddered. "It was awful. Forceful."

"It's a perversion of our own gift. Think of the song on New Year's Day. That is the gift in its purity. You will learn the gift in time, whether you want it or not. It's important you know what not to do with it. Lest it be corrupted."

Ana leaned over the oiled wooden railing of Zora's covered porch, listening to the downpour roll in. Her mind was flooded with questions. "What about the other gifts, like numbers?"

Magdalena smiled. "That's not a gift. Well, not a magical one. It's a perceptual phenomenon related to neurological functioning."

"But my friend says he can see numbers like they're laid before him on a timeline."

"He probably can," she said.

Ana paused. "Okay. I'm just trying to wrap my head around all of this. Is this why they want to kill my family?"

"Yes."

"They're worried it'll shift the balance of power?"

"Yes."

Ana was quiet for a moment. "They'd kill my entire family and everyone on this island just to hide history."

"To keep power."

They sat in silence after that, watching the rain fall. When it stopped, Ana went back to Zora's, her mind buzzing.

ANA HAD BEEN on the island for two weeks today. So far, she'd learned a lot of history, some theory on healing, and watched Magdalena heal a handful of people. There had been a little girl with scoliosis and a man with a scratched cornea just today.

"Tell me exactly what happened during the challenge," Magdalena prompted her.

Ana went through every detail with Magdalena. When she got to the healing part, Magdalena smiled knowingly. "It sounds like you will be a very powerful healer, Ana. Your Mother would be proud."

Ana bristled in the way she did anytime someone mentioned her mom. It's not that she wanted to forget her. It just felt like someone poking an open wound.

"Would it be okay if I leave early today?" Ana asked. "I promised my friend Ophelia that I would forage for plants while I was here. She's counting on me."

"It is good to honor our commitments."

Ana nodded. "Exactly."

"I'd be happy to help you. The flora is well known to me."

Ana was excited when she found the stargazer lily growing against the back of a large tree.

"You say this is the plant you used to heal your friend?"

"Yes!"

Magdalena let out a long, throaty laugh.

"What's so funny?" Ana demanded.

"Oh, how the young are stubborn. This plant did not heal your friend. Could not. The petals aren't the medicinal part. It's the root you want." She laughed some more. "You healed that boy all on your own. Tell me again how it happened."

Ana recounted her story.

"Do you love this boy?"

Ana turned bright red. "I don't know. Why are you asking me?"

"I'm sorry. I forget how embarrassing such vulnerability is for young people. Forget romantic love for a moment. Do you care for this boy? Is he a close friend? Do your hearts know one another?"

Ana thought of how she felt when she thought Adam might die. As if she would lose a piece of herself, too. "Yes, I think so," she admitted.

"That is how you did it. That is the key—love, empathy, vulnerability, and yes, pain too. It all comes together. You cannot take one part and leave the others. It is a bittersweet fruit."

She was talking her usual nonsense.

"You said you sang for him. That's important too. Many connect to the gift that way in the beginning. It's a part of our tradition."

"What are you carrying, Ana? What is so heavy that you cannot look at it?"

Ana didn't answer. Instead, she left Magdalena standing alone in the jungle, the plant dangling in her hand. She felt a surge of anger. Magdalena could be the most pushy, confusing, and intrusive person she had ever met.

ANA RETURNED THE NEXT DAY, grudgingly.

Magdalena was waiting on the porch as usual, but she stood when she saw Ana approaching. "Let's walk today. I want to show you something."

Ana felt relieved. Perhaps she'd be getting a reprieve from the emotional poking and prodding today.

The two women walked in silence. At first, Ana enjoyed the breeze. There was no rain today, and the sunshine felt nice on her skin. Then, after fifteen minutes, she began to wonder about the old woman's motives. Why were they going so far away?

They stopped at the stone archway that stood in the waves. It reminded Ana of the star portals Samuel studied. It was old and ornate.

"Step into the waves and approach the doorway, but do *not* pass through. Do you understand? If you push through, you will not be able to return the same way. This is a star portal, one of the only ones left functional on the planet. It will show you what you need to see."

Ana rolled her eyes but pushed up her pant legs and waded in. By the time she reached the doorway, she was up to her thighs.

To her surprise, the view changed.

She saw her mom—her familiar lopsided smile, her deep brown eyes that crinkled at the corner, and her long, chestnut brown hair. She looked so real. Ana reached out a hand, but the illusion rippled like skipping a rock across a calm pond. She pulled her hand back in, praying her mother would return.

She did.

"Hi mom," she whispered.

"Hello, little one."

Ana froze. She couldn't believe it. Was this really happening? How was it possible?

Her blood turned cold. And then her heart exploded like spring. She thought this was like a photo. "M-mom?"

"Yes, darling. I'm here."

She seemed so very real. She knew it wasn't true, but then, anything was possible. She had seen spaceships, magic, and... body doubles. A spark of hope ignited in her chest until her whole body blazed with it. "Are you alive?"

"I'm so sorry, darling, but no."

Ana was too numb to cry. Instead, her thoughts moved to everything Magdalena had taught her. "Why?"

"Why what?"

"Magdalena says all Halts can heal. If that's true, why" — the dam burst and tears flowed down her face, mixing with the salty mist of the ocean— "why did you die? Why did you leave us?"

"You already know the answer. To protect you."

"There must have been another way," Ana said, crossing her arms over her chest.

"Sweetie, I know you're still too young to understand this,

but I am only human. I may be your mom, but I'm not flawless or invincible. I'm not always brave, and I don't always make the right choices. I did what I thought was best. I hope that one day you can forgive me. I hope that one day that's all you ask of yourself, too."

Her picture began to fade, and Ana could see the ocean through her as if she were looking through a ghost. "No!" she cried. "Please. Please don't leave."

"I'm already gone. You know that. I'll always love you."

Ana stood staring at the empty spot where her mother had just been. She watched the gently lapping ocean waves beyond. She felt hollow inside.

Numbly, she walked back to the shore. She passed Magdalena without a word. Magdalena did not try to follow.

Ana refused to return to Magdalena's, choosing instead to mope around Zora's home. She watered the graybeasts and stroked their down. She picked weeds from around the grove. She lay in the hammock and zoned out.

Magdalena had tricked her. If Ana had known what was in that gate, she would have never stepped in. She didn't know how it worked, but she was sure it was some sort of trick.

Over dinner, she asked Zora, "Can we go see the real Madame Bali tomorrow? Please?"

Zora calmly chewed her food and nodded. "We can visit the bluff, if you see Magdalena one more time."

Ana put it off for a week, but finally, she knew there was no avoiding it any longer. She needed to meet the real Madame Bali.

When she arrived, Ana stood off to the side, refusing to make eye contact with Magdalena. She had been coerced into coming here, and she had agreed. But no one had said anything about talking.

"You remind me of an oyster. They clamp down so hard to protect their pearl. That pearl is formed through a painful grit of sand."

Ana glared at her, still refusing to speak.

"Ana—" Magdalena said softly. "—humans don't form pearls when they conceal their pain. They form diseases of the mind, body, and spirit. Please let me help you remove that sand."

Ana crossed her arms over her chest. No information was worth this. She'd find Madame Bali on her own. She didn't need Magdalena or Zora's help.

Without another word, she turned her back on Magdalena and stormed off. She'd ask Zora one more time. Then, she'd start her own search for Madame Bali's house tomorrow. She already knew it was on a bluff, and there were several nearby.

ANA'S PLAN was interrupted by an unexpected visitor at the house. "Samuel?" she exclaimed. "What are you doing here?"

"Behaving like a damn fool," Zora said.

"The sailor's life is...not for me. I was told there would be rum. I've experienced enough chanties and folklore to last me a lifetime. Besides, I hate chores." His eyes swept over Ana, and he smiled.

"You could get sick," she warned.

"I'm sure I'll be fine. I'm an honorary Halt, right?"

"I'm not sure honorary counts in this instance."

He waved off her concerns.

Ana went to get a shower and help Zora prepare dinner. Samuel went to read in the hammock.

When they met again, he was looking a little queasy.

"Maybe you should go back to the ship."

"Nah, it was just the fish I ate at lunch. Grimes made it. Didn't look right."

THE NEXT MORNING, Ana went to the beach. Something she'd been doing a lot of lately. She had a routine down now. She'd trek across the orchard, through the jungle, and out to the nearest beach.

So far, the beach had always been deserted. Zora's orchard was far away from the more populous parts of the island. Ana didn't mind. She wanted to be alone. Far away from the prying questions and careless nudging of Magdalena.

She had a routine now. She'd lay her towel across the sand and sunbathe for a few hours. Then, she'd break for lunch and a shower. As a result, her usually fair skin had turned light brown under the golden rays of the sun.

Ana was almost asleep, listening to the crashing waves and soaking up the rays of sunshine, when she heard a noise. It sounded like someone pushing their way through the jungle overgrowth.

She squinted through the bright sun, expecting to see an animal or a bird. Instead, she saw Samuel. He was dressed in ratty grey chino shorts and a white t-shirt. His thick, dark hair was pulled into a messy bun. A single dark lock had escaped and was sticking to his forehead with a sheen of sweat. The shadow of a beard had appeared on his face, giving him a rugged, natural look that seemed to fit the jungle setting.

She flipped onto her stomach and waved. Then, she watched as he crossed the dunes, his calf muscles working against the sand.

"What are you doing out here?" he asked.

She shaded her eyes and looked up at him. "I could ask you the same question."

"But I asked first."

"Sunbathing."

He raised an eyebrow. "I can see that much."

She blushed, remembering she was wearing Zora's canary yellow swimsuit. She sat up and pulled her towel around her.

He offered her a hand and pulled her to her feet. "Should we go sit in the shade? Your shoulders are starting to look a little pink."

She nodded.

They found a spot just under the cover of the jungle and sat together, staring out at the waves.

"So, what are you doing out here?" he asked again.

"I'm taking the day off. And you?"

"I was looking for you. Why a day off?"

Ana frowned. "Honestly...I'm avoiding Magdalena."

"What? The old woman who is supposed to be teaching you?"

"That's the one."

He studied her for a moment. "What did she do?"

Ana considered for a minute whether she would answer. Finally, she asked, "Did you know there's a star portal here?"

Samuel, who had been studying star portals all year long looked at her with narrowed eyes. "She didn't make you look through it, did she?"

Ana nodded.

Samuel swore under his breath.

WHEN THEY RETURNED from the beach, Samuel went to nap, and Ana showered. Then, they all met back for dinner. When

Samuel arrived at the table, he was pale and sweating. He stumbled, and his knees crumpled underneath him.

Zora, who had been cautiously observing, swooped in to catch him. Almost as if she had been expecting this. Maybe she had been. Having lived on the island for most of her life, she had seen the outsider's sickness before. "Ana," she said through the physical strain of holding him up, "run for Magdalena. Don't make any stops."

Ana nodded and hurried out the door. As her feet hit the sandy soil of the orchard, she ran flat out. She hadn't needed Zora's warning. She wouldn't stop if her own hair was on fire.

Magdalena looked up at Ana's panic-stricken face in surprise. "What's wrong, child?"

Ana wiped sweat from her brow. "It's my friend Samuel. He's got the sickness."

Magdalena nodded and stood creakily from her chair. She reached for her walking stick and began to slowly make her way out of her hut. "Take me to him."

She could feel her bitterness toward Magdalena begin to fade. "He's all the way at Zora's."

Ana tried to be patient as Magdalena slowly closed her door, but she felt like anxiety was dancing up and down her spine and nerve endings. What if something happened to Samuel? What if they were too slow?

They left through the back of the hut and went straight into the jungle. When they reached the orchard beyond, it was all Ana could do to stop from dragging the old woman across the sandy soil.

"Peace, Ana. No one has ever died from the sickness in a mere half an hour."

"But you can help him? There is a treatment?"

"There is a way. One that has not been used in a generation. A way that visitors can come to the Island and not suffer the sickness that plagues those who are not born here. A flower petal that, when mixed with several other local herbs and heated gently over a flame, will allow the drinker to visit. But not for long. To share this is a great risk. We are a target. Are you sure that he is worth the risk?"

Ana nodded emphatically.

When they got inside, they found Samuel sitting up in bed. His eyes were mostly closed, although she could see he was trying very hard to keep them open. They blinked slowly every few seconds. His cheeks were flushed and a sheen of sweat coated his forehead.

Magdalena took one look at him and said, "It is the sickness. It's not very often I treat an outsider with the sickness."

"It's not very often one is foolish enough to come to our shores," Zora said.

"You can help though? Right?"

"Zora, please bring some water to a slow rolling boil in the traditional manner. Ana—" Magdalena had to repeat herself because Ana was not listening. Her attention was fixed on Samuel, listening to his steady if shallow breathing.

"You'll not help by hovering," Magdalena said. "Go to the jungle and fetch me the following items." She handed Ana a slip of paper with several plants sketched on it for her reference.

"Can't you just sing for him?"

"It would help, but it would take the voice of many to make him truly well. The outsider sickness is potent. Only a Halt would have a chance at doing it." She gave Ana a long look. "Now off you go."

Ana didn't argue. She went at top speed, and only slowed to a walk to better select the herbs Magdalena had requested. For the first time in days, Ana forgot her obsession with Madame Bali and seeking out her namesake here on the island.

Ana felt certain that Samuel was the sort of patient who would moan and be melodramatic. This subdued behavior worried her more than she wanted to let on. Hadn't people died from the island's sickness?

ANA SAT in the wooden chair by his bedside until the light fell from the windows. Finally, she fell asleep with her chest leaned forward on the bed. When she woke, she had a crick in her neck, and shadows danced in the corners of the room.

Sleepy, and no longer caring about propriety, she crawled into bed beside Samuel and fell asleep with her face turned toward his.

For one moment, she thought about singing for him but decided it would only wake him. She didn't have the gift. No matter what Magdalena said.

She listened to his now steadier breathing, and it calmed her. She fell asleep in minutes.

When she woke, the bright morning light was flooding through the wooden shades, and she was boiling. No, Samuel was boiling. She sat up quickly, remembering where she was and saw Samuel was already awake.

He was staring at her with glassy eyes.

"How are you?"

He smiled wanly and said, "I knew you couldn't resist my allure forever. I've seen those vampire novels that sell so well on Earth. It's my pallor that's attracted you."

She sat up and reached over to feel his forehead. "You're burning up. That must be your delirium talking."

He tried to smirk but fell short. Instead, he gave her a weak smile and closed his eyes to rest.

She stretched and left to find Magdalena. From the hallway, Ana could hear Zora and Magdalena talking in the living room.

"What a fool," Zora said in a low voice. "Coming to the island. Catching the sickness."

The older woman replied, "Why would he come?"

"There is only one reason a man takes such a risk." She jerked her head back toward the hallway.

"Ana?"

"It's clear he is fond of her."

Zora snorted. "More. That boy is in love."

Ana felt her heart stop and then jolt forward in double time. Samuel… loved her? No, it wasn't possible. They were only pals.

She thought of the way he had pulled her to his chest on the ship. The way he had leaned down, his breath on her lips. Had he been about to kiss her?

Ana cleared her throat, and the two women looked up.

"How is he?" Zora asked.

"Burning up."

"That's to be expected at this stage."

Magdalena took a black kettle off the heat and poured it into a small bowl. "He'll need to drink this. It steeped all night and should be in its optimal state now."

"Ana, I'll need you to lift his head."

She started to put a hand under and then realized she and Magdalena couldn't both stand to the right of the bed. She felt awkward and clumsy.

"Is it okay if I—" she gestured awkwardly.

He blinked at her in confusion.

Finally, she settled on crawling back into bed and cradling his head in her lap.

His dark curls were damp in the back from his fever. She ran a hand through his hair absentmindedly.

He sighed and closed his eyes.

She felt better knowing she had helped him in some small way. If only she really were a healer.

Magdalena sat and raised a wooden spoon to his lips. "Drink

this, young man," she urged as he slurped the liquid from the spoon. "Our princess needs you well."

After taking his medicine, he fell asleep, leaving Magdalena and Ana alone for the first time in days. "He'll be alright," Magdalena assured Ana. "Though it will be several days yet before we can move him to the ship. He's in no condition to travel."

"Magdalena, I appreciate what you're doing. I truly do, but you should know, I'm not coming back to lessons anymore. I'm sorry you couldn't help me."

Magdalena nodded but said nothing.

Ana rested her head back on the bed and looked over at Samuel.

Magdalena stood from her chair. She looked pointedly between Ana and Samuel. "I have a feeling you're going to be just fine. But remember, Ana, you have to feel it all."

Ana lingered by Samuel's bedside for the next 24 hours, dozing in the chair with her head resting on his bed. She was very well practiced at bedside manner from her mother's battle with cancer. She pushed those unwelcome thoughts from her mind.

This was different. Samuel would be fine. Magdalena had amazing healing gifts, even if Ana did not. If he had to do something stupid, he was in the best place on the planet for treatment.

Not that she'd tell the Fleur scientists that. While Ophelia and her aunt were interested in helping others with new discoveries, there were plenty of others who wouldn't care for any new competition... that couldn't be monetized.

23
THE REAL MADAME BALI

Several days later, Samuel seemed to be doing much better. He was sitting up in bed, reading, and making snarky jokes. Yes, to Ana's astonishment, he had carried a knapsack full of books to the island.

Zora said he would be ready to move that evening once the sun was down and the weather was cooler.

He was napping now, so Magdalena sent Ana for all the herbs they would need to continue his treatment. She refused to tell any but Ana the remedy, insisting she was entrusting Ana with the safety of the entire island.

Ana foraged. And as she did so, she found herself closer and closer to the bluff. The one Zora had promised to take her to. The one near the real Madame Bali's house.

From the cliffside, Ana could see it. She was so close.

Madame Bali's house was modern, standing on stilts with glass overhanging the water. It was shaped like a shell.

There was a problem. Ana wasn't sure how to get down from the cliff to reach the house. She stepped onto the rocky bluff to get a better look, and then with a tectonic groan, it began to lower.

She stifled a small scream as the rock floated downward. Zora had told her the main boulevards on the island used magnetic energy. It was easy to forget that technology was advanced here, just in a different sort of way than she had seen in the capital. Older.

She soon landed gently on the sand and made her way to a set of black metal stairs that twirled up to a doorway underneath the shell-like home. It reminded her of something a posh snail might adopt as a home.

When she reached the door, it opened, and a woman stared politely out. She looked nothing like Madame Bali.

"Hello, princess. I wondered if you would come," she said. "Please come in."

Ana crossed the threshold.

"Why didn't you come to see me then?"

"I wasn't sure if you'd want to see me."

Ana followed her out to an observation deck overlooking the sea. It was dark and churning today, but mist hung low in the distance. A vast improvement from the conditions during her arrival to the Island.

Nothing had changed. And yet she couldn't stay here forever. Samuel was proof of that.

If she wanted to hide, she would have never come to Bellaton in the first place. She preferred to face her enemies head-on rather than wait for them to strike.

Madame Bali looked at her appraisingly. "The government contacted me, of course. They had many questions. I was even summoned to the mainland for a short time."

"What did they ask?"

"The same things I suppose you want to ask me. I am the real Madame Bali. I can provide identification. I am from the island. My family goes back many generations and served yours often. That's all in the records too."

"They're sealed," Ana said.

"From you?" She raised an eyebrow.

"I'm not yet a full member of the council."

The real Madame Bali pursed her lips. "You have had every right to sit on that council from the moment you arrived. There is no other to take your place."

She seemed so indignant that Ana really believed she meant it. "Thank you. Do you know who the fake Madame Bali was? Surely they showed you video footage."

"Yes," she said, a small sad smile playing across her lips. "Her real name was Terra Rorre."

Ana's heart stopped.

Terra.

Her name was Terra.

So, it was true.

"My dear?" Madame Bali asked. "Are you alright?" She placed a gentle, aristocratic hand on Ana's elbow and led her to a chair. "Won't you sit? This must all be a shock to you still. After all, she tried to kill you. It must bring back bad memories."

"It's not that," Ana choked out. "Well, not entirely. But tell me about her." She looked at Madame Bali, and their eyes met. "Please," Ana said desperately. "Anything you know. Everything you know."

"Well, there isn't much, I'm afraid. Terra and I were classmates at the Royal Conservatory but little beyond that. Because of my family's long association with yours and leadership on the island and in its local governance, I was allowed a position. Most of the students were of the Seven or, like me, closely tied in politically. However, there was one girl who did not fit the mold. Her name was Terra Rorre. She was a serious, quiet, and determined little thing. She rarely made eye contact with anyone, studied ferociously, and shook like a leaf if you snuck up on her.

"The boys thought that was funny. They made a sport of

jumping out at her. Though in retrospect, I suppose it was fairly cruel. But that's teenagers for you.

"Anyway, they didn't laugh for long. By her second year, Terra had shown a strong affinity for a chosen specialization —poison."

Ana sucked in a breath. Of course. The chocolates. The arrow.

"What kind of poisons did she study?"

"Are you familiar with the drug known as Lights Out?"

Ana nodded.

"It is a derivative of Elysium. That one seemed to be of particular interest to her. She got more and more obsessive, working long hours and trying to speed up the trial. They say she nearly blinded a test subject. She was nearly dismissed from the conservatory."

And then it slid together like a puzzle piece. Terra had been studying the poison that the Fleurs ingested. She wanted to cure them.

"And then things got worse, one of her guardians died. A Mr. Fleur, I believe. Though I can't remember which. There were questions over whether she would be allowed to stay on, whether the signatures and paperwork would be binding after his death.

"She stopped talking to everyone after that, including me. It was the last time I talked to her for years.

"That combined with her dark hair and quiet nature led to a lot of cruel rumors around the Conservatory."

"Like what?" Ana asked.

Madame Bali considered. "Awful things, really. That she was a witch. That she had killed her mother and father. That she was learning the art of poison making to seek out her next victim."

A knot tightened in Ana's chest. She remembered what it was like to walk the halls of her high school when the whispers followed her.

"Of course, she looks sad. Her mom died."
"I can't even imagine it."
"She's in foster care now."
"Nobody wanted her? Where's her dad?"
"He abandoned them."
"Abandoned or ran away? It's *like she's cursed."*

She felt angry with herself. She would *not* feel sorry for Terra— Madame Bali—whoever she was. *She would not.*

"I can't tell you which rumors were true and which were not. But her parents were out of the picture somehow. She had been adopted by the Fleur family."

That was okay. Ana already knew the truth. She had seen it through her own eyes. Terra's mother and father had both been murdered.

"What happened after that?"

"Terra grew increasingly more isolated. The boys no longer picked on her but ignored her entirely. The girls did the same. She worked silently and solitarily. Even the teachers seemed to leave her to her work. It continued that way until graduation."

"And after?"

"I heard nothing from Terra Rorre for three years. Her last communication came out of the blue. A request for information on plants grown on the Island. We corresponded and eventually, she made it clear that she wished to apply for a research visa. They were extremely rare even then, and outsider sickness was a tremendous risk. I agreed to ask, and surprisingly, her request was granted. She was to sail here that spring. But in late winter, the Oceania sunk, drowning twenty-eight Halts."

Ana froze. "What was the name of the ship again?"

"Oceania, my lady. It was ruled an accident, but no one believed it. The island went on strict lockdown by order of your grandmother. All visas were revoked. All ships were stopped.

Even communications were reduced to monitored and vital comms only."

"And that was the last I heard of Terra Rorre... until this summer."

Ana made a few more pleasantries and then left to be alone with her thoughts. She found herself thinking through the details.

How long did the poison take to kill? What if Mrs. Fleur was still alive? And, if she was, she might hold the answers Ana needed. She might know where Terra was hiding and maybe, just maybe, who had hired her?

Ana wasn't sure anyone had hired Terra anymore. She seemed like she had her own ax to grind. But why would she have been discovered with cash? Or had that been a lie? Could she be working with the Rockwells?

On her way back to the top of the bluff, Ana's infotab buzzed to life in her tote. She pulled it out. Did she actually have a signal from this height? Dozens of messages flooded through.

One blinking on the screen. Unavoidable.

I've been expecting you.
-36.67512, -73.532969
-M.B.

THOSE NUMBERS. What were they? A date? A code? Then, it clicked. Coordinates. It was a location.

Madame Bali was ready to meet.

Good. Ana was ready to end this game of cat and mouse. She was sick of being the mouse. She was ready to be the cat.

There was nothing left for Ana on the island. She was only hiding. She didn't want to confront her feelings with

Magdalena, and she no longer believed in her ability to manifest the gift.

Sticking around would only hurt others like it had Samuel. Who would be next while Ana ignored Madame Bali's summons? Ophelia? Holden? Her brothers even? If she thought about that too much, she found she could hardly breathe.

Anger was easier than fear, and she let it overcome her.

Whether she was dead or alive, it was time to find Madame Bali. It was time to face the woman who was haunting her. The fixture in all of her nightmares.

IN HER ROOM, she tossed her things into a duffel. It was half full when she realized she couldn't carry it with her. If she left this room with a duffel bag, she would attract everyone's attention. They would try to stop her.

She wanted to leave, but she couldn't do so in good conscience without at least checking in on Samuel one more time. He was still on bed rest, and she found him sitting up and eating toast.

"How are you feeling?" she asked.

"Like I've been trampled by a graybeast."

"Choices have consequences."

"Thanks for that."

She laughed. "You always say that stuff to me."

"True. I had no idea how insufferable I was."

"I don't mind."

"Then I guess we can be insufferable together. I just feel sorry for the bystanders."

"Ms. K is the only bystander, and she's more insufferable than either of us."

"True."

"So, you're really feeling better? "

"Definitely. I'd be out of this bed, but Zora insisted I rest today."

Hmm. Anas's mind had moved back to her mission. Which door should she go out? Which would be least likely to attract attention?

"Ana? Hello?"

"Oh sorry."

He looked at her with narrowed eyes. "You okay?"

"Yeah. Definitely. I just want to talk to Magdalena."

Samuel nodded.

She left his room, shutting the door carefully behind her. She made her way to the back door of the house and slid out without being seen. She was careful to shut it without a sound.

She made her way across the orchard and into the dense jungle greenery. Finally, she made her way to the spot Magdalena had shown her. The portal. It could show you anything you needed to see or take you anywhere you needed to go. She was counting on the latter.

The roar of the ocean was loud today. She couldn't even hear the call of sea birds. The wind whipped her hair around her face and neck. She waded through the still ocean water toward the magnificent stone archway. All she had to do was step through, and she would be at the address instantly.

Then again, would it be wise to show up without a weapon? Madame Bali had tried to kill her the last time they met.

She needed to gather supplies first. But from where? She was only familiar with four places on Bellaton: the island, Rockwell Manor, the academy, and the capital. The island had no weapons cache that she was aware of, and she couldn't exactly ask Zora for its location. She couldn't go to Rockwell Manor without Adam. The DNA-based security measures would probably kill her. And heading straight to the capital seemed like the stupidest thing she could conceive. So, that left the academy. It was risky too, but it seemed smarter than going to meet Madame Bali unarmed.

She stepped into the archway. In the split second before her transport, she heard someone in the distance shouting her name. It was too late to turn around.

Ana felt a rush of energy. There was darkness punctuated by a pulsing aura of light. It was wonderful and terrible and over in seconds.

She stumbled onto the academy grounds and landed on her knees on the frozen grass. It was still early morning. The campus was quiet. She looked around, hoping no one had noticed her sudden appearance. Luckily, there was no one in sight. A single call to the council, and she would be in a different sort of trouble.

She shivered, wishing for a sweater. The temperature difference between the island and academy had to be thirty degrees. She had almost forgotten it was December now.

She got back on her feet, but before she could make it ten paces, she heard a loud thud behind her.

24
A DESPERATE RACE

She turned and saw a pale Samuel sprawled on the grass. He didn't move.

So, he was the person she had heard calling for her. She couldn't believe he had followed her through the jungle and into the portal. He was still recovering.

She rushed to his side. "Samuel," she breathed.

"I'm okay," he croaked. "Just got the wind knocked out of me." He sat up, but his heavy breathing didn't escape her notice.

She managed to get him to his feet, and they made their way to her dorm together.

"You idiot. Why did you follow me? You should be in bed."

"I'm fine." He leaned on her shoulder. They both knew he wasn't fine. "What are you doing here? Why didn't you tell me you were leaving?"

She didn't answer.

As she drew closer to her dorm, she was surprised to find the door unguarded. The sentinel was gone. She wondered how much trouble he had gotten in when she had disappeared. Probably a lot.

With a grunt of effort, Ana shifted Samuel's weight and held out her palm. The door opened automatically at her touch. Then, she wrapped it back around his chest and dragged him across the threshold.

She thought about moving him on the couch but decided against it. It would be harder for her to sneak back out. She was still leaving. Dealing with a sick Samuel was just a pit stop.

She hauled him all the way to his bedroom and helped him down to the bed.

He was limp and pale and sweating. He lost consciousness for a moment as she laid him down, but his eyes fluttered back open.

"I have the things to make the treatment. Wait here," she said firmly. She didn't think he *could* follow her this time. She went to the only person she could trust with this task. Ophelia.

To her credit, Ophelia came and asked very few questions. When they returned to the dorm together, Samuel was sleeping. Sweat stuck strands of his long dark hair to his cheek.

"Why don't you take him to the infirmary?"

"He has the island sickness."

Ophelia looked alarmed.

"Don't worry. I have the remedy. He's been taking it for days. He just pushed himself too hard."

"There's a remedy?"

"Yes, but it's an absolute secret. Swear on your life you won't tell."

"I swear it. I'm just relieved. The longer he's away from the island, the healthier he will get," Ophelia said. "At least that's what all the field journals say."

"I'll get the remedy started. Come watch if you want."

"You trust me with the remedy?"

"I trust you with my life."

Ophelia's cheeks turned pink. "Thank you. All the same. I think I'll just sit with our patient. I wouldn't want to get you in any trouble."

"I'll be back in fifteen."

While Ana waited for the water to boil, she thought about her next moves. She had been in such a hurry to get off the island she hadn't thought things through yet. First, she needed transportation. And weapons. And probably a bunch of other stuff.

She added in the leaves, and the water began to change colors. She stirred. When the color had changed, she poured it into Samuel's favorite coffee mug. She left the kettle on the stovetop to steep. The tea would be more potent this evening.

Ana hurried back to the bedroom and handed it to Ophelia. "Make sure he drinks all of it. There's more steeping in the kitchen."

"Where are you going?" Ophelia asked.

Ana considered for a moment. Then, she showed Ophelia the message on her infotab. "I know where to find Madame Bali."

"You're not really going, are you?"

"What choice do I have? She's out there." Ana gritted her teeth. "She spied on me last year and stalked me this year. She almost killed Adam. If she hadn't tampered with the dome, Xan would still be alive!"

Ophelia nodded. "I won't try to stop you, but won't you at least take Adam?"

"Maybe."

"You'll ask him?"

"I'll think about it. But if I'm going, I've got to get moving. I need to get to the combat classroom before classes start. I need to borrow a few things."

She remembered the headmistress words. Borrowing without asking is stealing. She brushed them off.

"Take care of him?" she added, a pleading note in her voice.

Ophelia nodded. "I will, but I'd feel better if I were going with you."

"I know. I'll be back though. See you soon."

Ophelia said nothing more, and Ana hurried to the door. She made her way down the hall and onto the grounds. The first light of day had broken, and the birds were singing.

To her surprise, the door to the combat classroom was already open. She was grateful. She hadn't quite worked out how she would get in, but this made things simpler.

She hurried through and nearly walked into Adam's chest. Beside him was Holden. Both of them were dressed in faded green fatigues, and it was obvious they had been on their way to morning drill.

"What are you doing here?" she exclaimed.

Adam crossed his arms over his chest and smirked. "What are *you* doing here?"

"Ophelia called you, didn't she?"

Adam and Holden exchanged a glance.

"We can't reveal our source at this time," Adam said.

"I don't want anyone else hurt because of me. I'm going alone."

"Sounds pretty selfish to me. What do you think, Holden?"

Holden nodded. "We all want to find Madame Bali. She shot Adam. She tried to kill you. If she hadn't messed with the safeties, Xan would still be here."

"We're going with you," Adam said with finality.

Ana didn't argue. She didn't see a way to win, and she didn't have time. Every minute on campus was a liability. At any moment, the council could be notified and haul her away for questioning. She couldn't lose this chance.

She ran down to the girl's locker room and changed into her combat suit, hoping it would give her some protection from elements and foes. Then, she pulled her hair back into a ponytail and went to join the guys.

Adam tossed her a gun. "We raided the weapons while you changed. Cool?"

"Yeah."

"Figured you wouldn't want the bulk of a rifle."

"You guessed right."

"Any idea how we're going to get out of here?" she asked.

"Funny you should ask," Adam said. "We already worked that all out...with a little help from Shay. Come with us."

The jet was small and sleek, built for two passengers—a pilot and copilot. It was military grade and intended to be used in emergency defense of the school only. Needless to say, students were not permitted in or even near the jets.

Holden crawled in first, snagging the pilot's seat. To his credit, Adam didn't protest but instead lifted Ana by the hips and gave her a boost into the craft. He followed, pulling himself up.

It was a tight squeeze. Ana sat in the middle on a small jump seat that Holden pulled down for her.

When Adam joined them, he practically sat on her, trying to get the door secured. "Couldn't you-know-who have gotten us a bigger vehicle?"

"Beggars can't be choosers," Holden said. "Now strap in, and let's get going before someone stops us."

"Agreed," Adam nodded.

Ana reached to pull hers from somewhere behind her shoulder. In the process, she managed to elbow Holden in the chest. "Sorry," she murmured.

"Ana, we need the coordinates, but—"

"Don't say them out loud," Adam finished.

She frowned. "Is written down okay?"

"Sure, but keep it obscured from that black dot right there." He pointed to a small camera lens.

"Can't they just track the jet? Even cars have anti-theft systems," she said, thinking of her brother Ryker's obsession with expensive cars.

"If things go well, our friend"—he looked at her pointedly—"is going to try to block everything they can for as long as they can."

Thirty minutes later, they were still in the clear. Whatever Shay was doing, it was working.

"Don't get too excited," Adam warned. "It's just a head start. Someone will notice eventually."

They were closing in on the coordinates now. The location was just a few minutes away. They were near the capital, just outside of the mountainous, protective ring that shielded it.

Even from the air, the house and grounds were enormous. A place to rival, maybe even exceed the grandeur of Rockwell Manor.

Holden circled.

"Adam, can you confirm the location?"

Adam grabbed the sheet of paper Ana had written on and looked at it, then at the system's dashboard. "Yes, this is it. Take us down."

"In the garden," Ana said.

Holden began to slowly bring them in but as he got close, the systems began to blink on and off. The engine sputtered. "Whoa," Holden said, lifting the nose back up. "Something's not right."

"She's got military-grade wards."

"Figures," Holden grumbled. "I guess we need to find a spot nearby."

"Isn't there any other way?" Ana asked. "If I'm caught, I'll be arrested. I need to see Madame Bali. It could change everything. Please."

Adam looked at her and sighed. "Holden, open the hatch."

"No way. I'm not letting you two go down there alone."

"We need an exit strategy more than a third, and Ana can't pilot this thing. It has to be you."

Worry furrowed Holden's brow, but he nodded. "Okay. I'll circle until you're ready." He pressed a button, and the door to the jet slid away, leaving a vacuum of rushing air.

"Be careful. And don't forget your glasses," he said to Ana.

She nodded, securing her backpack. "I never leave home without them," she said with a nervous smile. "Thanks, Holden." She patted him affectionately on the head.

Adam turned toward her. "Ana, we're going to have to jump. Last chance to decide you don't want—"

She smirked at him and stepped forward. She felt a pull at her stomach as she was sucked outward.

25
LIGHTS OUT

Bright metallic parachutes expanded behind Ana and Adam as they made their descent into the gardens below. They landed with a thud.

Adam looked over at her with a huge grin etched across his face. "You okay?"

"Oh, you are such an adrenaline junkie," she laughed.

"Guilty. Need help with your chute?"

She nodded.

"Pull down on both of your sleeves simultaneously," he instructed.

She did, and her parachute retracted back into her combat suit.

Ana took in the landscape around her. They were inside a large formal garden, but to Ana's surprise, the layout was unfamiliar. She had expected everything to look just as it had in her dreams.

But she knew that was irrational. Two decades had passed. Changes were bound to be made. Still, she felt ready.

A bright flash caught her eye, and she looked up. Across the gloomy winter sky, light erupted through the clouds. She had seen this twice before, once at Lauren's birthday and once at Xan's wake. With one noticeable difference. This time, there were no celebratory words. Instead, a bright, scarlet letter *A* caught fire, blazed, and turned to ashes.

To Ana's surprise, real ashes fell like snow in their hair and on their combat suits. Who did the A reference? Ana? Adam? Was it possible that Madame Bali knew they were both here?

In its place, cruel words spidered across the atmosphere like lightning.

Anabella Halt, you are a liar.

Then, a video began to play. Ana recognized it at once. It was from the challenge. Ana was sobbing. She reached into her pocket, pulled out a petal, and pressed it into Adam's mouth.

Her stomach dropped. Someone had captured it on film, after all. This video was a death sentence. She was more determined than ever to reach Madame Bali now. If she didn't, this video would be the end.

The scene changed. Ana stood in a crowded bar. She was wearing that stupid lavender dress, and she knew what would happen next. She fell forward, and her hands pressed to Samuel's chest. He was dressed in a dark tuxedo and a smile. Their faces were inches apart when Ana claimed his lips.

The clip ended, and the sky returned to overcast.

Ana's eyes flicked over to Adam. He was still staring up at where the feed had been.

"I can explain," she started.

He shook his head as if removing water from his ears. "No. Not here. We have to keep moving." His adrenaline-junkie smile was gone now.

The trellis archway from her dreams had been replaced by a towering hedgerow maze. It was so tall it obscured the view of the home entirely. "If we follow the hedgerow maze, it should lead us to the back entrance of the house," Ana explained.

"I don't like it," he said, glancing around. "She already knows we're here. Now, she's pushing us forward."

"She's taunting us."

"Well, there's no turning back now. Let's keep going. We'll see who has the last laugh."

They walked toward the maze, keeping an eye out for lurking dangers.

"Could we try to go around the maze?" Ana asked.

Adam thought for a moment. "No. If it's like Rockwell Manor, there will be DNA-activated landmines."

Her eyes widened. "Maze it is, then."

"Once we go in, let's stick close together. Pay close attention to the shrubberies. We don't want anyone jumping out at us."

Ana nodded. "Agreed."

Together, they stepped into the maze, and at first, everything seemed fine. No one was waiting inside. At least not yet. They continued until they reached the first turn.

"Which way?" he asked.

"I don't know. Let's just keep making lefts until we can't anymore. At least, then we'll know which way we came."

"That makes sense. Keep your eyes out for threats."

On their second left, they reached a squared clearing with shaped topiary inside the perimeter.

"Looks like somebody is trying to give you Rockwells a run for your money," Ana said, nudging him. "These are even creepier than yours. Look at that one. It's got jagged teeth."

She walked into the center of the space and turned to look at all the fearsome, carved creatures. "I'm just grateful they're plants." She laughed.

But as she twirled around, she stopped. The more she looked, the more she wanted to look away. The beastly topiary's teeth were covered in a dark, thick red liquid. It couldn't possibly be—She looked down at the topiary's clawed feet and saw two flying lops lying dead on the ground. Their little wings were broken, and bright red pools of blood surrounded them. Freshly slain.

Ana grabbed Adam's arm. "Look," she hissed, pointing to the macabre scene.

Adam looked at the rabbits and then down at their feet. Ana followed his gaze. Vines were reaching toward them from the perimeter. When Ana spun back around, their entrance was rapidly closing.

"It's Carnivorous Quick. We need to move faster."

She didn't need to be told twice. She remembered this plant vividly. The Fleurs had allowed it to overtake the hallway and cover her dormitory door when she had first arrived at the Royal Academy.

They took off at a run.

Two left turns later, Ana bent over to catch her breath. Those topiaries and their teeth. It was like something out of a horror novel, and thinking of it again made her stomach turn. Standing upright, she said, "I'm starting to get a bad feeling about this."

"Starting to? I've had one since we landed. But the only way out is through. Holden can't land until we turn off the barrier."

"Is there a way to pass through the hedges?"

"Maybe, but it wouldn't be safe, and it wouldn't guarantee an exit either. It could just lead us into another part of the maze."

While they talked, a vine had begun to creep toward Ana's ankle.

Adam pulled his gun and shot it. "Come on."

As they jogged, she said, "I had no idea Carnivorous Quick could be that deadly."

"It's usually not. It was probably altered."

Ana moaned, "Oh no."

His eyes flicked toward her. "What?"

"I forgot to tell you. Madame Bali is a botanist. She trained at the Royal Conservatory."

"Shit," he said. "We have to get out of this garden now."

They broke into a run. Ana watched their left, and Adam watched their right. They hit their first dead end and turned back. They turned right this time and reached another room. They didn't linger, pressing forward.

A few yards further, Ana heard a strange sound behind them, like a sword blade whistling through the air. She pulled at Adam's sleeve and hissed, "Do you hear that?"

"Turn on three. Weapons drawn," he said in a low voice.

He held up three fingers, two fingers, and finally one. They stopped and whipped around to face their attacker. Only, no one was there.

A curved, metallic blade the size of an SUV hung threateningly in the air behind them. As they stared, it began to swing to and fro like the pendulum of a clock. There was no accessible clearance above it or below it. Going around it was only possible by stepping into the carnivorous hedges.

"Maybe we can outmaneuver it. Lose it," Adam said. "Run. All lefts."

She turned and ran. The blade had no trouble keeping pace. They made it to the first turn, and it followed with ease.

Adam swore under his breath.

At the next turn, Ana pulled a sweater from her backpack and tossed it to the right while they went left. The blade was not fooled. It was getting closer now, closing the gap between them. Ana could feel her pulse quicken.

"Can we shoot it?" she asked desperately.

In spite of everything, Adam rolled his eyes. "It's a gun, Ana. Not a furnace. It can't melt metal. At best, we'll put a hole through it. At worst, it'll deflect our own shot at us."

"Well, do you have any ideas?" she panted.

"Maybe, if we timed it just right, we could slide under while it swings to the other side. Hand me something you don't need."

She frowned and passed him an energy bar from her backpack.

When the blade reached its furthest point to the right, Adam leaned down and slid the energy bar across the grass. The blade adjusted speed and sliced the bar in half.

Ana's eyes widened. "So, I think that's a no to sliding under."

"Forward then and fast."

They sprinted now, and all conversation between them died.

Then, the hedges ahead closed in. They had reached a dead end. Just ahead, the ground was black. No, it wasn't ground at all.

Ana grabbed Adam's collar and jerked him back just in time. Ahead was nothing but a large hole in the ground, probably six feet wide she estimated.

Why did all of this seem so familiar? She didn't have time to dwell on it. She had a choice to make: be diced by a giant blade or jump to her death.

"How deep do you think it is?" she asked.

Adam pulled a cartridge from his gun and dropped it into the pit. There was no sound. The blade was now only a few yards away. Ana got on her knees and reached a foot tentatively into the pit. Her eyes lit up. "There's a ledge! Come on!"

"What if it's a trap?"

"And the alternative?" she prompted.

"Ledge it is."

They jumped down and landed a few feet below on a narrow ledge.

"Maybe the blade will pass us by, and we can climb back out," Adam whispered.

"Maybe," she said. "Can you feel anything on the walls?" She spread her palms on them; they felt cool and earthy.

"Nothing. I'm not sure if we're in a big hole or a service tunnel."

Then, they heard the unmistakable swish of the blade above.

Dirt rained down on their heads. The scythe had not given up so easily. It was swinging to and fro now like the pendulum on a clock, slashing through the dirt above.

They only had one foot of clearance above their heads. They needed a solution, and they needed it now.

Then, she saw it. A pair of dining chairs were floating just below them. A sick and disturbing pattern was emerging in Ana's mind. First, the strange hedges and then the blade. It all felt familiar.

She grabbed Adam's hand. "We need to jump."

"Are you insane? We have no idea how deep this thing is."

The blade had worked its way closer. They had only inches to spare now.

She jumped, and to her relief, he followed.

For one horrible moment, Ana thought she was wrong. But then, the anti-gravity system kicked in and their descent slowed to gentle floating.

They passed the dining chairs, a golden skeleton key, and several teacups.

They stopped their descent and floated in midair by a table draped in ivory linens. Behind her was a candelabra with lit candles. Wax dripped gently down the sides. At Adam's ear, there was a sugar cube. They had all the makings for high tea.

If there hadn't been a blade steadily making its way through the earth, inch by inch, toward them, she might have enjoyed the weightless sensation. Maybe even the novelty of seeing *Alice's Adventures in Wonderland* recreated.

However, soon enough, the blade would reach them. On the table, there was a single glass vial with a paper attached. Ana reached for the candelabra behind her and then for the bottle. She made out the label, *POISON*, in fairy tale script.

Yes, there could be no coincidence now. *Alice's Adventures in Wonderland* had always been one of her favorites. She could still hear Alice's words echoing in her ears. "If one drinks too much from a bottle marked poison, it's almost certain to disagree with one sooner or later."

She had a feeling it was the answer. The way out of this mess. But the blade was still six feet above her head, and she wouldn't do it if it wasn't necessary. She looked around. "Do you see anything that can help us?"

"Nothing. This feels like an access tunnel. That means there should be service stairs or a lift. There should also be a gravity switch. If we can find it…" he trailed off, looking back up at the blade.

"What does that bottle say?"

"You don't want to know."

He took it from her. "Poison. She wants us to kill ourselves? Not likely." He put it back on the table and resumed his search for stairs and switches on the surrounding walls.

The blade was now two feet above them. Ana could feel the breeze against her hair. It was now or never. "I think one of us has to drink this."

"Are you mad?"

She could barely see his face through the candelabra's glow, but his tone was incredulous. "I'm pretty sure it's Lights Out. If we drink it, we'll be able to see the way out."

"Now I know you're mad. If it *is* Lights Out, big if, it has a 1 in 20 chance of blinding us."

"What do you think our chances are against that blade?"

He grabbed the bottle. "Fine. I'll do it."

Ana panicked. "No!"

He moved to pull the cork, and Ana did something impulsive. With a grimace, she brought the candelabra down across Adam's forehead with a crack. For just a split second, his eyes went wide, anticipating the blow. He crumpled, and she caught the vial.

"I'm sorry, Adam," she whispered. "But I won't let you step in front of my arrow this time."

The truth was Ana didn't think this was Lights Out. She thought it was Elysium—the undiluted poison. She could see how that would fit Madame Bali's twisted sense of justice.

She had seen firsthand what Elysium could do to its victims — blindness, seizures, debilitating nerve pain, and eventually, death. Adam's chances of surviving a head blow in Bellaton were much, much higher.

The blade was less than a foot away now. She pulled the cork out and tilted the bottle back. The liquid burned pleasantly as it slid past her lips and down her esophagus. In just seconds, she could feel it affecting her body, sending euphoric jolts through her nervous system. Her pupils began to dilate, and the promised benefits began to kick in.

She could see in the darkness. It was like someone had turned on a blacklight. The candelabra's warm glow was now a bright neon green. More colors hovered in the periphery, but she ignored them and searched the tunnel. It was concrete at this depth, and the anti-gravity switch was just inches to her left.

Several feet below it was a ledge.

She wrapped her arm around Adam's torso and positioned them both over the ledge. Then, she flicked the switch. They fell three feet and landed safely on the ledge. The skeleton key clattered beside her on the ledge, and she hurried to grab it as it teetered near the edge. She picked it up and placed it in the locked door. It opened, and she dragged Adam across the threshold.

Ordinary light blinded her, and she remembered why people took this drug at outdoor parties at night. She couldn't see anything. Her retinas burned. Ana grunted in frustration. They had come all this way only to be stuck again. She edged a foot slowly forward, trying to determine if it was safe to step.

This was stupid. Anything could be waiting for her.

She remembered her gun and reached into her backpack for

it. She could, at least, be armed. But her hand was in the wrong pouch. Before she could retract it, her fingers grazed plastic. Something round. Sun-glasses.

Triumph flooded her as she pulled them on and switched the dial to night mode. Suddenly, she could see again.

Just ahead was a small elevator. No way, she thought. No way. But to her surprise, there was an ornate set of steps too. She propped Adam against the wall and attempted to drag a pedestal and house plant in front of him to camouflage him. It wasn't great, but it was the best she could do under these circumstances. It was probably safer than where she was going.

Back at the academy, Samuel had woken. The distance from the island, and the medicine were starting to kick in. He felt like he had a hangover. His head pounded. His hands had a slight tremor.

He looked up and saw a small girl with icy blonde hair sitting next to his bed in a wooden chair. Ana's friend—Ophelia.

"Um, hello," he croaked. His mouth was dry.

She smiled down at him. "Hello. How are you feeling?"

"Thirsty and confused. Where's Ana?"

Ophelia frowned. "Let me get you a glass of water."

Samuel sat up in bed, rubbing his aching temple.

Ophelia returned with the water, and he downed it without taking a breath.

"Do you want more?" she asked.

"Ana," he repeated. "Where is she?"

"She had to step out, but you should lie back down."

"I have to know. Please tell me."

Ophelia sighed and handed him a slip of paper. She had

copied down a set of coordinates. "She's gone to find Madame Bali. She thinks she's at the Fleur Estate."

Samuel stared at the coordinates in horror. He scrambled from his bed, leaving the cover pooled on the floor. "This isn't the Fleur Estate."

26
THE SPIDER

At the top of the stairs, Ana found a small hallway with several doors. She walked to the nearest, turned its ostentatious knob, and threw her shoulder into it. There was no resistance. She burst through the door, panting and clutching her side.

She had imagined many things on the other side of this door—Madame Bali's botanical lab filled with poisons and tinctures, a cyborg army, and even a hologram to taunt her failure.

What she found was a palatial sitting room, adorned in marble and luxurious drapery. In front of an ornate arched window, there was a velvet settee. A gray-haired woman was resting on it with a cup of tea next to her, growing cold. Her hands and ankles were bound, and her mouth had been gagged with a strip of ripped cloth. The woman's eyes widened at the sight of Ana.

"Lady Jacobs?" Ana choked out. She swiveled around, searching for lurking danger. She found none and hurried to remove the cloth from Lady Jacobs's mouth. "Are you okay? Where is she? Where is Madame Bali?"

With the gag removed, Lady Jacobs sucked in a breath of air

and said, "She's gone to check the perimeter. She's been doing it every half hour. We have maybe half of that time."

Ana nodded. "Then we better remove these restraints on your hands and ankles. I've got a knife in my backpack. Wait just a moment." She swung her backpack onto her hip and began to rummage through its contents. When she finally located her utility knife, she looked up.

Something was odd.

Lounging on the settee, Lady Jacobs lifted a teacup to her lips and took a long sip.

Ana stopped dead in her tracks. "Your tea. How did you free your hand? How did—"

Lady Jacobs smiled as a cat does when it has its paw on the mouse. "I see you've figured out my little trick."

"What are you—is Madame Bali keeping you here? Where is she?" She could hear doubt creeping into her own voice.

Ana looked closer. Lady Jacobs didn't appear as if she had been in any sort of struggle. Not a hair was out of place on her head. Each curl was pinned perfectly in place. Her legs were neatly hooked at the ankle. There wasn't so much as a run in her stockings. Her countenance was composed. But there was something unsettling in her eyes. Something Ana hadn't noticed before.

Samuel's words echoed in her mind. "And Lizzie Borden kinda disliked her parents.... If my family didn't scare you, you'd be an idiot."

The children's rhyme echoed hauntingly in her mind. *Lizzie Borden took an ax, gave her mother forty whacks. When she saw what she had done, she gave her father forty-one.*

She shuddered. What had Samuel meant? Was his grandmother actually dangerous? Was she a killer?

"Oh, I do love to watch a mind turn. Have you figured it out yet?"

"It's you," Ana sputtered. "You're working with Madame Bali. You're together. But why? Why all of this?"

"I suppose you could call me Mr. Hyde."

"What is wrong with you? Why all these games and riddles? Why the maze?"

"No maze would need have been erected had you come alone, but I so tire of unwanted company. Those Rockwells are all extraordinarily dim-witted. Brawn does not equal brain, I'm afraid. As a council member, the drop-ins, even from one's own family, can be very tedious. So, I found a way to make them…a bit more entertaining."

"What kind of monster are you?"

"I sat in the sun on a bench; the animal within me licking the chops of memory."

Ana breathed out in frustration. *More riddles.*

"Fine. You wish to cease the games?"

Ana nodded.

"Then, let us be who we truly are, Anabella Halt. Two ruthless women. One who would trick, trap, and torment. Another who would bludgeon a lover and leave him propped up with the houseplants."

"That's your fault, not mine," Ana said, her voice rising.

She raised an eyebrow. "Am I mistaken? Are you not the one who hit him with the candelabra?"

"If you wanted to kill me, why bother with"—she gestured widely—"all of this?"

"Who said I wanted to kill you? I never kill people who are useful to me."

"But Madame Bali, is she here?"

"Alas, Terra Rorre is no more." She smiled at her own little rhyme.

"But I thought you said you don't kill people."

"Oh, I never said that. I said I never kill those who are useful to me. Little Terra was no longer useful, just a liability." Her tone sent shivers down Ana's spine.

"But she tried to kill me. How can it be you?"

"She bore you quite a grudge, I'm afraid. But your death was never my goal or hers. She wanted the money, and I have more money than god."

Ana grimaced. Everything about this woman was detestable.

"Little Terra had a case of cold feet. However, I assured her a poisoned arrow would be no match for a true member of the Halt line. It should have never killed you. Unless, of course, you were an imposter. In which case, the killing would be lawful. However, you've made it nearly impossible to be sure."

"I can't heal, but I am a Halt."

"The law of contradiction says otherwise."

"The what?"

"Simply stated, these two things cannot be true simultaneously."

Ana was losing patience. Somewhere, a level down, Adam was lying in need of medical treatment. She put her hands on her hips and squared off against Lady Jacobs. "Are you going to kill me or not?"

Lady Jacobs examined her manicured fingernails. "Not. I have a business proposition for you. Sit, won't you?"

The woman was mad if she thought Ana would sit. "If you're not going to kill me, then maybe I'll kill you," she snarled.

"Unlikely. If I die, you will never know all the answers you so desperately seek, and let's not forget the Elysium is still coursing through your veins like a freight train."

Ana scoffed, but she knew it was true. She could feel it. The euphoria was overwhelming. It was like the first bite of chocolate cake or the thrill of an unexpected kiss but so, so much better. Breathtaking color exploded all around her. Each object in the room had its own unique aura.

Even in this situation, a part of her wanted to smile like an idiot, but her fear was keeping it at bay. She was fairly certain she had taken Elysium, not Lights Out. Elysium was deadly. 100% of the time.

"What answers could you possibly have that I want?" Ana growled.

"All of them." She smiled. "Who came after you on Earth. Who ordered Samuel's arrest. Who freed him. Who killed off your family line. The whereabouts of your father. And so, so much more. Won't you have a seat?"

Ana sat.

"Well, don't be shy. After all, you don't have much time left. That was a rather large dose of Elysium."

"Why did Madame Bali help you?"

"Revenge and money. As you know, her adoptive parents were poisoned. Terra was swimming in loss, anger, and guilt. So, she made it her raison d'être to cure them, but she was running out of time. Mr. Fleur was on the brink of death. Terra had only one hope—the island. She believed a plant there held the key to unlocking the cure. She applied and received a research visa. However, when the Oceania sunk, your grandmother halted all travel. Terra's visa was revoked, and her trip canceled. Mr. Fleur died the following week. She blamed your family."

"But I didn't have anything to do with that," Ana said.

"As I said, it was irrational."

"What about the money?"

"She wanted to fund new research. After nearly blinding one of her test subjects, she was having trouble getting financial backers. She felt there was still time to help Mrs. Fleur."

Ana's arms were beginning to tingle, but she ignored the sensation. She pressed on with her questions. "And the dreams? Were they real? Did you do that?"

"Terra was a commoner. She had no formal education, only home learning. As such, she was severely underprepared for the

Royal Conservatory. Out of desperation, she made a mistake many others made before her. She purchased a neural chip mod. It helped her catch up on years of schooling in weeks. But at a cost."

In horror, Ana realized she had wanted one of those chips herself. She had seen them when she and Ophelia were back-to-school shopping. Ophelia had said, "Once you create a pathway, you can hardly be surprised when someone else uses it."

Lady Jacobs continued, "Terra came to me willingly. She took the job spying willingly. But when it came to killing, she really dragged her feet. I mean… poisoned chocolates. How pathetic. A toddler would know better."

Ana felt stupid. If only Lady Jacobs knew how close she had come to eating them.

"Once I found out about the neural implant, I began to make suggestions. Subtle ones. She probably didn't even know she was being controlled at first. I was waiting for just the right moment."

"But she figured it out. She removed the chip, a painful process, I assure you. Neural chips are ingested, you see. After many weeks, they attach to the brain. Memories, especially strong ones, can become embedded over time. What you saw were breakthroughs of her most vivid, most precious memories. The last ones to slip away."

Ana had a sinking feeling she knew the answer to her next question, but she asked it anyway. "How? How do I have her memories?"

She smiled like a shark. "Oh, I think you already know the answer to that. I can tell from the expression on your face. You're correct. That chip is now inside of you. You ingested it. It was Terra's last little act of defiance. She was feeling guilty. She knew she might die in the dome. She was desperate for you to understand why she did what she did."

Ana felt her stomach sink. But she kept going. "And the ghost?"

She laughed. "Oh, that was me! What a lark. I never imagined it would send you toppling into the sea."

"And Madame Bali's death?"

"The entire planet believed you had manifested the gift, but despite my hard work, I was unsure. After a year of careful planning, that blasted Madame Bali botched her shot. Though I suppose it's wrong to bear ill will against the dead, especially when you are the one to kill them." She smiled like a shark.

So, it hadn't been General Rockwell, after all.

Ana wanted to run. Even through the warm hug of Elysium, every instinct in her body screamed at her to run. This woman was a murderer, and she appeared to hold no remorse whatsoever for her crimes.

Despite that, Ana remained on the ornate velvet sofa. She uncrossed her legs and set both feet firmly on the floor, in case she needed to bolt.

"I frighten you."

Ana didn't see the point in lying about it. "Yes."

"Why? Am I not civilized? Is the tea not to your taste?"

"That makes it even scarier," Ana choked.

"I suppose I see your point. It's much easier to spot someone unhinged like that Delphi DuBois. What a showboat. I am what you might call a sociopath. A highly functioning one, of course. But there is a silver lining."

"Oh yeah?"

"I only strike if it is advantageous to me. Murder does nothing for me like these sick fetishists. I only do what is necessary. Stay on my side and to my advantage, and I shall never need to kill you or your little friends. It's all very simple."

The tingle in Ana's arms had become a burning sensation now. She ran her hands nervously up and down her arms, trying to soothe the pain. "Perhaps, you've already forgotten, but you poisoned me half an hour ago."

"Heal yourself. Anytime is convenient for me."

Desperate to avoid prolonged silence, Ana asked the question on the tip of her tongue. "Why did you kill her?"

"She had information on me and a conscience that wouldn't rest, the tortured woman. The moment she failed at her task and the crowds descended on the dome, she was a liability. Not an asset."

"But why pretend she was alive?"

"An old woman needs some entertainment. The council is very dull, and I do get sick of answering fan mail. My pen pal died. Besides, I wanted to test your mettle."

"What for?"

"I'm not ready to say just yet, but I will be in touch, Ana. And when I am, your answer had better be yes."

Ana swallowed her discomfort. "How did you even meet Madame Bali?"

"I'm not a Fleur, but I do have an interest in things that are useful to me. Like poison. Some might even call me an amateur botanist." She smiled serenely as though sharing a private joke with herself. "People who can be useful to me tend to find their way to me. Not unlike yourself."

The pain was intensifying with every ticking minute, but Ana gritted her teeth. "Who attacked me at the bus stop?"

"My son and his wife, unfortunately. Idiots the both of them. Brash. Lacking forethought. It doesn't suit them well in their business dealings either. Hence why I continue to hold this tiresome council seat. I long to be dethroned."

"But why?" Ana pressed.

"They wanted revenge. They felt your mother and grandmother had brainwashed and stolen their son."

"Samuel wasn't stolen."

"Well, of course, I know that. And you know that. And, on

some level, they do too. But it's much easier to blame you, you must see."

Every single one of Ana's nerve endings was firing on all cylinders. The pain was enough to make her see stars. "W-what about the rest of my family?"

"Ah an answer you will not care for, I'm afraid."

Ana blinked and fell to her knees in a wave of pain. It felt like she was on fire. She opened her eyes a slit and croaked, "Who was it?"

"Whom my dear. There was not one but a conspiracy. But I must interrupt. I can tell you're about to go into seizures. I really do recommend healing yourself now, to avoid additional discomfort."

"I can't," Ana shouted.

"Can't or won't? If you do, in fact, have the gift of healing, you should have no trouble overcoming a simple poison. If, however, the dome was a setup, then you lied to the council. In which case, I'm merely enacting the punishment for treason." She loomed over Ana's crumpled form and whispered, "Between you and me, I'm rooting for you to live."

"It would be easier to heal if I weren't losing consciousness."

"Would you like me to poison someone else instead? Perhaps, my eavesdropping grandson. You can come out, Samuel."

"No!" Ana gasped.

"Ah, so you truly are fond of him. How sweet."

"You would poison your own grandson?" Ana asked through now chattering teeth.

The hallway door swung open, and Samuel entered the room.

"I have dozens of grandchildren. I think I can spare just the one."

"What a lovely way to walk into a room. A pleasure as always grandmother." Then, he saw Ana on the floor. His eyes widened, and he rushed forward. "What the hell have you done?"

Another wave of pain came, and Ana blacked out. She saw her mother's face, just as beautiful as the day Ana had seen her in the star portal. Ana thought of her words. "To protect you."

When she regained consciousness, it felt as if she was being electrocuted. She convulsed on the floor. Samuel was beside her, trying to hold her body still. Tears slid down his cheeks.

She didn't know why, but something about it shocked her. She realized if she died, Samuel would cry. Others would too. They would feel pain just like she had when her mom died.

Her mom had died to protect her family. She had died doing what she thought was best. Who was Ana protecting by dying? Only herself. Tears leaked out of her eyes and down her face. She couldn't wipe them away, even if she wanted to. She no longer had control of her own arms.

And then everything went dark. Ana had no vision left for the sun-glasses to alter. She was blind. She had never felt more alone or frightened. Magdalena's words rang in her ears. "You have to feel it all, Ana. The good and the bad."

So, as she shook on the floor, Ana finally let go. She felt everything she had been holding back for so long. After she released her anger, she felt the emotions that lurked beneath—guilt and sadness.

Her mom had done her best. And now, Ana had to do the same. She felt a deep sadness but also acceptance. She was glad that even if she did die, she would be at peace with her mom.

And if she lived, she would stop lying to her friends and family. She would let people get close to her again.

She couldn't sing, but she imagined she could. She imagined the song she would sing. She thought of her mom's lullaby, and she sang it over and over again in her mind, thinking of her mom and her brothers. Of the happy times they'd had together. Moments she treasured. She thought of seeing Samuel's face again. She knew he was here, even if she couldn't see him. He was always by her side.

Almost as if flipping a switch, the pain disappeared. If only she could see. Everything remained dark. All she could see was a moon in the sky.

Wait a minute. Why could she see a moon? Then, she remembered. She was wearing sun-glasses. She pulled them off and realized her vision had returned. She looked around the room in wonder and ran her hands along her face and then her arms. She was alive.

She could heal.

SAMUEL ROSE to his feet and loomed over his grandmother. "Give me one good reason why I shouldn't kill you."

"I can give you six. The people who want the Halt family line extinguished. There was a conspiracy, crossing multiple families, and I will gladly hand you every name. But as you know, my dear," she said, addressing Ana, "everything has its price. Are you willing to pay?"

Ana clenched her jaw. "What is the cost?"

"Nothing you can't afford. A favor."

"What sort of favor?"

"I'm not ready to ask yet. But when I do, I'll expect a yes. And it's not just the names I can give you, I need a successor. And amongst my many children and grandchildren clamoring for my endorsement, I believe Samuel is the most fitting."

Samuel let out a harsh laugh. "You have to be kidding."

"Not at all."

"I hate this family. I hate you."

"That may be so, but you're still young. I'd rather see you tear it down and rebuild it in your own image than watch some weak-minded, controllable puppet take my seat. Your strength of will is impressive, grandson."

He scoffed. "Your preference means nothing. The seat is decided by wealth. Do you intend to bequeath yours to me?"

"You know as well as I that inheritance cannot make up more than 50% of assets when filling the Jacobs seat. I'd be happy to provide the 50%, and while I can do no more, I can invest. If you were to have a profitable idea. For instance, the control of all intergalactic travel in the foreseeable future. Then, I could provide my countless resources to that task."

"So, you know I solved it."

"I know most things."

"It's still theoretical."

"Everything starts as theory. Make star portals a reality. Then, you'll have my seat."

"Let me make myself clear, grandmother. I will never, ever work with you," he spat. "At this very moment, I am debating whether to kill you where you sit."

"You're being emotional, Samuel. Don't let it cloud your judgment. If you want to protect her, you need names and you need power. I am offering you both. Don't be a fool when you could be a prince instead."

"We are leaving. If you so much as breathe in Ana's direction, I will make sure you die a most unpleasant death and that your council seat goes to the most idiotic family member I can find. We will decide whether to contact you. Understood?" He turned toward Ana who was still sitting dazed on the floor. "Ana, is that okay with you?"

She stood. "Give me the first three names now."

Lady Jacobs smiled like a shark. "Here's a young lady who knows how to bargain. I knew I liked you, Anabella Halt."

"The feeling is not mutual."

27
TERRA'S FAREWELL

"We have to get Adam."

"And Ophelia," Samuel added.

"What?" Ana gawked at him. "You brought Ophelia?"

"I wouldn't exactly say brought. She couldn't be stopped."

"Where did you leave her?"

"In the hallway. She wanted to see the gardens."

"We have to go. Now." Ana started moving quickly toward the door, and Samuel followed.

Ana stopped to turn and scowl at Lady Jacobs. "Turn it all off. Every last thing. I need my jet to be able to land and have one of your servants bring up Adam Rockwell. Unharmed. Do these things or there will be no deal."

"With either of us," Samuel echoed.

"It's all been off from the moment Ana crossed through the doors. You needn't be so dramatic."

Samuel looked like he wanted to stay and argue or maybe hit an old woman, but Ana grabbed his sleeve. "It's deadly out there. We have to go."

They exited outside of the maze, and Samuel dragging his

grandmother along for insurance. Ana surveyed the lush grounds and spotted Ophelia.

She was sitting on a large tree whose branches were splayed over a brook. She stared at the water as if mesmerized.

"No. Please no," Ana moaned.

"What?"

"We have to hurry," Ana yelled, running toward her. She recognized this scene. It was from Hamlet. She remembered it because of the macabre paintings she had seen online after reading the play in school.

As they closed in, Ana grew more desperate. From here she could see the look of deep melancholy on Ophelia's fair face. Her cheeks had no color. Her crystal eyes were downcast. And she was still, so still. Was she even breathing?

She must be. She was still sitting up. It was as if she was in a trance.

"Undo it. Now!" Ana screamed, shaking Lady Jacobs. Right now, she didn't care about information. She felt willing to shake her until she answered…or was incapable of doing so ever again.

"I can't. It's already begun. Only she can stop the scene."

Ana stepped onto the branch, and Samuel grabbed her arm. "What if it pulls you in too?"

"There's no room for two in a clamped mousetrap."

Samuel released her arm, and Ana made her way down the branch. "Ophelia," she called in what she hoped was a cheerful tone.

Ophelia did not look up. Although there was no logical reason why she wouldn't have heard Ana. She continued to stare at the ripples in the pond.

Ana looked down too and saw shadowy reflections swimming there. She looked up, afraid of what the reflections might show her. She wondered what Ophelia was seeing.

Ophelia hunched over, bending her head closer to the water.

The branch began to creak. It was so narrow out there. It could snap at any time.

The water wasn't fast-moving. Would Ophelia have the will to swim?

"Ophelia," Ana grabbed her arm. "Snap out of it!"

Ophelia jerked out of her reach and nearly fell into the glistening water below. But though the branch swayed, she did not fall. Through no effort of her own, of course. She was still immobile.

Ana changed tactics. "Ophelia, whatever you are seeing, it's not real. You can beat it."

Ophelia blinked slowly as if stirring from a daydream. But she still wasn't moving

"You are my dearest friend. Please come back to me."

Ophelia's connection to the water seemed to be breaking. She lifted her head.

"I can't lose you," she admitted.

Ophelia's head jerked like a marionette, and she gasped for air. "Ana!"

"Ophelia! Take my hand. You have to hurry. This branch isn't stable."

"How did you do it?" Samuel asked.

"I recognized it. I can't believe you didn't. It was a scene from Hamlet. The beautiful Ophelia commits suicide because of her father's death and the cruel words of Hamlet. I thought maybe if Hamlet had been kinder, things might have been different."

Servants approached with a now conscious Adam in tow. He shook off their grasp. "Get off me," he shouted.

"Adam!" Ana screamed. She rushed over to him. "Are you okay?"

He rubbed his forehead, where a large whelp had formed. "I've been better."

"I'm so sorry. The vial was Elysium, and I didn't want you to drink it. I panicked."

"It was what? Are you okay?"

"I'm fine. I did it. I healed myself."

Samuel looked between the two of them with great interest. "Did you take a swing at Rockwell?"

Ana ignored him because, on the other side of the garden, a jet was quietly making its landing. Holden jumped from the cockpit and ran toward them. He gave Ana a bear hug and clapped Adam on the shoulder.

"Where is she?" Samuel said, looking around.

"Who?" Ophelia asked.

"She's gone," Samuel said.

"It doesn't matter now." She looked at Holden. "You need to get Adam to a hospital. He could have a concussion. And take Ophelia with you, too."

"What about you? We can't leave you here."

"Three was snug as is."

"I'm not leaving you here."

"I'm healthy and happy." She flashed him a winning smile.

"You're lying."

"You're right, but I will be." She gave Holden a hug and waved as their jet took off from the property. "You really should go. I have one more thing to do, and it's not dangerous. I swear."

"YOU WANT TO GO WHERE?"

"The real Fleur estate. The one in this picture." She pulled her drawing from her backpack, the one she had made months ago.

Samuel raised his eyebrows. "Why?"

"There's someone I need to see."

On the ride over, Ana thought of what Magdalena had once said to her. "It will heal you or destroy you."

When they arrived, Ana was quiet. The house and gardens were in a state of decay. The sight of them broke Ana's heart a little, or maybe it was Terra's heart breaking.

"Hello," they greeted with suspicion creeping into their voice. "The lady doesn't receive many visitors. Who might you be?"

Ana pulled herself to her fullest height and effected an air of grandeur. "I am Anabella Halt of the Council, and this is Samuel Jacobs, the grandson of Lady Jacobs of the council."

The servant swept into a bow so deep he nearly toppled over. "Please let me escort you. The lady is just taking in the day from her gardens. Please be aware she does not have a lot of her memories anymore. She doesn't always know what year it is or any of the current affairs."

Ana assured him it was only a social visit and that they would find the lady themselves. He bowed again, and they proceeded.

As Ana stepped into the garden, memories overtook her. This place was too powerful of a trigger. She rested her hand against a nearby trellis. A flood of images and emotions flashed through Ana's mind.

A summer garden with plump, luscious roses.

Lady Fleur's hopeful, soft smile.

The feel of damp soil as Terra put a plant into the ground.

A message certifying her approval to visit the Island.

A feeling of light in the darkness.

The image of a sinking ship on the holovision.

A flurry of messages.

Mr. Fleur's gray face staring unblinking up from his bed.

Anger, bitterness, pain, regret.

Then, the memories slowed and settled.

Terra rushed up the steps. Ana could feel her fear pulsate through her own body. Terra was desperate, afraid to go in but more afraid not to. The room was empty. The bed was empty. A man should be here. A man with a pale, lined face and a smile that moved his mustache when he laughed. The bed was mussed. Something was terribly wrong. Ana could feel it. He was dead. Terra knew it, so Ana knew it.

Ana realized what she was seeing and felt her gut lurch. She had lived through a moment just like this one. It was her worst memory. A secret she had told no one. Not even her brothers.

Ana had gotten the call from the hospital. Her mother wasn't going to make it. Like Terra, she rushed to the bus stop and frantically waved down the driver. She made it all the way to the hospital parking lot. And then, panic overwhelmed her. She couldn't do it. If she went in, it would be admitting her mother was dying. She couldn't face it.

Tear-streaked and shaking, Ana ran.

She made it back onto the bus and four blocks away before she pulled the rope to stop the bus. She got off and sprinted back toward the hospital. But by the time she arrived, it was already too late. Her mother was gone.

The nurse handed over her mom's blanket and a small bag of personal items, and that was it. That was all the goodbye she would ever have. It haunted her to this very day.

Her memories tangled with Terra's.

Terra who was now hitting the floor, her heart ripping in two, awash in guilt.

Terra really believed it was her job to heal him, Ana realized. It was ridiculous for her to put that burden on herself. To find a cure for a substance that had been hurting people for decades.

She could feel a seed of bitterness plant in Terra's chest. She could have done it. If only the Halts had welcomed her onto the isle. If only.

. . .

ANA BLINKED, and it was over. Really and truly over. She had seen it all. Everything she was supposed to see. And she knew what Terra wanted. She knew why she had fed Ana the chip.

Her final wish.

That someone who brought so much light into the world should die without any is a cruelty I cannot bear. I will find the cure. No matter the cost.

She wanted Lady Fleur to be saved.

"Whoa," Samuel said, bracing her. "What's going on? Are you okay? Is it the Elysium? Do we need to get you to a hospital?"

Ana took a deep breath, remembering who she was and where she was. She wiped the tears from her own cheeks. "It's a very long story, and it involves an inherited neural chip."

THE GARDENS WERE in a state of ruin and so was the woman sitting in them. She was in her wheelchair with her face tilted toward the winter sun.

"Hello!" she called out in a rickety voice. "Is someone there?"

She was both like and unlike the face Ana remembered so well. She wondered if perhaps Terra had loved her so much that she had made her face more beautiful. Now, it was lined from a life of hardship and heartbreak. She appeared to be unable to move without the aid of her servant and wheelchair. Her eyes were unseeing.

"Terra," she called. "Is that you?"

Ana felt like she had been socked in the gut. She neared the wheelchair and kneeled down beside it. "No," she said in her softest, kindest voice. "My name is Ana, and beside me is my friend Samuel. I think- I *know* I can help you." She reached for the woman's hands and held them in her own. Her skin was so thin it was nearly transparent.

Ana held a hand over the woman's eyes. She remembered the love Terra had felt for Lady Fleur. The warmth and happiness in the garden. The sorrow of seeing her beginning to lose her vision. She felt it all— the good, the bad, and in spite of it, she was okay. She was still here. She could feel warmth flow from her hand, and she knew it was working. Her magic felt more controlled than when she had healed Adam and herself.

She pulled her hand back, and the woman blinked. Her eyes looked different. They were no longer milky white. Her pupils had returned, and her irises were a pale green. Lady Fleur blinked in the sunlight and the gardens.

"Why? How?"

"Terra sent me."

Tears leaked out of the woman's eyes. "Terra," she whispered. "My Terra."

Ana nodded.

The old woman clasped Ana's hands and kissed her cheek. "Thank you."

When Ana and Samuel reached the gate, Ana turned around to look back at the garden one more time and whispered, "Goodbye Terra."

28
THE BOARD IS SET

Ana turned to Samuel with a resolute expression. "We're not going back to the academy. Not today, anyway."

"We're not?" he asked, cocking his head to the side.

"Has your island sickness cleared up, or do you need more treatment?" She looked at him up and down for signs of infirmity.

"No, I'm fine."

"Good. Then, do you think you can find us some lodging for two weeks, incognito, of course?"

"Sure. Do you want to be close to the academy?"

"No. The capital."

He raised an eyebrow. "What for?"

"I have a ball to attend."

Several weeks later, Ana and Samuel emerged from a shabby flat two miles from the center of the capital. Their attire didn't match their surroundings. Ana was dressed in an emerald green silk dress with silver chandelier earrings. Her hair was intricately curled and pinned with crystal orbs. Samuel wore a black tuxedo and polished shoes. His hair had been recently cut, and he was freshly shaven. His homeless Earth persona had been shattered.

Samuel hailed transport, and a black car hovered to a stop above them. It lowered, and they stepped in. The transport was empty, operated by A.I. "To the capitol, please."

THE COUNCIL always met before the Winter Ball. It was one of the few occasions where they were in the same place at the same time. Generally, they exchanged formal well wishes for the upcoming year, finalized a few pre-agreed upon documents, and departed for the main event. Last year, the council had used their time to meet and interrogate Ana.

This year, she had plans of her own.

She grabbed General Rockwell's arm as he was about to turn into the makeshift council chambers, a board room several floors above the ball itself. "General Rockwell, can I have a moment of your time?"

He turned. "Certainly. However"—he tapped his watch—"the meeting is about to start."

"I know, but I wanted to tell you this first." She fought the urge to look at her feet. "I've already talked to Adam. We've decided to end our engagement."

"Don't be ridiculous," he scoffed. "Even if you get your own crown, do you think it will protect you?"

"No, sir. I don't."

"Then, why would you do something so foolish?"

She squared her shoulders and steeled her nerves. "You

wanted an ally, General. That's still on the table. But I won't be bullied or coerced."

He narrowed his eyes as if measuring her resolve.

"Take some time," she offered. "Think about it."

MOMENTS LATER, Ana entered the council chambers with Samuel a few paces behind. He moved to take a spot close to the wall. At the sight of her, the already seated council erupted.

"Stolen jet!"

"Ignoring a summons!"

"Insolent girl!"

She waited for the worst of it to die down. She ignored their words and focused on her task. Ana pushed a long leg through the slit in her emerald ballgown, revealing a sheathed silver dagger. She removed it and held it aloft for them to see.

The room quieted, waiting to see what she would do next.

"If you mean to threaten us, you'll need far more than that little blade," Arkwright spat.

Ana held her hand aloft and ran the blade against the soft flesh of her palm. She tried not to wince at the sharp pain. She had a role to play. Weakness had no room here. Not if she were to do this right.

She stepped forward and up to today's acting chairman, General Rockwell. She held his gaze and let her blood drip across his papers. He stood his ground and looked at her appraisingly. She did the same stepping to each council member individually an unspoken challenge in her eye. DuBois recoiled in disgust at the blood. Noble peered closer. Fleur's expression held a disturbing and unquenched blood lust. Jacobs smiled her shark's smile. Arkwright looked red-faced. Like he might be working up to a rant.

She returned to the center of the room and closed her eyes. She concentrated on healing her hand. She knew she could do it now. She knew her mom could do it, too. And she accepted that. One day, she might even forgive her.

Ana could feel the pain leaving her hand and a warm tingle as new skin grew to cover the wound. She opened her eyes and held her hand aloft.

"I am the rightful heir to the Halt crown, and I've come to claim my council seat."

29
HOW TO KILL A KING

Samuel stared at the board in front of him, lined with alternating white and black squares. "Bellaton has many unique games," he protested. "How can you possibly think Earth's are superior?"

Ana looked at him with incredulity. "Monopoly, Candy Land, Settlers of Catan. Stop me when I reach something that isn't awesome."

He laughed.

"Besides," she muttered. "I haven't exactly had much time to play games since I got here."

"True." He twirled a queen between his thumb and forefinger. "But chess, this game belongs to Bellaton. It's elegant and strategic. A power struggle played out in miniature." His lip quirked upward. "And how do you become a king?" He swiped his queen ruthlessly across the board. "Why, you kill the sitting one."

ACKNOWLEDGMENTS

Thank you to all of the wonderful patrons on Kickstarter who made these special editions possible!

Celestial Crown

Alaina Danielle
Nathan Morgan
Xiomara Reyes

Tea with the Villain

Ambi C
Lauren

Moonlit Majesty

Aeriel Diaz
Alexandra Corrsin
Amanda Eschmeyer
Ashton Smith
Billye Herndon
Caitlyn Price
Claudia M.
Courtney R Delgado
Cristal and Flavio Juarez Lopez
Elly Walter
Hannah Conrad
Jennifer Vittetoe
Julie.mckenna16

Karisa Jones
Katherine Malloy
Kelsey Lieberman
Matthea W. Ross
Meilene Lin-Plebuch
Nicolas Breton
Nijeara "Ny" Buie
Rachel
Sarah L. Linser
Shanon M. Brown
Skylar Charbeneau
Tanya Young
Zabe

Sunrise Seeker
Alicia Guess
Claire Lee
Emika March

Royal Guardian
Amanda Balter
Ashley Cook
Azi
Caitlin Baxter
Caitlin Millsaps
Cherelle H
Connie H
Danielle Craig
Elizabeth
Elizabeth W.
Eron Wyngarde
Gianna C.
Heidi Moone
Katherine Shipman

Kathryn Parson
Kitsune James
Leslie B.
Lisa Watson
Maria Mejia
MF Caram
Morgan G.
Rebecca Hill
Summer Austin

Starry Wanderer
Cate
Elif Çağla Kurt
Jennifer Willcock
Jordan Rivet
Leslie Twitchell
Michelle L

Beta Readers
With special thanks to my beta readers, Marta and Justine, who stuck with this series from the very beginning, giving me valuable insight on how to make each of these books shine! Also, thank you to my other beta readers who joined later in the project, AJ, Carl, Dot, and Lark. You're all so appreciated!

ABOUT THE AUTHOR

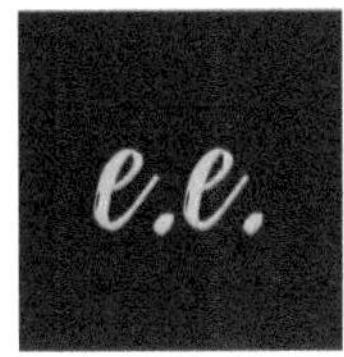

E.V. Everest is a sci-fi and fantasy author. Ever since she discovered the summer reading program, she's been unstoppable. After all, if books contain worlds, she's pretty much an intergalactic traveler, right?

When she's not visiting other worlds or inventing her own, Evelina enjoys drinking too much coffee, playing her trombone, and hiking with her four fur babies.

Join E.V.'s Newsletter Book updates, giveaways, and exclusive content. Join and get a free short story!

https://www.evelinaeverest.com

https://www.facebook.com/groups/evelinasbooks

https://www.instagram.com/evelina.everest

https://www.evelinaeverest.com/subscribe

ALSO BY E.V. EVEREST

Shadows & Starlight

Seven Crowns

The Botanist's Game

Rule of Shadows

Fallen Kingdom

Enemies Ever After

Kissed by Songs of Lilies

Anthologies

Ink & Incantation

Flights of Fantasy

www.ingramcontent.com/pod-product-compliance
Lightning Source LLC
Chambersburg PA
CBHW020339310726
48979CB00015B/2429/J

* 9 7 8 1 9 5 7 4 9 8 0 7 2 *